W9-AXF-634

DISCOVER
READ
EXPLORE
LEARN
NEW HANOVER COUNTY
PUBLIC LIBRARY

DETECTIVE FICTION

DETECTIVE FICTION

WILLIAM WELLS

THE PERMANENT PRESS
Sag Harbor, NY 11963

This is a work of fiction. Names, characters, places, and incidents either are products of the author's imagination or are used fictitiously. Any resemblance to actual events or locales or persons, living or dead, unless explicitly noted, is entirely coincidental.

For information, address:
The Permanent Press
4170 Noyac Road
Sag Harbor, NY 11963
www.thepermanentpress.com

Library of Congress Cataloging-in-Publication Data

Wells, William—
Detective fiction / by William Wells.
pages; cm
ISBN 978-1-57962-431-6 (hardcover)
1. Serial murder investigation—Fiction. 2. Suspense fiction.
3. Mystery fiction. I. Title.

PS3623.E4795D48 2016
813'.6—dc23 2015034964

Printed in the United States of America

For Eddie and Lucy

"Our perfect companions never have fewer than four feet."

—Sidonie-Gabrielle Colette

Acknowledgments

Naples is a real city on the Southwest Florida Gulf Coast. The year-round population of about 22,000 residents doubles during the winter months, also known as "The Season." This creates a town-and-gown kind of situation. The permanent residents dislike the overcrowding during the winter, but the local merchants depend upon the snowbirds and tourists to survive.

Not everyone who resides in Naples is over-the-top wealthy, of course, but if you are doing a PhD thesis on the growing income disparity in America, Naples is one of the places where you should do your fieldwork.

As with most, if not all, of the coastal regions of the Sunshine State, overdevelopment and overcrowding threaten the tranquility and natural beauty of the region. But it remains a very nice place to live and a lot of the unpleasant stuff is made up. During the year I was writing this book, residential property values did increase by 25 percent.

My gratitude to Martin and Judith Shepard of The Permanent Press in Sag Harbor, New York, for publishing my first effort at detective fiction; to Judith, and to Barbara Anderson, for excellent editing; and to Lon Kirschner for his good cover design.

And thanks also to the pioneers and current stars of the detective fiction trade, whose work has provided not only countless hours of great reading over the years but also a master class as I was writing this book.

"When in doubt, have a man come through the door with a gun in his hand."

—Raymond Chandler

1.

The Detective

The cold winds of a late October storm front howling in off Lake Michigan drove a cold rain through the skyscraper canyons of Chicago, painting the cityscape with a coat of glistening wetness that made the old city look new, at least for a while.

The city shrugged its big shoulders and thought: At least it's not snow, not yet.

A flash of lightning ripped across the evening sky, illuminating the figure of a man standing on a South Side street corner beneath a streetlamp whose bulb had long been broken, as were all the others in the vicinity, because it was that kind of neighborhood.

The wind-driven rain drenched the man—Detective Lieutenant Jack Stoney, to be precise—like he was a stockyard side of beef swinging through a car wash. Hatless, his black hair dripped water down his neck. He shivered, turned up the collar of his well-worn Burberry, and reflexively reached into an inside pocket for a pack of the unfiltered Lucky Strikes he'd given up a year ago when, during his annual departmental physical exam, the sawbones showed him a gray, diseased lung floating in chloroform in a jar.

Nothing in the coat pocket but an empty pack of Juicy Fruit and an old Illinois lottery ticket. Not a winner, or Stoney wouldn't have been standing there at all, not in that neighborhood, and maybe not in that city, with winter on the way.

Well, Stoney thought, at least I've still got Mr. Jack Daniel's to comfort me in times of need—that is, until the doc shows me a ruined liver in a jar and spoils the party completely.

A clog of leaves broke loose up in the gutter of the tumbledown four-flat he was staking out, releasing a swampy Niagara of dirty water that gushed down the drainpipe and spilled onto his shoes and pants cuffs.

I was too friggin' old for this drill three mayors ago, he thought, as he shook the rainwater off his coat and stomped the wet leafy crud off his shoes, like a hunting dog coming up out of a marsh.

He looked up at the windows of the building's two second-floor apartments. The lights were on in both, but shades blocked the view inside. I have choices, Stoney thought:

A, keep standing out here like a fuckin' mook.

B, call it in, let a SWAT team do the heavy lifting, head home, fill a glass with Black Jack on the rocks, and catch the Bulls against the Lakers on TV.

Or C, go inside and up to the second floor, kick in both apartment doors if necessary, and then try to persuade one Marcus Lamont, if in fact that shit-for-brains loser is really up there, that the Criminal Code of the City of Chicago is not to be taken lightly.

Stoney's plan had been to spend the evening at the Baby Doll Polka Lounge on West Cermack. He liked the Baby Doll for its generous pours, the kielbasa with kraut sandwiches, and the antique Wurlitzer jukebox, with its flashing rainbow of neon lights, and its stack of 45-rpm vinyl discs embedded with old Chicago bluesmen like Muddy Waters, Howlin' Wolf, Willie Dixon, and Buddy Guy.

Stoney was seated on a stool at the Baby Doll, sipping his drink and chatting up a waitress named Doris when a snitch he knew named Jake The Snake slid onto the stool beside him. Jake had a last name, like everyone, but he'd been called The Snake so long maybe even he'd forgotten it.

The Snake offered Stoney the location of Marcus Lamont's hidey-hole in return for his usual fee: A shot of Four Roses with a beer back and a favor in the bank for when The Snake got into trouble, which he always did, sooner or later. Usually sooner.

Lamont had robbed the Jewel Supermarket at Division and Clark two weeks earlier. That, by itself, was not enough reason to leave the convivial warmth of the Baby Doll on a nasty night.

Homicide detectives didn't chase robbers. But Lamont had shot and killed an off-duty cop working as a security guard at the Jewel. And that, my friend, is a definite no-no.

Stoney knew the cop: Lenny Wadkins, good guy, wife and three kids, a departmental Medal of Valor, eight months from retirement, with plans to move down to Vero Beach to fish and play golf. So Lamont had to go down, with "Dead or Alive" implied, if not printed, on his wanted poster.

There had been no leads on his whereabouts until The Snake's tip.

"I know a guy who knows a guy who told me that Lamont is at his girlfriend's place as we speak," the snitch had said. "Her name's Lucinda. Strips at the Funky Monkey. Lives in an apartment at Saginaw and Ninety-Third, second floor. Don't know which of the two units, though."

Good enough. Stoney took a twenty from his wallet and slapped it onto the bar.

"Thank you, my man," The Snake said as he made the bill disappear with a magician's slick sleight of hand.

Stoney put down another twenty for his drinks, took his trench coat from a hook by the door, and went outside. He was driving his classic red 1963 Corvette Stingray convertible, and not the department's unmarked brown Taurus that had his shotgun and Kevlar vest in the trunk.

You took drinking money and a roll of Tums to the Baby Doll, and your service revolver, but not a Kevlar vest and a shotgun. The first and last time some asshole had tried to take all the fun out of happy hour at the Baby Doll, by walking in with a sawed-off shotgun concealed under his coat, demanding the contents of the register and the customers' pockets, it had not ended well for the perp.

Leon Kramarczyk, the owner, who'd been a paratrooper with the Polish army, had shot the dickbrain through the neck with the Vis 9 mm pistol he kept near the cash drawer. Word got around the neighborhood that there were much easier ways to make a living than by sticking up the Baby Doll Polka Lounge.

Stoney looked up at the second floor again. The rulebook called for choice B. Call in backup. Why be a hero? At some point, when you're burned out by the job, divorced, middle-aged, and gun-shot on three occasions, enough should finally be enough. The citizens he'd sworn to protect and serve, as it said on the sides of the squad cars, didn't care about the daily life of a cop. Instead of gratitude, you got a shield, a service sidearm, and a salary that paid for three hots and a cot, as they said in the marines. But no more than that, unless you counted the adrenaline high you got from the job, sometimes. The times when your life was on the line.

If you survived the mean streets, and the inevitable Internal Affairs investigations about your conduct, you also got a pension. Maybe you would save enough to chase the standard-issue cop dream of moving somewhere where the sun shined year-round and you were safe from the bite of The Hawk, which is what Lou Rawls called the winter wind off the lake.

One cop Stoney knew did end up owning a bar in Reno, but he'd been on the take and put his added income into tax-free municipal bonds.

None of that for Jack Stoney, however. Honest and poor, that was his fate, he had concluded early on. He knew that he'd never get rich on the public payroll, but what the hell, it sure was fun prowling the city streets with a badge and a gun.

Stoney reached under his coat and touched his Smith & Wesson Distinguished Combat .357 Magnum in the leather holster clipped to his belt. The department had issued him its standard 9 mm Sig Sauer, which he used exactly once and returned to the armaments clerk when a shot through the thigh failed to stop a badass dude high on crack cocaine coming at him in an alley off West Madison.

Apparently the perp's central nervous system was so anesthetized by the drug that he didn't even realize he'd been shot until Stoney put another round into him, center mass. That finally stopped him. He looked down with terminal surprise at his chest, a red stain blooming on his white tee shirt. He dropped to his knees, saying "Ohhh fuck me . . ." and toppled over frontward, dead before his head bounced off the pavement.

After filling out his after-action report, and being interviewed by Internal Affairs, Stoney had gone home and found the Smith &

Wesson wrapped in an oilcloth at the bottom of his old USMC trunk, beneath the proud uniforms of his youth.

The S&W was only a six-shot versus the semiauto Sig with seventeen rounds in its clip. But the big-bore bullets would always do the trick, whether the dickweed was stoned or sober, creating an exit wound you could drive a Ford F150 with double-wide tires through.

Stoney looked up and saw a shadow move past one of the second-floor windows of the front apartment, too big to be a woman. Maybe that wasn't Lamont, but The Snake has never given me bad info, so he's up there, Stoney thought. Warm and dry and gettin' it on with some poontang whose taste is as bad as her luck while I'm out here freezing my sorry butt in the goddamned rain.

He decided. Choice B. Call in the badass young guns of SWAT. This time, the rulebook had it right. He fished his cell phone out of his pocket. But then he paused, sighed, and put the phone away, thinking, what the hell, I'm already here, I'm already wet, that cock-sucking, motherhumping Lamont killed a cop and maybe he'd be gone by the time the SWAT boys arrive.

So lock and load. It's C.

He moved up the three cement steps to the front door of the old building, named The Lakeview Apartments, a sign mounted on the brick wall beside the door announced, even though the lake was nowhere in sight.

He found the door locked and shouldered it open, easy enough given the weakness of the rusted lock and the decayed wooden frame.

He stepped into the lobby: peeling, puke-green paint on the walls, worn brown linoleum on the floor, and one bare-bulb light fixture hanging from the low ceiling. There were doors to the right and left for apartments 1A and 1B, and a stairway leading up to the second floor to 2A and 2B.

Stoney left the outside door wide open, just in case he'd need to exit the building in a hurry, and started up the creaky wooden stairway, straddling his feet onto the outside of each step so as to reduce the sound of his footsteps. That was part of the tradecraft a cop had to learn if he wanted to make it to that boat and bar down south.

He paused in the second-floor hallway and unscrewed the lightbulb in the wall fixture so he wouldn't be backlit when he made his move. The S&W came out, held barrel down along his right leg.

He touched the thin fabric of the black tee shirt under his trench coat where his Kevlar vest should be. Well, you play the hand you're dealt, he reflected, which pretty much summed up his philosophy of life.

The Snake hadn't known which second-floor apartment. So roll the dice: 2A or 2B? If Stoney guessed wrong, maybe he'd give a family having dinner one hell of a surprise.

He mentally flipped a coin, turned toward 2B, and gave the door a prodigious cop-kick with his size twelve hand-tooled cowboy boots, like a pizza delivery boy from hell: Anyone here order a large sausage and mushroom, motherfucker?

The door flew inward and hung open. By way of greeting, a shotgun blast from inside ripped through the air, splintering the wood of the jamb, telling Stoney he'd guessed right.

He pressed himself flat as paint against the hallway wall and rubbed his right cheek with the back of his left hand. It came away smeared with blood. Just a flesh wound from the flying wood splinters, and not the shotgun pellets, but it'd hurt like hell when shaving.

All right Lamont, now you've gone and done it, Jack Stoney thought. You've put me in a real bad mood.

He raised the S&W, crouched low, and rolled into the apartment, firing as he went . . .

2.

Shoot Me And I Bleed

Spoiler alert: Jack Stoney will survive that gunfight because he's a fictional detective, and he needs to be around to appear in sequels to the novel you've just been reading. A character made of ink and paper does not die unless the author wants him to.

But I do bleed when shot, and have, on more than one occasion. So, unlike Detective Stoney, I would not blast my way into Apartment 2B, Lone Ranger style. I'd call in a SWAT team with their full body armor, flash-bang and tear-gas grenades, assault rifles, and bring-it-on attitudes, while I hung back, way back, and supervised.

In fact, in a strikingly similar situation, I did exactly that. While staking out a real Chicago South Side four-flat, and seeing the bad guy I was after walk past a window, I pulled out my cell phone instead of my gun. It seemed like half the precinct turned out to catch the cop killer, who didn't survive the "arrest attempt," which was how the official after-action report described what was essentially an execution. You want your constitutional right to a fair trial, don't kill an officer of the law, at least not in Chi Town.

Because of prudent decisions like that one, I am alive and sitting in the galley of my houseboat in Fort Myers Beach, Florida, a red Sharpie in my hand, reading through the manuscript of *Stoney's Last Stand*, which is William Stevens's new Jack Stoney novel.

Bill Stevens is the *Chicago Tribune*'s veteran police reporter. He has me edit his best-selling books before they are published to help him get the cop stuff right. I get a nice fee for this work, but I'd do it for free because I have a vested interest. The stories are all based upon my own career as a Chicago homicide detective.

If Bill gets something wrong, as he did a few times before asking for my assistance, he inevitably receives letters from readers taking him to task. For example: Jack Stoney's 1911 model .45-caliber handgun was a semiautomatic, not a revolver, wrote one reader from Minneapolis; Jack Stoney could not have driven a 2012 Ford Crown Victoria with the police interceptor package because Ford stopped making that model in 2011 and switched to the Taurus for law enforcement work, commented a retired cop from San Diego; the Chicago Police Department calls it the Homicide Division, not Robbery-Homicide as they do in some other cities, explained a man in Prague. How in the world a man in the Czech Republic knew that arcane fact is beyond me, but he was, in fact, correct.

I considered making a note in the margin of Bill's manuscript describing how that South Side stakeout actually went down. But I decided against it. Jack Stoney *would* have kicked in the door and gone in alone. Nobody wants to read about a hero who plays it safe.

It's a cliché, I know, all those cops you read about in detective novels. They are inevitably cynical; burned out after too many years on the job; recovering alcoholics struggling to stay on the wagon; divorced, because their ex-wives finally couldn't take the drinking and the stress of the cop life anymore; estranged from their kids because they put the job first and weren't around for the school plays and soccer games; mavericks, always in hot water with their captains/police chiefs/mayors, but (just barely) tolerated because they have the best close rates in the department.

Allow me to introduce myself. I am Mr. Cliché in the flesh, aka Chicago Homicide Detective Sergeant Jack Starkey (retired). You've just read my résumé.

After being shot for the third time, once while a marine involved in an overseas operation that didn't officially exist, and twice more while on the payroll of the City of Chicago, I retired on full disability to the little town of Fort Myers Beach on Florida's Southwest

Gulf Coast, where I own a bar and live on a boat. Living the cop dream, and loving it. And no, I wasn't on the take. Bill Stevens makes a lot of money from his novels. He is my partner in the bar, The Drunken Parrot. He put up the cash and I manage the place.

Bill's other novels have titles like *Stoney's Revenge*, *Stoney's Honor*, *Stoney's Day Off*, and *Stoney's Killshot*. He makes my alter ego larger than life. Jack Stoney is taller (six two to my even six); braver (he won the Silver Star as a captain in the marines and three Chicago PD citations for above-and-beyond, while all I got as a marine lieutenant were the usual sharpshooter's and good conduct medals, plus a Purple Heart, and no police departmental citations because, I believe, the powers-that-be didn't want to endorse my maverick behavior); and meaner (Stoney believes in vigilante justice, not trusting the screwed-up legal system to keep the bad guys off the streets, while I only did that sort of thing as a last resort). Stoney is a detective lieutenant; I was a detective sergeant.

Stoney is a handsome devil with a thick shock of salt-and-pepper hair; muscular; with piercing green eyes; and a killer smile that melts the hearts and dissolves the resistance of the ladies who cross his path. Here, again, Bill has enhanced the real me, although I've always had a date for the prom.

Stoney likes his women fast and loose, a wham-bam-thank-you-ma'am kind of guy. He once said, "After an hour in the sack with that leggy blonde, I wished I had two johnsons for double the fun." I'd never say anything like that, although, I'll admit, the concept is rather intriguing.

It is widely reported that readership of books is way down because of the blizzard of electronic sensory inputs people get via their TVs, smartphones, tablets, computers, and now smart watches. But, according to Bill, there is clearly a large appetite among those who do still read books, either in paper or e-book form, for hard-boiled crime fiction, and he plays into that with his novels. All of them have been best sellers.

My relationship with Jack Stoney brought me a measure of fame in my hometown. That caused me a lot of razzing down at the station house and in the cop bars, and it didn't exactly endear me to the top brass in the department. I guess that Detective Stoney's behavior reminded them what a pain in the butt I could be.

I keep a stock of the Jack Stoney books in The Drunken Parrot and give away copies autographed by both the author and me to any patron who asks—I consider this to be a marketing tool for the bar—and to some who don't, especially if they are female and pretty. Pick-up line: "Hi, do you like detective fiction?" Actually, that was before I met my current lady friend. Now I just thank the fans and buy them a drink.

Bill visits periodically to check on his investment in the bar and to fish. Business is good because of our generous pours, the best hot wings and sliders on the beach, authentic Chicago-style hot dogs (a Vienna Beef tube steak on a poppy-seed bun dressed with mustard, onion, tomato slices, a dill pickle spear, bright green relish, celery salt, and sport peppers), and a happy hour that runs from our ten A.M. opening until last call, which is whenever I feel like locking up.

The previous owner of The Drunken Parrot had a parrot named Hector who liked to stroll up and down the bar, dipping his beak into customers' beer glasses and then staggering and doing a very good imitation of a burp. Hector said things like, "What's a dumpy broad like you doing in a classy joint like this?" to the female patrons, and "You've been over-served, bucko" to the men. He could also sing the opening lines of "Danny Boy."

In Hector's honor, I keep a framed eight by ten of him on the wall. When I bought the bar three years ago, Hector was not included, although I would have been happy to have him stay on. But his owner purchased a motor home and set off to see the country, with the bird riding shotgun. Maybe the guy will write a book: *Travels With Hector*.

I thought of changing the bar's name to The Baby Doll Polka Lounge South. The Baby Doll is my favorite Chicago bar, and also Jack Stoney's. Leon, the owner, wouldn't have minded, but I knew that my customers wouldn't catch the reference, and Hector had created a certain amount of equity in the existing name.

You might wonder if it is a good idea for a recovering alcoholic to own a bar. Maybe not, but I make it work. My drink of choice these days is Berghoff root beer, a custom brew made by the famous old German restaurant of that name in the Windy City. My beverage distributor brings it in. If I ever get tempted to revert to Gentleman Jack, I have only to look at the faces of the hard-core drinkers who shamble into the bar, and the urge goes away. I do what I can to help these poor souls with advice, which they usually don't want, and coffee and a hot meal, which they usually do.

Fort Myers Beach is one of those Florida, girls-gone-wild, spring-break kind of towns. For years, three pals I've known since we all went to Saint Leo's Academy, a Jesuit high school in Chicago, and I would head down here for vacations. We'd rent a boat from Salty Sam's Marina and troll the backwaters of Estero Bay for snook, red-fish, sheepshead, and ocean perch. Sometimes we'd head north to Boca Grande Pass in pursuit of tarpon. At night we'd hit the bars along Estero Boulevard, including The Drunken Parrot, trolling for women above the age of consent, or at least those who had IDs saying they were (not that we'd ever intentionally buy a drink for a minor).

The Drunken Parrot occupies a ramshackle, single-story building with weathered, white-wooden siding and a green tin roof. It is located right on the sand, with a big back deck, a straw-roofed, tiki-hut bar, and beach volleyball nets. On weekends during spring break, we have wet tee-shirt contests. A thousand pardons for any antifeminism involved, but the girls are volunteers and it's good for business. One time, a beefy Iowa State right guard entered, and he won by unanimous acclaim from the customers, proving that our contest is not sexist. Inside, there is a long, curved mahogany bar with a brass rail, college and pro sports team memorabilia on the walls, a small stage where blues and jazz musicians play weekend nights, and a serviceable kitchen presided over by a veteran short-order cook. I make certain that the restrooms are always spotless, as if ready for a Marine Corps inspection.

One night while drinking at The Drunken Parrot with my Chicago buddies, I gave my detective's business card to the retired navy chief petty officer who owned the establishment and told him to call me if he ever wanted to sell. Dreaming that cop dream, you understand. It was mostly the alcohol talking. By the next morning, I'd forgotten all about it.

But the owner did call me. I was in my Wrigleyville duplex at the time, recovering from that third gunshot wound. I took a .380-caliber round in the right shoulder, through and through, that limited my range of motion so badly that the department's physician said I was unfit for duty—not the first time I'd been told that by the brass, but this time it was for a purely physical reason.

The perp was a guy wearing a ski mask who ran out of a credit union on La Salle Street in the West Loop and bumped right the hell into me, surprising us both. He took early retirement from the armed robbery game when he shot me and I reciprocated with three rounds from my Smith & Wesson Distinguished Combat .357 Magnum—the same gun Bill Stevens puts in the hand of Jack Stoney—dropping him to the pavement like a marionette with its strings cut.

I am dating a lovely woman named Marisa Fernandez de Lopez. Her father came to Miami from Cuba as a boy via the Mariel boatlift. Her mother was Venezuelan. She is about ten years my junior; I don't know much about women, what man does, but I do know enough to not ask their ages.

Marisa is drop-dead gorgeous, with lustrous, shoulder-length black hair, flashing dark eyes, and a killer bod, which she maintains by running marathons and practicing power yoga. She owns a small real estate agency in Fort Myers Beach and does very well because waterfront property values are astronomically high. I don't know what she sees in me, and I'm not inclined to ask in case it would make her wonder about the same question.

Marisa has never read any of the Jack Stoney novels. She prefers literary fiction, books like *The Light Between Oceans* by M.L. Stedman, which she just finished, and *The Goldfinch* by Donna Tartt, which she is reading. "Why would I read about a fictional detective when I have the real deal?" she once told me. Can't argue with that logic.

Other than editing Bill's books, I don't read detective fiction either. Busman's holiday. The books on my shelves are mostly nonfiction: *Homicide: 100 Years of Murder in America* by Gini Graham

Scott; *Bartending For Dummies* by Ray Foley; *Shooter's Bible Guide to Firearms Assembly, Disassembly, and Cleaning* by Robert A. Sadowski; *City of Big Shoulders: A History of Chicago* by Robert G. Spinney; and *The Confessions of Saint Augustine* by the Saint himself (a Saint Leo's textbook I saved for some reason). And of course *Semper Fi: The Definitive Illustrated History Of The U.S. Marines.*

My home is a forty-six-foot Voyager houseboat named *Phoenix*. Generally, I despise cutesy names for boats like *Dad's Dream*, *Lazy Dayz*, *Nauti Girl*, and *She Got The House*, all of which I've seen. In that same unfortunate category are pretentious designer names some parents give their children. But *Phoenix* seems appropriate for my new home. I hope, with this new life of mine, to rise from the ashes of my earlier years, like the bird of Greek mythology.

I bought *Phoenix* used—its original name was *Takin' It E-Z*—with part of the proceeds from the sale of my Wrigleyville duplex. I keep it moored at Salty Sam's. "Moored," as in nailed to the dock. *Phoenix* is as seaworthy as The Drunken Parrot, I believe, an opinion I never mean to test.

I met Marisa when I walked into her real estate office, located in a block of commercial buildings on Miramar Street, looking for a place to live. She asked me what my ideal residence would be. "A boat on a budget," I told her. Her MLS listings pulled up *Takin' It E-Z*, which was owned by a woman from Syracuse who'd gotten it in a divorce. According to my realtor, the woman was a "highly motivated" seller. I made an offer, it was accepted, and I moved out of a motel called The Neon Flamingo, my temporary quarters, and onto the boat.

I had the amusing but unserious thought of getting a pet alligator, like Sonny Crocket had on his sailboat *St. Vitus Dance* in the old *Miami Vice* TV series, which I love. I decided instead on a cat. Actually, the cat decided on me. One morning, after I'd been in residence aboard *Phoenix* for about three months, I awakened in my bunk with the feeling that someone was staring at me. Someone was: a very large feline, calico, with the scars on his ears and face of a street fighter, a condition that we share. Maybe that's why I took to him immediately.

All I could think of to say to the cat was, "Welcome aboard." He looked at me and meowed; maybe he was trying to tell me that he was the captain now, like that Somali pirate in the movie *Captain Phillips*.

The cat didn't seem inclined to go ashore anytime soon, so I went to the galley, opened a can of tuna and put it in a bowl on the deck for him. He took a few bites and then looked at me and meowed again, which I took to mean, "Not bad, but I prefer fresh." I made a pot of coffee while he finished the tuna. Then he strolled into the stateroom, hopped onto the bed, curled up, and went to sleep. We've been together ever since.

My aunt, who had six cats, had an embroidered pillow on her sofa that said, "Dogs have owners, cats have staff." I soon found that to be correct. But it is a relationship that works for Joe and me. I named him after my brother. He apparently decided it was time to settle down with a permanent gig and, for some reason, picked my boat. Maybe he is prone to seasickness and liked the fact that the *Phoenix* was obviously never going to sea.

3.

The Rich Are Different

It was just after nine thirty on a balmy winter evening, the temperature in the midseventies in Fort Myers Beach, and three degrees with wind-driven snow in Chicago. One of the pleasures of moving to Florida from a northern climate is comparing the winter temperatures in your old and new hometowns, which I do regularly via an app on my cell phone. This is less fun during the summer months.

Marisa and I were lying in bed aboard *Phoenix*, relaxing after a good dinner followed by some very passionate lovemaking. "Lovemaking" is a hopelessly old-fashioned term I know, but then, I'm a hopelessly old-fashioned kind of guy. I'm not criticizing casual sex, but I like Marisa very much and consider myself past the age for hooking up with any target of opportunity, as I tended to do in my youth.

Marisa is an excellent cook. I'm great at ordering take-out and can put together a very tasty bowl of cereal. Bill Stevens makes Jack Stoney a gourmet chef. After a hard day of crime fighting, Stoney goes home to his Wrigleyville apartment and whips up some incredible meal for himself and his date from whatever is in his refrigerator.

My fridge does not contain truffles, or leeks (whatever they are), or fresh Parmigiano-Reggiano, all of which Jack Stoney added to eggs for an omelet after he got home from a gunfight in the last novel. As I recall, he even baked some crusty bread, and had just the right wine on hand. I have an onion or two in the larder, plus a few cans of tuna and some dry cat food for Joe, a box of Frosted Flakes, a loaf of Wonder Bread, and a block Velveeta that has a longer shelf life than wood, plus a few other odds and ends in cans, jars, and boxes. As far as I'm concerned, use-by dates are for sissies. My wine cellar, aka a refrigerator shelf, consists of a six-pack of beer for guests and Berghoff root beer for me.

But tonight, Marisa brought groceries and prepared a delicious *ropa vieja* (shredded flank steak in a tomato sauce), black beans, yellow rice, plantains, and fried yucca. Dessert was a caramel flan. She lives in a Key-West style pink stucco cottage on Mango Street with a professional-grade kitchen, where she really rocks.

Glenn Gould's classic 1955 recording of Bach's *Goldberg Variations* was playing on the Bose sound system I installed on the boat. It was Marisa's CD. My musical tastes run heavily to classics like Led Zeppelin, The Ramones, Bob Seger, and The Dead, as well as the same Chicago bluesmen Jack Stoney likes: Buddy Guy, Muddy Waters, Howlin' Wolf, Freddy King, Arthur "Big Boy" Crudup, Sonny Boy Williamson (father and son), and others. Last Christmas, Marisa gave me a box CD set titled *Best Of Chicago Blues*, bless her heart.

I was feeling quite content. All was not right with this troubled world, but there, in bed with Marisa, my little corner of the planet was doing just fine.

"What are you thinking?" she asked as she lay with her head on my chest and her hand exactly where I would have requested she put it if I needed to, which I didn't.

"I was just thinking about the Beach Boy's *Pet Sounds* album," I told her. "It was really Brian Wilson's project after he quit touring with the band to focus on his composing . . ."

"The relevance to the present moment being exactly what?"

"It's obvious. They used a harpsichord on *Pet Sounds* and Bach wrote the *Goldberg Variations* for the harpsichord." That latter was something Marisa told me, and which, oddly, I remembered.

Not content to quit when I was ahead, an attribute of my poker game, I added, "The Beach Boys also used bicycle bells and dog whistles on the album, which, in my view, provide a nice counterpoint to the main themes. I'm surprised Bach didn't think of that."

Jack Starkey, world-class wise guy.

My wise guyness was one item on the long list of personal attributes that annoyed my ex-wife. It was right up there with leaving the toilet seat up, burping during a meal (she didn't buy the argument that this was considered a compliment to the cook in China, or maybe it was India, pointing out that we were dining in the United States), and not putting a coaster under my beer bottle (I was still in my drinking days then, which was one more thing on her list).

Maybe Marisa was also making a mental list of my shortcomings. But if she was, she kept it to herself, bless her hot Latina soul.

"Define the concept of counterpoint in musical composition," she responded.

She had me there, as she knew she would. Following the example of politicians when stumped, I simply changed the subject: "How about those Cubs? I need to remember to order tickets."

I've been a lifelong Chicago Cubs fan. Some people follow the White Sox. There is no accounting for (bad) taste.

She follows soccer, where twenty-two players in shorts run around kicking a ball that hardly ever makes it into the goal. That is compared to the intellectually stimulating, heart-stopping action of The Great American Pastime, where an entry is made in the record books on every play. You could look it up.

"You'd think I'd have learned by now that I shouldn't ask you what you're thinking," she said.

I was trying to come up with a clever response to that when I heard the sound of someone stepping from the dock onto the *Phoenix's* deck. I wasn't expecting a visitor, so I instinctively reached for the .38 snub-nosed Smith & Wesson revolver, my backup piece from my days on the job, that I keep in my bedside cabinet.

Joe was sleeping on a quilt on the floor as he did whenever Marisa occupied *his* place on the bed. I made the mistake of buying a cat bed for him once. He ignored it and I deposited it into a dumpster at the end of the dock.

Marisa looked at me, said, "I cook, you repel boarders," and pulled the sheet up to her chin.

From outside the cabin, a voice shouted out: "United States Coast Guard! We know about the contraband Cuban cigars, and the underage girl in your bed!"

"Bless him for that last," Marisa said.

It was Cubby Cullen's voice. Clarence "Cubby" Cullen is the Fort Myers Beach police chief. He is short and stocky, with a silver crew cut and substantial beer belly. Think Rod Steiger in *In the Heat of the Night*. He is a former deputy chief of the Toledo Police Department who got bored in retirement. He applied for the Fort Myers Beach job when it opened up and was advertised in a Fraternal Order of Police newsletter.

I went to the Fort Myers Beach police station to introduce myself to Cubby soon after I arrived from Chicago. This was a professional courtesy, one cop to another, and also to get an application for a Florida concealed carry weapons permit. Cubby was disappointed to learn that I didn't drink, but that didn't prevent us from becoming pals, trading war stories, and backwater fishing on his Smoker Craft skiff. That's why I didn't have to sweat the local ordinance regulating bar-closing time.

I did have a box of Cohibas aboard; Cubby knew that because he gave it to me. He got several boxes while on a fishing trip to Lake of the Woods in Canada, a country that enjoys free trade with Cuba. I told him the story about how JFK sent his press secretary, Pierre Salinger, down to Cuba to bring back a large supply of Antonio y Cleopatras just before signing the Cuban trade embargo. Rank definitely does have its privileges. I read about that in a book about Kennedy. You couldn't attend a Catholic prep school or college without learning a lot about the nation's first Catholic president.

"It's just Cubby," I told Marisa. "Back in a sec."

I slipped on my boxers, khaki shorts, and a Cubs tee shirt and went out onto the deck.

"Hope I'm not disturbing you," Cubby said, referring to the possibility that Marisa might be aboard.

"Not a problem, Cubby. Let's go into the galley."

He followed me inside. I'd closed the door to the stateroom, protecting Marisa's modesty. I took a bottle of Blue Moon ale, Cubby's brand of choice, out of the refrigerator, along with a Berghoff for me. I also found an orange, cut a slice for Cubby's Blue Moon, and poured the beer into a tall glass with the orange slice, which is the only way to serve it, as every bartender knows.

I joined Cubby at the galley table. We sipped our drinks and he said, "Do you ever miss police work?"

I pondered this for a moment, then said, "Once, about six months ago. But I lay down and the feeling went away."

Which was not completely true. I did miss the job sometimes, especially the adrenaline rush you got from being in harm's way. Just like military combat in that regard. "Nothing is so exhilarating as to get shot at without result," Winston Churchill said. Although, as I've reported, three times there was a result for me; it was all the other times that were exhilarating.

Cubby took a long drink of his Blue Moon, put down the glass, wiped foam off his mouth with the back of his hand, and said, "I know you were a good homicide detective, Jack. One of the best, according to people I know in the Chicago department. When it came to clearing cases, you apparently were a rock star."

I winced at the past tense, as Cubby knew I would. Clearly he wanted something other than a late-night beer and chitchat. He took another hit of the Blue Moon and said, "Thing is, the police chief down in Naples, Wade Hansen, is a friend of mine. We had lunch today. He told me he needs help with a tough case. I worked late tonight and decided to stop on the way home to tell you about it."

I felt a hit of adrenaline surge into my bloodstream at the mention of the words "tough case." An old firehorse hearing the bell.

Naples is a small town about thirty miles south of Fort Myers Beach on Florida's southwest Gulf Coast. It is one of those places where the superrich congregate to spend the money they made somewhere else. Marisa told me that Naples, unlike Palm Beach, for example, is the home of "quiet money." The city employs a New York PR firm to keep its name *out* of the news, and especially off those "best places to live" lists, she said.

Quiet money? I guess that means they don't grab people like me by the lapels and shout, "I'm rich and you're not!" But when you see their penthouse condos and waterfront mansions, and their Bentleys, Porsches, Maseratis, and Ferraris, the effect is the same. Maybe the residents worry that, if the hoi polloi knew about all that wretched excess, they might form an ugly crowd, arm themselves with farm implements, storm the iron fences surrounding the palatial homes, and set up a guillotine in a downtown park. To a kid from Wrigleyville, Naples might as well be on the far side of the moon. The first time Marisa and I went to dinner in the city, I was concerned that the maitre d' might size me up and say with a sneer, "Deliveries to the rear."

F. Scott Fitzgerald wrote, "Let me tell you about the very rich. They are different from you and me." Credit that literary knowledge to Brother Timothy, my English lit professor at Loyola. Interesting guy. He was a semipro boxer before becoming a Jesuit priest. "In the ring, I got the crap beaten out of me and the sense beaten into me," he once told our class. "Some pugs see stars as they hit the canvas. I saw Jesus."

"WHAT KIND of help does your buddy need?" I asked Cubby, trying to sound nonchalant.

"Call it consulting," he said. "Wade has a couple of possible homicides. His department doesn't have much experience with that kind of thing. So I mentioned your name. The idea being for you to just take a look at the case files and tell him what you think."

Homicides? Now that fire bell was really clanging.

"What do you mean by *possible* homicides?" I asked. "You get a corpse with a bullet hole in it floating in the Chicago River, or someone in a dumpster with a kitchen knife in the gizzard, and know you've got an actual murder."

"One of the deaths was an apparent heart attack, apparent because there was no autopsy, and the other was a fall down a staircase. Wade suspects that those two deaths might have been murders. Something about the circumstances. He wasn't specific about that with me. He just said he could use a set of experienced eyes to review the case files. If you're interested, you have an appointment with him and the mayor in the mayor's office in city hall tomorrow morning at eight thirty."

"You already made an appointment for me?"

"If you don't want to go, I'll call Wade to cancel before I go the airport." He smiled and added, "He said they'd have coffee and doughnuts."

What cop, or even an ex-cop, could resist an offer like that? Cubby had me at murders, even possible ones, but the coffee and doughnuts greased the skids, as he knew they would.

"Okay, Cubby, I'll go to the meeting, just to hear what they have in mind. But I might not do anything more. I'm out of the cop game and I've got the bar to run."

"Fair enough. Wade understands that."

When Cubby was gone, I went back into the stateroom, which is a pretentious term for a bedroom on a little houseboat like mine, but that's the proper nautical terminology, so I use it. Marisa and Joe were both sound asleep. I joined her in bed and soon sunk into the sound sleep of a person who'd put his ass in harm's way and survived, and now got a monthly check in the mail for his trouble.

I didn't know it at the time, of course, but that conversation with Cubby Cullen was about to propel me into the heart of a mystery that would challenge the abilities even of Detective Sergeant Jack Starkey, and possibly bring an end to my idyllic new life.

4.

A Double Homicide, Maybe

At seven thirty the next morning, I was cruising south on Estero Boulevard toward Naples in my red 1963 Corvette Stingray convertible, not coincidentally the same kind of car Jack Stoney drives, and also, not coincidentally, the same kind of car Tod and Buz drove in the old *Route 66* TV series I loved as a boy.

I never did know why their names, which I saw in the show credits, were spelled in that unusual way, dropping the final "d" from Todd and "z" from Buzz. But that didn't matter, because the car was the real star of that show. I dreamed of someday owning one like it, and now I did.

I'd driven down from Chicago in my Jeep Cherokee, which was good for the long winters. A bad-weather "beater," such vehicles are called. In Florida, I didn't need four-wheel drive, so I decided to realize that boyhood dream.

I bought the classic 'Vette at an auto auction I saw advertised in the *Fort Myers News-Press* which was held at the Sarasota County Fairgrounds on Ringling Boulevard. I did my homework; using *Kelley Blue Book* and *Hemmings Motor News* as guides, I determined that the values of vintage Corvettes run between $54,000 and $130,000, depending upon the model, options, and condition. My 'Vette was not the pricier ZO6 model; it had a 340 horsepower V8, standard transmission, air-conditioning, AM-FM radio, red leather seats, and power windows. It was in good condition, having been driven 80,000 miles by its original owner, according to the fact sheet.

I maybe paid too much at $63,000 because of a bidding war with some elderly gent wearing an ascot and Panama hat. Maybe he was a savvy collector, or a shill for the auction house. You know what they say: If you don't know who the sucker is in a poker game, it's you. Boys and their toys.

As soon as Bill Stevens learned that I'd bought the 'Vette, he had Jack Stoney, not to be outdone by his flesh-and-blood counterpart, sell his 1974 green Pontiac GTO convertible—that Goat being a sweet ride in its own right—and get the same model Corvette too. He paid a bargain price at an auction, of course.

The sparkling waters of the Gulf of Mexico were on my right and Estero Bay on my left as I drove over the Lovers Key Causeway. I'd violated the laws of classic car restoration by adding a nine-speaker Bose audio system, similar to the system I have in the *Phoenix*. It was cranked up loud, playing the haunting strains of "Hotel California" by the Eagles.

Sorry, Marisa, but Bach has no place in a Corvette.

On the gulf side of the road, mostly Spanish-style minimansions stood among smaller ranch-style houses and cottages, as well as some rundown shacks. Many of the latter two categories had for-sale signs out front. These were teardowns; an owner could get a million plus just for the beachfront dirt. Some of the for-sale signs were from Marisa's agency, Paradise Realty. Each transaction earned her a commission several times my annual Chicago PD salary.

Seagulls wheeled and cackled above the azure waters; overhead, a canopy of fluffy white clouds drifted across the sky. An osprey plunged head first into the gulf, like a dive-bomber attacking a carrier, coming up with a wriggling silver fish for breakfast. I slowed as a snowy egret strolled on spindly legs across the roadway, taking its own sweet time.

I drove south on Estero Boulevard to Bonita Beach Road, swung left for a mile, and then right onto Vanderbilt Drive to Vanderbilt Beach Road, where I turned left near the entrance to a palatial Ritz-Carlton beachfront hotel. I came up behind a yellow Rolls-Royce Corniche convertible, sticker price about 450K. Marisa told me that

Judge Judy has a condo in Naples and drives a car like that. Maybe it was her. If I paid that much for a car, I'd have to live in it.

I hung a right onto US 41 South and made the fifteen-minute drive to Fifth Avenue South, the downtown Naples equivalent of Worth Avenue in Palm Beach and Rodeo Drive in Beverly Hills. I turned right onto Fifth and rolled past the ultrachic restaurants, art galleries, jewelry stores, and clothing boutiques, as well as a great many banks, stock brokerage firms, and trust company offices. When Willie Sutton was asked why he robbed banks, he said, "Because that's where the money is." Which is why all those pricey eateries, shops, and financial institutions are here. With the top down, I could almost hear the dry rustling of bonds maturing and the ka-ching of stock dividends accruing.

Which is not to say I wasted any energy envying the wealthy residents of Naples. My police department pension, generous book-editing fees from Bill Stevens, and profits from The Drunken Parrot were more than sufficient to meet my needs. We are who we are. To paraphrase another Willie (Shakespeare), jealousy is a green-eyed monster.

NAPLES CITY hall is located on Riverside Circle, a quiet street lined with banyan, royal poinciana, and palm trees just south of the downtown shopping area. I turned into the parking lot, pulled into a visitor's spot, and went inside.

I was wearing a navy blue blazer with brass buttons over a white, open-collared shirt, tan slacks, and Top-Siders, no socks. If I washed ashore on Martha's Vineyard, I could stroll right into the nearest cocktail party and ask for a towel and a gin and tonic. But even in my yacht club uniform, I didn't feel that I belonged in Naples. As they say at the Baby Doll Polka Lounge, you put lipstick on a pig and it's still a pig.

I found the information desk in the lobby and told an older, smartly dressed woman with tortoise-shell reading glasses hanging on a gold chain around her neck, and her grey hair in a bun, that

I had a meeting with Mayor Charles Beaumont and Police Chief Wade Hansen.

She told me the mayor's office was on the second floor and gestured toward a stairway and an elevator. Unlike many Florida residents, I still had all of my original joints, so I took the stairs, two at a time, just to impress the woman.

I turned right down a hallway, came to the mayor's office, opened a double glass door with the mayor's name painted on it in gold lettering, and stepped into the lobby. A very pretty young woman sat behind the reception desk. I introduced myself and said I had an appointment with Mayor Beaumont and Chief Hansen.

She told me that her name was "Kathi with an i," and that they were expecting me. I guess she was accustomed to providing that spelling to everyone she met for the first time, just to clear up any confusion if they ever needed to write her name.

Kathi with an i stood, led me down a hallway, knocked on a closed wooden office door, opened it without waiting for a reply, and stepped aside, allowing me to enter a large, well-appointed corner office with a view of a big jacaranda tree in full bloom though the window. Marisa knew all about trees, as well as flowers and plants, and would often point to them and tell me their names. In return, I offered to teach her what I knew about firearms, which is a lot, but she declined.

A man was seated behind a desk and another on one of two club chairs, drinking coffee from china cups. They stood when I came in. As promised, there was an open box of Dunkin' Donuts on a coffee table. I'd overslept and skipped breakfast. I spotted a jelly doughnut with my name on it and hoped it had strawberry filling, my favorite.

I had no trouble telling who was who. I am, after all, a trained detective. The mayor was obviously the taller guy in his early seventies with a full mane of slicked-back silver hair, wearing an outfit similar to mine, but made of better fabrics. A patrician. The police chief was of medium height, bald and muscular, with a square jaw and a tattoo of an eagle, globe, and anchor on his left forearm bearing the motto "*Semper Fi.*" A former marine, like me.

He was wearing a starched white uniform shirt with epaulets and a gold badge, blue twill pants, and a wide shiny black leather duty belt holding a pair of silver handcuffs, a can of Mace, and a Beretta semiauto pistol in a black holster.

I wasn't carrying. I was accustomed to having to walk through a metal detector when entering a municipal building, and, even though I had a concealed carry permit, the people didn't know me here, so I didn't want to cause a fuss. But this was Naples, not Chicago. There'd been no metal detector in the lobby, or any visible security at all. I could have strolled in with a shoulder-fired, surface-to-air missile, unless the reception lady was a lot tougher than she looked.

"Jack, I'm Charles Beaumont and this is Chief Wade Hansen," the mayor said, walking to me. "We appreciate your coming to discuss a possible situation we have."

We all shook hands and hizzoner gestured me into one of the club chairs. Hansen took the other chair. Beaumont sat on the sofa and asked if I wanted coffee, which I did. He poured a cup for me from a pot on the coffee table and didn't mention the doughnuts, which left me conflicted. Would it be impolite to help myself this early in our relationship?

I said to both of them, "I don't know if I can be of any help, but I'm happy to hear about what's going on and tell you what I think."

"That's all we expect, Jack," Hansen answered.

Now that we were friends, I decided to go for it. I stood, walked over to the doughnut table, picked up the jelly doughnut, and took a bite. It was strawberry. Remembering my mother's admonition to not speak with my mouth full, I took a moment to chew and swallow as I returned to my chair, then looked at Hansen and said, "I assume you've got detectives on your force, chief."

"We have two, and they're very competent," he answered. "But they've been here their entire careers and have no experience with this kind of situation."

"Which is?"

The mayor stood, walked over to his desk, picked up a sheet of paper and a pen, and handed them to me. "Before we tell you more, I need you to sign this confidentiality agreement," he said.

I scanned the agreement. It required me to keep everything I was about to learn an absolute secret in perpetuity or the City of Naples, Florida, could remove my testicles and make me eat them—or words to that effect.

By now, I was curious. I signed and handed the document back to Beaumont. He glanced at it, maybe to make certain I hadn't signed it "Eleanor Roosevelt," which is, in fact, how I'd first signed my divorce papers, and put it back into the drawer.

The mayor nodded at the police chief, who began by saying, "Six months ago, a woman drowned in her swimming pool while doing laps. She was seventy-eight years old. She was a widow, and her son and daughter, who live in Boston and Philadelphia, didn't want an autopsy. The death was ruled as being due to natural causes. Maybe a stroke or heart attack."

"And you think it wasn't one of those?" I asked.

"Something about it bothered me," Hansen said. "Read the file and see what you think."

I finished the doughnut. A dab of strawberry jelly dripped onto my shirtfront. I left it there, so as not to call attention to this egregious faux pas.

"Ten days ago, a seventy-two-year-old man broke his neck by falling down a staircase in his home," Hansen told me.

"Old people trip sometimes," I said, deductively.

I'd tripped stepping onto the deck of the *Phoenix* a few months ago, bruised my shoulder and sprained my ankle. And I'm not all that old. It was midnight on a moonless night; a heavy rain had made the deck wet and slippery and I was wearing cowboy boots. Boaters' tip: always wear deck shoes when boarding a boat after a rain, even when stone-cold sober.

"They do," Hansen responded. "But, again, it just seemed to me that something wasn't right . . ."

Beaumont interrupted him. "We haven't had a homicide here since a woman put cream, Splenda, and cyanide into her husband's morning coffee. She was his third wife, twenty-eight to his seventy-nine. His other heirs got a court order for an autopsy. The wife got thirty years in the Lowell Correctional Institution instead of his

$200 million estate. That was fifteen years ago, so we're a bit out of practice in the murder area."

"We're hoping you'll come on as a paid consultant," Hansen said. "Read the case files, look into the backgrounds of the two victims, and see if anything seems suspicious to you."

"Sure," I said, rather flattered that my detecting skills still had some market value. "I can do that."

"Good," the chief said.

The mayor nodded his agreement and looked pleased. I stood and took another doughnut, this one chocolate-coated with sprinkles. Now that I was part of the team, I didn't think it impolite to have another. No one had mentioned my fee, but I wasn't above working for doughnuts and the chance to get back into the "murder area."

"What if these two deaths turn out to be something other than accidental?" I asked as I returned to my chair. "Murders happen . . ."

"Let me be frank," Beaumont said. He sighed and ran his fingers through his hair. "It's my job to make certain that the beaches have enough sand, that mosquitoes are controlled, and that nothing threatens property values. We don't want to be like Detroit, where the average home price is less than the cost of a steak dinner. Murder is something that isn't supposed to happen here."

Or like Chicago, I thought. Obviously there was no way anyone would ever equate Naples to Chicago or Detroit, crime wise, absent having a band of drug-crazed killers riding motorcycles along Fifth Avenue South and spraying people on the street with automatic weapons fire. But I got his point: A murder in this town would go over like a turd in a punchbowl, as they would say at the Baby Doll.

"How soon can you start?" Hansen asked.

I looked at my watch. I had nothing pressing to do for the rest of the morning. I figured that I could read the files, make some notes, and be back in Fort Myers Beach in time for lunch. "Now is good," I told him.

"We'd prefer that you not take the files out of the building," Hansen said. "I'll set you up in a conference room down the hall."

In case I felt the urge to turn the files over to the *Naples Daily News*? But they were writing the checks, so they made the rules. We stood and Beaumont asked, "Would a fee of $5,000 for this initial phase be acceptable?"

Acceptable? Be still my beating heart. "That'll work," I answered, trying not to salivate.

I wondered what he meant by "initial phase." More than just reading the files and offering an opinion? Whatever it was, I was being extremely well paid for doing it. When the check cleared, I could have my boat repainted, take Marisa on a Caribbean cruise, and have money left over for a ring job on my 'Vette.

5.

Follow The Money

I was seated at a polished mahogany table the length of Soldier Field located in a second-floor conference room near the mayor's office. There were two three-ring binders on the table plus a fresh cup of coffee and another doughnut, this one powdered sugar.

Floor-to-ceiling windows overlooked a park. On one wall of the room was the Seal of the City of Naples. It contained a drawing of city hall and the words "City of Naples, Florida, On the Gulf." There were seven stars along the bottom. I guess dollar signs would have been considered garish, even if appropriate.

The park was nicely landscaped with flowerbeds and palm trees. A fountain whose bowl was shaped like a seashell spewed a stream of water from the mouth of a stone fish. A Chicago friend had a statue in his backyard of a cherub with the water coming out of his penis. It's all a matter of personal taste.

Through the window, I also could see a single-story concrete building across the park; a sign on the front lawn said this was the Naples Police Department. I used to work out of a Chicago PD station house on South Wentworth Avenue on the city's South Side, in Chinatown. The atmosphere there was very different from where I now was; not nearly so picturesque, but the Chinese food was better than any you could find in Naples.

Joy Yee's Noodles, where I often ate lunch, was a favorite among cops, and also FBI agents whose offices were nearby on West Roosevelt Road. One noon hour, when I wasn't there, a man who must have been new to the city attempted to rob the place. Like the guy who tried to stick up the Baby Doll Polka Lounge, but worse. Talk about a bad day. Bill Stevens used both scenes in his Jack Stoney books.

The binders contained reports from the uniformed police officers first on the scenes of the two Naples deaths, from a detective named Samuels who arrived later, from the Naples crime scene investigator (idea for new TV series: *CSI Naples*), and from the Collier County coroner. Everything was professionally done. I was not at all certain I could add anything to what seemed to be a very complete and competent investigation. Except for the fact that Wade Hansen wasn't buying it. He had good credentials, so I gave a lot of weight to his instincts. He'd been the chief of police in Fall River, Massachusetts, before taking the Naples job. Like Cubby Cullen, he'd learned the job up north, packed up his skills and his sidearm, and set up shop amongst the palm trees. I guess I was now in the category too.

The first victim was a woman named Eileen Stephenson. As Hansen said, she was seventy-eight years old when she died. She was found floating facedown in the swimming pool behind her house by the pool cleaner at ten A.M.

Her son told police she swam laps at seven every morning. There were photos of the pool and of her body, at the scene and in the morgue. She had short brown hair and looked to be in very good shape for a woman her age, presumably from the swimming.

Also in the file was a copy of her obituary from the *Naples Daily News*. It reported that Eileen Stephenson won a bronze medal in the breaststroke at the 1956 Summer Olympics in Melbourne. I guessed it was this fact that caused Hansen to be suspicious of the death, especially in light of the absence of an autopsy and the fact that there was no evidence that she had any medical issues. A Detective Samuels had interviewed her doctor, who reported that she'd had an annual physical two months before her death, and she was in good health. She could have had a heart attack or stroke while swimming but, given her medical condition, as well as her swimming background, I could see why Hansen suspected murder.

The obituary said that Mrs. Stephenson's husband, Bruce, had died four years earlier and was the founder of a company called

Stephenson Industries, which manufactured such things as titanium missile parts and engine casings for motorcycles. It must have been very successful because, according to the obit, the Stephensons had been philanthropists, donating large sums of money to worthy causes in Naples and back home in Indianapolis.

Hmmm.

Rule number one of investigative work is to follow the money. There's a rule number two, but I'd been off the job awhile and had forgotten it. Something about sex, I think. Presumably, Mrs. Stephenson's son and daughter were her primary heirs. I made a mental note to see if I could get a complete list from her will. Whoever they were, they could now afford nicer cars.

I turned to the second file. The deceased was a man named Lester Gandolf, who would never be older than seventy-two. The police report stated that his wife, Elizabeth, age sixty-eight, found him at one A.M. lying at the bottom of the marble staircase in their house. She said that she and Lester had gone to bed at ten that night. Lester was reading when she fell asleep. She was awakened by a noise, saw that he wasn't in bed, and went looking for him. She said that it was not his habit to get up like that and go downstairs, or anywhere but to the bathroom, as old men do during the night.

My Chicago friend with the statue once told me, while we were sitting on his back porch drinking beers and watching the cherub relieve himself, "I remember a time when urgency and frequency referred to sex, and not urination." Not a condition I looked forward to. His one other pearl of wisdom was, "Remember Jack, nice girls like it too." Maybe not as deep as a saying by Confucius, but useful nevertheless.

Elizabeth Gandolf did allow an autopsy, which found her husband to be in good health—except for the fact that he was dead from a broken neck. She told the coroner that Lester had no history of dizziness or of any other medical condition that could cause him to trip. His medical records reflected that as well.

Of course Lester could have gotten up that night, decided to go down to the kitchen for a ham sandwich, and tripped on the stairs.

But still, something did seem possibly rotten in the State of Denmark, as Hansen had suggested.

Lester Gandolf's newspaper obituary was also included in the file. Like the Stephensons, the Gandolfs were very wealthy. Billionaires, in fact, rich enough to hit the annual *Forbes* magazine list of the nation's Upper One Percenters. Lester's grandfather started a meatpacking company in Chicago, which grew into a multinational company called Gandolf Foods. I'd heard of it. It owned many recognizable brands found on supermarket shelves.

Lester and Elizabeth Gandolf were prominent philanthropists, too; they supported many of the same Naples charities and arts organizations as had the Stephensons. The Gandolfs were also major contributors to, and fund-raisers for, the Republican Party. I suppose you could have held a caucus for the Collier County Democratic Party in a phone booth, if there were still any phone booths. If not, a broom closet would do.

If Eileen Stephenson and Lester Gandolf, both apparently in good health when they died, had been murdered in a small town like Naples and their deaths made to look accidental, any competent investigator would try to find all of the connections between the two victims because that might suggest a single killer and uncover a motive. An obvious connection was that they were both rich and moved in the same social circles. Someone would have to dig deeper. Maybe by saying "initial phase," the mayor meant that the someone was me.

After reading the files, I had a revelation. I wanted that third doughnut. Powdered sugar is not my favorite kind, but one must adapt to the circumstances while on duty. I ate it while I drank the rest of my coffee and contemplated what I'd just read.

Hansen entered the conference room, sat at the table, and said, "Well Jack, what do you think?"

"I think that both of these cases bear further investigation. I can see why they're troubling you."

"Will you lead that investigation for us?" he asked, as I suspected he would. I hadn't decided what my answer would be.

"I have a business to run," I told him.

"Your bar in Fort Myers Beach."

"That's the one."

"The city budget has a large contingency fund for use at the mayor's discretion. Mayor Beaumont considers this matter to be of very great importance, as do I. We will make certain you are well compensated for your time, plus expenses, and have any resources you need. That's in addition to the $5,000 you've already earned for giving us your opinion about whether there is, in fact, anything to investigate."

As I said, I was living a very comfortable life. I didn't need the money that Chief Hansen was offering. But, I realized as I was reading those files, the part of my brain that controlled deductive reasoning, think of it as the Sherlock Holmes lobe, had been dormant for too long. And Sam Longtree, the Seminole Indian who was my bartender, was a very competent fellow who could pick up any slack created by my detective work. He was well named because he had the physique of a Sequoia: Six foot five inches of pure muscle.

"I still don't know if I can add any value to your investigation, chief," I said. "And I don't want to cause you any trouble with your detectives. You know, who's the hotshot asshole from Chicago?"

"Let me handle my people. Part of the reason we brought you in is so we can keep the investigation confidential. Word gets out we think there's maybe a serial killer bumping off the citizenry, we'd have a major-league cluster fuck, ending up with both the mayor and me unemployed."

"Okay," I told him. "I'm willing to give it a shot."

Shot, as in the old college try. Not as in gunfire, I hoped. I didn't want any more holes in my hide.

6.

If The Mountain Won't Come To Muhammad

Marisa and I were having dinner at the Tarpon Lodge on Pine Island, a relatively undeveloped barrier island in the Gulf of Mexico connected to the Florida mainland by a causeway near Fort Myers.

The lodge provided a real taste of Old Florida. It was built as a hunting and fishing hotel in 1926 and has been preserved pretty much in its original condition, which is why I like it. So much of coastal Florida has been bulldozed, paved, and overdeveloped that, but for the water and palm trees, you might be in any part of America. But parts of Old Florida still remain; you just have to know where to look.

It was a balmy, moonlit evening as we sat at an outdoor table on the covered porch, which overlooked the calm waters of Pine Island Sound. White tablecloths and candles. A light wind rustled the palm fronds, and the jacaranda trees on the property were in full, purple bloom. There is a reason that this stretch of gulf-front land, running from Fort Myers to Naples, is called The Paradise Coast.

I was enjoying my fish tacos and Marisa her blackened grouper, which she accompanied with a nice pinot grigio. It was an odd time and setting to be talking about murder, but that's just what we were doing. By the time the dessert course arrived, key lime pie for me and crème brûlée for her, I'd told her all about my new assignment in Naples.

That was a direct violation of the confidentiality agreement I'd signed. But I trusted Marisa implicitly; she was a very smart lady, and

I wanted her insights and opinions about the case, especially because my detecting skills were somewhat rusty. Rusty in the sense that I'd been on the case for a while and hadn't a clue about who had done what to whom. That's not the kind of situation report—sit rep, we called it in the corps—you want to give to your superiors: Sorry fellas, I haven't got Clue One about what's happening, and here's my invoice.

"So what's your next step?" Marisa asked, putting me on the spot.

"I don't have enough hard evidence yet to hold up in court, but it's clear to me that Colonel Mustard did it in the library with the candlestick."

Marisa smiled. "So you've got nothing."

"That would be correct," I admitted under her withering cross-examination. "One of Hansen's detectives, a man he trusts to keep it quiet, is pulling together backgrounds on the lives of Eileen Stephenson and Lester Gandolf. Obviously I can't go around Naples knocking on doors and asking about them. Other than that, I'm keeping my options open."

"I may have an idea."

That sounded promising, so I said, "Tell me."

"If the mountain won't come to Muhammad, Muhammad must go to the mountain," Marisa said, enigmatically.

"I see," I said, sagely, even though I didn't.

She continued: "The answer to the mystery might lie within the confines of Naples high society," she explained. "I'm suggesting that you must get inside that rarefied circle in order to figure out what's going on."

"You mean, like, going undercover?" I'm a quick study when someone gives me the answer.

"Right. Those people aren't going to open up to Detective Sergeant Jack Starkey, retired, owner of The Drunken Parrot, and resident of a houseboat in Fort Myers Beach," she said, running her finger around the rim of her wine glass, causing that high-pitched, squeaking sound.

I'd once seen a man appearing at the Illinois State Fair play "The Battle Hymn of the Republic" and other patriotic songs on water glasses using that same technique. It was highly entertaining, if you were having a slow day.

"I see," I said again, still not.

"So you'll need to do a Jay Gatsby number on them," Marisa said, taking a sip of her pinot.

I'd read *The Great Gatsby* but I still wasn't following her idea.

She took a dainty bite of her crème brûlée and dabbed at her mouth with the white cloth napkin. "You should pose as one of them, a rich guy," she explained. "Move among them and see what you can turn up. I assume that the mayor and police chief can help you do that. And maybe an instructor in etiquette."

I was much impressed by her idea. If she ever tired of the real estate business, maybe we could be partners in a private investigation firm: "Starkey and Fernandez de Lopez, No Mystery Too Tough, No Injustice Too Small." She could be the brains and me the brawn.

"That's a brilliant plan," I said. "Dinner's on me."

"It already was," she said. "I require something more."

"Shall we adjourn to the *Phoenix* and see what we can come up with?"

"Works for me, big guy," Marisa said with a seductive smile. In fact, all of her smiles were seductive.

I caught the waiter's eye and said "Check, please," wondering if I could put this dinner on my new expense account, now that Marisa had all but broken the case. If I'd thought of that earlier, I'd have had the lobster.

7.

My Name Is Frank Chance

I awoke to the sound of seagulls cackling outside an open window and waves washing up onto a beach. I opened my eyes and saw lace curtains being blown inward by a warm breeze. I was lying in a canopy bed between lime-green satin sheets.

For a brief, surreal moment, I could not remember where I was. Certainly not aboard *Phoenix*, because I don't own lace curtains, a canopy bed, or satin sheets. Before I met Marisa, I slept in a sleeping bag atop my bed. It saved on laundry. She bought some sheets for me at Target.

I sat up, yawned, and stretched, just like Joe did every morning, and looked around the bedroom. It was bigger than an average-sized 7-Eleven. There was antique furniture, an Oriental rug over a parquet floor, large framed oil paintings on the walls, and a high ceiling with a painting of fat little cherubs romping in the clouds.

I am not homophobic, but it all did seem rather gay. Had I been reborn as Little Lord Fauntleroy?

I swung out of bed, padded in my boxer shorts over to the window, and looked out at manicured English gardens and a lawn that ran down to a beach on the Gulf of Mexico. Marisa had instructed me that location was the most important thing in real estate. This was surely the mother of all locations.

I yawned and stretched again, clearing my head, went into the bathroom, and turned on the shower. As I waited for it to warm up, I looked into the mirror and mentally recited my new identity:

My name is Frank Chance, playboy extraordinaire. I have every material possession a person could want. My father made his fortune as a currency trader in New York and I've been doing my best to deplete it all my life. I'm a bachelor. Both of my parents are deceased. I am staying here in my aunt's house while looking for a place to buy in Naples . . .

I paused, gave myself a wink in the mirror, and added: And I'm a hunka hunka burnin' love.

That last wasn't a part of the undercover identity that Marisa and I cooked up. But when you have the opportunity to reinvent yourself, why not go whole hog? Jack Stoney, eat your heart out.

It was my idea that my undercover name be Frank Chance. As any true-blue Chicago Cubs fan knows, he was the Hall-of-Fame first baseman for the 1908 team, the last to win a World Series, and also part of the famous Tinker-to-Evers-to-Chance double-play combination.

Maybe, with proper instruction from my new aunt on how to behave like a swell, and wearing my new uncle's wardrobe, I could actually pull this off.

Undercover cops pose as criminals trying to entrap the bad guys. I'd done that a few times myself. But I liked it this way much better, even if I was more at home among the criminal element of the City of Chicago than I'd be in the rarefied world of Naples high society I was about to enter.

I tested the shower water, stepped in, and sang a few bars of Steppenwolf's "Born To Be Wild" as I soaped up. In the marines, we called our morning routine the three S's: Shave, shower, and shit. When Claire and I were living together before we got married, I said that to her one morning, explaining the meaning. I thought she'd find it to be clever. She didn't. She reminded me that I was no longer a marine and I should leave that sort of lingo behind if I wanted our relationship to continue until breakfast.

My shower finished, I dried myself with a thick, white terry cloth towel and entered a large walk-in closet that looked more like a ritzy men's clothing store than one person's wardrobe. There were racks of soft tropical wool suits; rows of more formal business and evening clothing; shoes for every occasion; and shelves containing stack upon stack of shirts in every hue of the rainbow.

Fortunately, my "uncle" and I were close enough to the same size that I could wear his haberdashery. I brought my own underwear, socks, toothbrush, and running shoes.

I stood before the casual section and selected a navy blue silk shirt, pleated white linen slacks, and black leather Gucci loafers, which I slipped on without socks. My uncle and I even had the same shoe size, twelve; by the look of the leather soles, this pair had never been worn.

I knew from investigating cases in the wealthy neighborhoods of Chicago that gentlemen of the highest social classes did not wear socks with this sort of casual outfit. In that regard, they were no different than the vagrants panhandling on the streets of the city, except that the dandies had no open sores on their ankles.

I'd once arrested a man for murdering his wife's lover. When I cuffed him on the porch of his Gold Coast row house, I noticed that he was wearing shoes without socks, a detail I found odd because it was February. A slave to fashion. I wondered if that guy would wear socks with his prison-issue sneakers at Stateville.

I admired myself in a full-length mirror. I'd cleaned up nicely, if I had to say so myself, which I did, because no one else was there. Good-bye Jack Starkey, retired homicide detective and bar owner; hello Frank Chance, trust-fund bon vivant.

I undid one more button on my shirt to show some chest hair, looked in the mirror, and then rebuttoned it. Frank Chance was a socialite, not a pimp. I was ready to begin my first full day of what might have been the most unusual undercover assignment ever.

It was time to head downstairs to join my aunt for breakfast.

8.

Uncle Reggie And Aunt Ashley

The mayor and the police chief were initially upset that I'd shared the details of my assignment with Marisa, but there are special rules for beautiful women, and this particular beautiful woman also had a good idea for solving the case.

I'd arranged for her to meet with them in the mayor's office so she could explain her plan. When the meeting was concluded, Mayor Beaumont thanked Marisa for her input, told her that her undercover idea was "brilliant," and said that he hoped she'd continue to advise us as the investigation moved forward. Chief Hansen nodded in agreement as he looked at Marisa's legs. Maybe she should have been a cop and me a realtor.

Mayor Beaumont and his wife were friends of my fake aunt, Lady Ashley Howe. She was the widow of Australian press lord Sir Reginald Howe, who died five years earlier when his private jet disappeared on a flight from Sydney to Hong Kong, never to be found. He owned a chain of tabloid newspapers in England, Australia, Canada, and the United States. Queen Elizabeth knighted him in the same ceremony in which Elton John received his title.

Lady Ashley was an American whom Sir Reginald met when she was nineteen. She was standing on a revolving platform beside a Lincoln Continental at the Detroit Auto Show, the mayor told me. Sir Reginald was a car collector, there to view the new models. Sir Reggie obviously found one he liked, and it wasn't the new Lincoln Continental.

Beaumont said that, after her husband's death, Lady Ashley—everyone called her "Ash," he noted—put their homes in Australia, Tuscany, Saint Moritz, and Cannes, and their apartment in Paris, up for sale and moved permanently to the Naples house.

After the meeting with Marisa, Beaumont approached Ash with the idea about me posing as her nephew. He told her that my undercover assignment was confidential, so he couldn't share the details with her except to say that I was a retired Chicago detective helping the city with an important and sensitive investigation. Her role would be to help me meet people in her social circle.

Ash told him she'd be thrilled to take part in the investigation, whatever it was about. She would not only introduce me into Naples society, she said, she would also tutor me on how to behave in her world. She thought I needed that because, I assumed, there was no book titled *Social Skills For Dummies.*

Marisa warned me not to get too friendly with any of the "society sluts" that I would be meeting. "Cougars," she also called them, "on the prowl for a handsome rich guy, with an emphasis on the rich."

I assured her that she had nothing to worry about because these women would spit me out like a bad oyster when they discovered my true identity. She punched me hard on the arm because that apparently wasn't the answer she wanted to hear.

I walked down the curved marble staircase from the second floor, resisting the urge to slide down the wide banister, and caught a view of the Gulf of Mexico, framed by palm and banyan trees through large Palladian windows.

Hanging on a wall at the bottom of the staircase was a painting of a small green footbridge going over a pond with flowering purple bushes behind it. I knew that it wasn't the Michigan Avenue Bridge over the Chicago River because it was too small, and the water didn't look polluted. A brass plaque on the bottom of the ornate wooden frame ID'd the painting as *The Japanese Bridge at Giverny* by Claude Monet.

The only artwork I owned was a watercolor of Wrigley Field by a Chicago artist, Paul Ashack, which my ex-wife, Claire, gave me as a birthday present one year. Even though it's an original, I suspected that this Monet fellow's painting was worth more to an art collector, even if not to me.

My painting hung above my bed on the *Phoenix* and was one of the things Claire didn't want in our divorce settlement. She also didn't want my softball bats, my Chicago PD marksmanship trophies, my bass lures, or my extensive collection of beer bottle openers. Freud admitted that he didn't know what women wanted. Me neither. Some of those beer can openers are collectors' items.

We're sure not in Wrigleyville anymore, Toto, I thought as I walked through the french doors leading out to the backyard.

I found Ash seated at a round, glass-topped, wrought iron table reading the *National Tattler*, one of Sir Reginald's newspapers. A big bold page-one headline revealed that Russian President Vladimir Putin was secretly gay. Apparently the *Tattler* had scooped the *New York Times*, the *Chicago Tribune*, *Pravda*, and *60 Minutes* on that one.

Beaumont introduced me to Ash the previous night over dinner at a fancy French restaurant called Provence. I was still dressed as Jack Starkey then. The other diners likely assumed I was Ash's driver or bodyguard, especially when I told the waiter to hold the black truffle sauce on my filet mignon and bring ketchup. Which I meant, and which he did. I guess the chef whipped up the ketchup from scratch because it didn't taste like Heinz, but I made do. I knew that I'd have to improve my table manners when posing as Frank Chance.

Over dinner, I could tell that Ash was excited about her role in the drama that was about to begin. She confessed to being a bit bored with her life in Naples, especially with her husband gone, and said that it would be "a hoot to scam the swells," even if she didn't know why we were doing it.

She was—I will avoid being condescending to a fine lady by adding "still"—a very attractive woman. At dinner, she wore her long blonde hair in a single braid down the middle of her back. Her hourglass figure was draped in a low-cut, red satin dress. She had green eyes, and the smooth skin of a much younger woman.

When I told her she looked much too young to be my aunt, she said it was all thanks to plastic surgery, a personal trainer who "works me like a rented mule," and "the miracle of Botox."

"When you get to be my age, sweetie, nature is not your friend," she said. "It needs all the help it can get."

When I approached the table, Ash looked up from her paper, smiled, winked, and said, "Well, well, the frog has been transformed into a handsome prince."

"Croak, croak," I replied, and sat down.

"Let's have some breakfast while we chat," she said.

She picked up a small crystal bell and shook it. A man appeared from the doorway to the kitchen pushing a brass cart like the ones hotels use for room service. He was somewhere in his sixties, with thinning hair and a pencil mustache. He was wearing a starched white jacket and neatly pressed black pants. The butler, I presumed. I wondered if his name was Jeeves.

"Thank you, Martin," Ash said. "We'll serve ourselves."

When Martin had gone back into the house, Ash said, "I asked Suzette, she's my cook, to make sourdough french toast topped with cinnamon sugar and plantains sautéed in butter and brandy, strong espresso to kick-start your motor, freshly squeezed OJ from trees on my property, side dishes of thick smoked bacon and grilled chorizo sausages, banana nut muffins, and a bowl of fresh fruit. I hope that's okay."

Okay? I began to salivate like one of Pavlov's dogs—and also like my Uncle Lou at family dinners. "That sounds great," I said. "I usually make do with drip coffee, OJ straight from the carton, and a Pop-Tart."

She served me generous portions of everything as I watched a gecko stroll along the marble balustrade surrounding the patio. As I tucked into my breakfast, Ash regarded me with a serious look. I noticed that she'd put only fruit and a bran muffin on her plate.

"Is this assignment dangerous?" she asked.

I got the feeling that maybe she hoped it was. "No, I don't think so," I told her. "And certainly not for you."

She smiled. "I have absolutely no doubt that Detective Jack Stoney will crack the case."

That surprised me. "So you know Bill Stevens's books?"

"Oh yes. I've read every one. I was amazed when Charlie told me they're based on you. I have a celebrity in my home! Too bad I can't tell anybody."

She picked up a ripe strawberry and took a bite. "Say, do you think that what's-his-face, the author, would ever base one of his characters on me?"

"I'll introduce you to Bill Stevens the next time he's in town," I told her. "And I'll suggest that to him."

"Goody," she said as she finished the strawberry. "And ask him to make me younger. I really turned heads three or four presidential administrations ago!"

"You still do, but I don't see why he wouldn't make you any age you want, Ash," I said. "After all, he improved upon the real me."

She leaned across the table and pinched my cheek. "Oh, hon, I'm sure you do fine just as you are."

Martin appeared to clear the breakfast dishes. This was my first meal served by a butler. I wondered how I'd ever done without one.

When he'd gone back into the house, Ash said, "Reggie brought him over some years ago from Boodle's, one of his London gentlemen's clubs. He's a dear. Suzette's from Strasbourg. Reggie hired her from his favorite restaurant, I forget the name, because she made such wonderful pâté de foie gras, which he ate with nearly every meal, including breakfast. That stuff goes straight to your arteries but, as it turned out, Reggie didn't have to worry about heart disease."

"So what's the agenda for today?" I asked her.

"We're lunching at my country club so you can begin meeting people. And I've invited a few friends for a dinner tonight in your honor. Think of it as your debutante coming-out party."

"Sounds like a plan."

"There is something you might enjoy right now, Jack. I assume you like cars from the Corvette you drove here."

"I do."

"Take a look in the garage. The keys are hanging in a box on the wall."

9.

Boys And Their Toys

The garage, like the main house, was a tan stone Tudor-style structure with a black slate roof. The house was nearly the size of Windsor Castle, or so it seemed to me; the garage was slightly larger than the residence of the archbishop of Chicago on North State Parkway.

I went in through an unlocked side door, found a light switch, flipped it on, and beheld a sight that made me glad I have a strong heart. Otherwise I might have needed a jolt from electric defibrillator paddles because there, on a floor made of large black-and-white tile squares, was parked Sir Reginald's magnificent automobile collection.

I'd seen a TV special about Jay Leno's car and motorcycle collection. This one was smaller, but no less impressive in its quality and variety. Reggie probably had more vehicles at his other residences. Maybe Ash had them auctioned off or they were in storage.

Boys and their toys.

I walked around admiring the cars, stroking their fenders like you would a pet. There was a red Porsche Carrera GT, a silver Stutz Bearcat, a black 300SL Mercedes Gullwing Coupe, a black Rolls-Royce Corniche, a blue Shelby Cobra with a white racing stripe, a green MGB GT, a yellow Duesenberg with a leather steamer trunk attached to the back, a pink Cadillac convertible, and a white 1953 Corvette convertible, which was the first year Chevy made them. And more. I was completely dazzled.

Framed posters from Formula One Grand Prix races around the world were hanging on the walls: Monaco, Germany, Spain, France,

Japan, Italy, and the US, with signatures on them of famous drivers. There was a photograph of Sir Reginald in a driver's suit, a broad smile on his face and a helmet in his left hand, standing beside a white Jaguar racing model.

The late Sir Reggie was a handsome man, tall, with an angular face, dark hair, and an athletic build. His broad smile revealed a set of perfect teeth, uncommon in the British Empire of that era. He was standing ramrod straight and resembled a photo I'd seen of Lord Mountbatten.

There, at the end of a row, was the car I knew I would drive that day. I found the keys in the cabinet, pressed a button on the wall to open the garage's big double doors and eased myself into the cockpit of an ice blue Ferrari F149 California with its hard top off.

Undercover detective work does have its moments.

I put the key into the ignition and started the engine. It produced a low, guttural roar like that of an awakening jungle cat. I drove out onto the brick pavers of the courtyard and let the beast idle as I closed the garage doors. A breeze coming off the gulf had blown fragrant violet flowers from a lilac bush into the Ferrari's cockpit. I brushed them off the driver's seat, got in, and blinked from the dazzling rays of the tropical sun. I noticed a pair of tortoise-shell sunglasses on the dashboard. Maybe this was the last car Sir Reginald drove while here. Or ever.

With a flip of the F1 paddle shifter, the car slipped into first gear and I roared off down palm-lined Gordon Drive, with the gentle, rolling waves of the gulf on my left and a row of palatial estate homes, equal to the grandeur of the Howe residence, on my right. I'd never driven a car with a paddle shifter, but I'm a motor head so I figured it out with a minimum of bucking and jerking.

I punched on the radio and found an FM station playing Bon Jovi's "Livin' on a Prayer."

The moment was dead-solid perfect. A rarity in this life, so you have to enjoy such moments when they come your way. I fished my cell phone out of my pants pocket and called Marisa. She answered on the first ring.

"How's it going so far?" she asked.

"Excellent. Got time to go for a ride in my new wheels?"

"As long as it's not a motorcycle. I'm nobody's biker bitch."

I got a speeding ticket on my way to Fort Myers Beach, but I didn't care. If you drove a car like that at the speed limit, you risked offending the ghost of Enzo Ferrari himself.

My ride with Marisa was short, just the distance from her office to the *Phoenix*. As much as I admired the body designed by Pininfarina coachbuilders for Ferrari, I liked the body designed by God for Marisa better.

After I dropped her back at her office, I drove to her house, used the key under a pot of geraniums on the back porch, and went inside to visit Joe. Marisa volunteered to take care of him while I was staying in Naples. She liked Joe and he liked her back. I could tell this by the fact that he'd never bitten her, which he was not above doing to someone who rubbed him the wrong way, or sometimes for no apparent reason at all.

I found him napping on the living room couch. Hearing the door open, he lifted his head, jumped to the floor, strolled languidly over to me, and began rubbing against my leg and purring. I scratched him behind his ears and said, "This is just a temporary arrangement. Enjoy the cuisine, and I'll be back for you as soon as I can."

I got another speeding ticket on the way back to Naples. Eighty in a forty mph zone, allegedly. This time, it was unavoidable because I was on a tight schedule. I had to be back in time for lunch, and time flies whenever I'm with Marisa, especially when we're in a horizontal position. In Chicago, the pols give out get-out-of-jail-free cards to their pals; get pulled over, show the card to the officer, and you're back on your merry way. Maybe my pal Cubby Cullen could fix both tickets so that my auto insurance premium wouldn't increase.

The young Collier County sheriff's deputy who pulled me over on the way back asked me, "Where're you headed in such a hurry, sir?"

I knew this was a rhetorical question, and any answer I gave wouldn't matter unless I said I was a bomb squad tech headed to an elementary school. So I didn't bother telling him that I didn't want to be late for lunch at a fancy country club, especially while I was driving a car that had cost enough to cover his salary for several years. No reason to aggravate one less fortunate, especially when he was wearing a .45-caliber Sig Sauer.

10.

The Men They Used To Be

A half hour later, I was driving with Ash up a long, winding road lined with flowerbeds, sculpted bushes, and palm trees, leading to the Olde Naples Country Club. I guess when you add an "e" to "Old" you acquire a touch of class. Maybe I should change my bar's name to The Olde Drunken Parrot and increase the drink prices.

I'd chosen the pink Cadillac from Sir Reginald's collection. Ash told me that the car was originally owned by Elvis and that the Ferrari I'd driven to Fort Myers Beach was once the personal vehicle of the great Ferrari Formula One driver Michael Schumacher, seven times a world champion. My Corvette was once owned by Tony Cavalari, a Tampa plumbing contractor, according to the papers that came with it.

On the way to lunch, Ash told me about the Olde Naples Country Club. In a town with many exclusive clubs, Olde Naples was the crème de la crème, she said, with a waiting list of seven years. This added to its cachet, she explained. It didn't matter who you were, you still had to wait your turn.

A story often told, Ash said, was about a past CEO of one of the Big Three auto companies, she forgot which one, who retired to Naples. One day he strolled into the club's membership office and said he was there to join up. If they did the paperwork right then, maybe he could get in eighteen holes before lunch, he said. He'd brought his checkbook and his clubs.

The membership director informed him that there was a long waiting list.

"Do you know who I am?" he reportedly asked her.

"Yes," she replied. "You are someone who will be put at the end of our waiting list."

And he was.

Most of the club's members were very old (olde), even for "God's Waiting Room," as Naples is called. Whenever a hearse goes by on the street, the joke goes, someone just moved up a notch on the Olde Naples waiting list.

I parked on a circular drive in front of the clubhouse, a sprawling, one-story, white brick building, and turned the car over to a valet who greeted Ash by saying, "Welcome back, Lady Howe. It's so good to see you today."

The maitre d' in the dining room, who also greeted Ash warmly and by name, had some sort of European accent and was named Philippe, according to the brass nameplate pinned on his jacket. Claire and I once saw the comedian Dennis Miller perform in a theater in Rockford, Illinois. I remember him saying that, if you wore your name on your shirt to work, you'd made a serious vocational error. Funny. At the time, I was a uniformed patrolman with my name on my shirt.

Philippe showed us to a table with a view through floor-to-ceiling windows of grounds that looked a lot like those at Ash's estate, except that they also contained a golf course. The green outside our window was the eighteenth, Ash told me.

"Do you play?" she asked.

"No. But if they have a bowling alley here, next time I'll bring my ball and shoes."

She laughed. "No bowling alley, but we do have a cricket field."

Of course they did.

The waiter arrived with the menus. His jacket told me his name was Michael. He also greeted Ash by name. With an initiation fee of $250,000 and annual dues of $25,000, figures Ash gave me on the ride over, they'd better know your name, and the names of your next of kin in case you keeled over while eating your poached salmon.

"What are the soups today, Michael?" she asked.

"Today we have vichyssoise and split pea with ham, along with our usual gazpacho and New England clam chowder," Michael told her.

I wondered what the staff at a club like this really thought of the members. Did they spit in the soup—or worse—before serving it?

"The vichyssoise and gazpacho are cold, the other two are hot," Ash told me, helpfully. So began my tutorial in the customs of Naples high society. I knew that the clam chowder and split pea were hot, but I may have made wrong answers on a culinary multiple-choice test about the other two.

Ash ordered a Cobb salad, dressing on the side. I really wanted a cheeseburger, the cheese not on the side but right on top. But I was Frank Chance, so I asked for the poached salmon and found it quite tasty, actually, even though it was healthy. No soup.

As we ate, I scanned the room. Ash was right about the age of the members. We might have been in a very fancy nursing home. She seemed to guess what I was thinking.

"One morning, you wake up and you're old and you have no idea where all the years went," she sighed. "At what point are you old? I think it's when you die and people don't say it was premature, they say it was about time."

She began telling me about the other diners:

"That guy over there by the window, sitting alone, founded a bathroom fixtures company in Wisconsin. I have his products in my house, including a super toilet that does everything but shine your shoes. His wife died two years ago. They had lunch here together every Monday and sat at that same table. The bowl at the place setting across from him contains a Waldorf salad, which his wife always ordered. The waiter brings it automatically. It's sad, but so very sweet."

She indicated another table with a nod of her head. "That guy with the knickers—the 1950s called and they want their golf pants back—and the mane of silver hair? He was an army general who became head of one of the big defense contracting companies. Everyone calls him General. I think he'd like them to salute. And the fellow over by the potted palm in the pink shirt and red slacks with three other guys was managing partner of the biggest investment-banking firm on Wall Street before he got indicted. He served a few years at one of those federal minimum-security prisons, Club Fed they call them. He said he improved his tennis backhand while he was there."

As we ate, Ash continued telling me about the backgrounds of people in the dining room, always saying who the men "used to be" and dishing dirt on the women:

"She's currently screwing the assistant tennis pro while her husband's playing hide-the-salami with that cute little waitress walking into the kitchen. Who am I to judge? It works for them.

"She's had so much work done, the only parts left of her original self are her internal organs, and maybe not all of them.

"The woman with brown hair over there was blonde last time I saw her and a redhead the time before that. I bet she can't remember her original color."

And so on.

She noted how the men had acquired their money. Some by hard work, some by luck, some by picking the right parents, and some by a combination of those attributes.

There was another route to Easy Street, one that my time as a detective made me familiar with. Balzac wrote, "Behind every great fortune there is a crime." An exaggeration for literary effect, no doubt, but I was probably lunching with a number of unindicted co-conspirators.

I told Ash that it seemed everyone here used to be somebody, past tense. Just like when Cubby Cullen said I used to be a good detective.

"That's right. They used to be rich and powerful. Now they're just rich. You'd think that'd be enough, but for many of them, it's apparently not. They were accustomed to having staffs and giving orders that were always followed. They had drivers. Their phone calls, which they never dialed themselves, were always answered, or returned promptly. Now they play golf and then sit in the barroom playing cards and telling stories about the old days that no one wants to hear for the zillionth time."

"Not all that different from the Fraternal Order Of Police lodge in Chicago," I commented. "Retired cops go there to drink beers and shots and talk about the old days too. One day you've got a badge and a gun, and the next you're just another civilian. If I hadn't moved to Fort Myers Beach, I'd be hanging out there too."

A cell phone rang in the dining room and all conversation stopped. The ringtone was John Philip Sousa's "Washington Post March." It was very loud.

I saw a man a few tables from us hurriedly find the ringing phone in the pocket of his golf slacks, take it out, and turn it off. He looked very embarrassed. His companions, another man and two women, were looking away from him as if trying to dissociate themselves from the offender.

A moment later, Philippe appeared at the man's table and held out his hand like a teacher taking contraband away from a student. The man surrendered the phone without protest. Philippe walked away with it, and only then did conversation in the room resume.

"The guy with the phone is James Cunnane, a former assistant secretary of state in the Reagan administration," Ash told me. "His wife, Edith, looks like she's about to disown him. Cell phone use is strictly prohibited in the clubhouse. You can have one out on the golf course in case someone in the group needs medical attention, but it must be on mute or turned off. It will cost Jimmy a $500 contribution to the Make-A-Wish Foundation of Collier County to get his phone back."

I wondered how much they'd fine me for a burp in the dining room. Fortunately today's special was not a kielbasa-and-kraut sandwich, a favorite of mine at the Baby Doll.

"What other rules should I know about?" I asked Ash. "I mean, if I'm ever invited here again."

She laughed. "You will be, dear boy. Hmm . . . You must always keep your shirt tucked in. You may not wear a hat inside the clubhouse. On the golf course, you must behave like a gentleman, follow the Rules of Golf to the letter, and maintain a good pace of play. Otherwise, you can feel free to sleep with anyone's spouse or cheat anyone in a business deal."

When we finished our meals, Ash walked me around the room, introducing me as her nephew, Frank Chance, to some of the used-to-bes and their wives, who were all very cordial. As we were waiting for the valet to bring Elvis's Cadillac, she touched my arm and said, with a mischievous look, "Whoever or whatever you're investigating, this is going to be great fun!"

11.

The Girl Told The Truth

Back at Ash's house, I had free time between lunch and the dinner party in my honor. I decided I'd use it by continuing my editing of Bill Stevens's book.

I met Bill when he was covering one of my cases for the *Trib.* I was after a woman who shot her husband one night in their bed because he couldn't—or wouldn't, as she claimed as a mitigating circumstance—stop snoring. She left him there, bleeding out, packed a bag, and went to her sister's house in Naperville, which was the first place I looked.

Generally, cops don't like reporters, but Bill and I hit it off, in part because we both were lifelong Cubs fans, and also because he was known as a guy who did his homework and got the facts right before putting them into print. Sometimes, after we got to know one another, he'd call me before deadline to double check the facts of a police story. That's where he got the idea for me to check his fictional stories, too, I suppose.

Bill still pretty much lives the life he did before becoming a best-selling author. He doesn't spend much on clothes, and he drives a white 1996 Ford Bronco, "a classic," he calls it, which he bought at a police auction. His one indulgence is a forty-one-foot Sea Ray motor yacht named *The Maltese Falcon,* which he keeps at the Belmont Harbor Marina. I've never known him to actually take it out onto Lake Michigan. Instead he uses it during the good weather as a floating writer's studio. During the long Chicago winter, the boat is hauled out and stored inside a boatyard building.

Bill lives in an apartment building he owns on Waveland Avenue, right across from Wrigley Field. Those buildings, and a number of others like it on Waveland and Sheffield Avenues, are known as "Wrigley Rooftops" because their flat roofs provide a nice view of the ball field. The owners installed seating and other amenities on their rooftops and sell tickets to watch Cubs games, with commentary from radios and TVs tuned to the broadcast.

Bill's rooftop has tiered bleacher seats for authenticity more than for comfort, a bar with a cold keg of draft Goose Island lager, soda on ice, and a gas grill for hot dogs, burgers, and brats. On a warm summer evening, with a game on, surrounded by friends, that rooftop is as close to heaven on earth as I've ever been.

A typical gathering during a ball game on Bill's roof included print and radio journalists (Bill hates TV "talking heads"), lawyers, judges, cops, tradesmen, restaurateurs, corporate execs, cabbies, and a number of ex-cons Bill met while covering their trials. In other words, the same demographic you'd find in the stands at Wrigley Field.

Bill allows the tenants of the apartments in his building to come up to see a game whenever they want. He has a night for Boy and Girl Scouts and residents of the Cook County Youth Home. I've been with vagrants up there too, and found them to be excellent and appreciative companions.

I still follow the Cubs and watch their televised games whenever I can. They are known as The Lovable Losers, and not without justification. They have not been in a World Series since 1945; the time since their 1908 win represents the longest such drought of any sports team in America. That was only five years after the Wright Brothers' first flight. Aviation has come a long way since then; the Cubs, not so much.

None of that is the team's fault. The problem is the Curse of the Billy Goat, placed on the team in 1945 by Billy Sianis. Billy owned the Billy Goat Tavern, which is still in business. It was made famous by a *Saturday Night Live* skit: "Cheezborger! Cheezborger! . . . No fries—CHEEPS! . . . No Pepsi—COKE!"

Billy always brought his pet goat to Cubs games for luck. He was asked to leave a World Series game in 1945 because the goat's odor was bothering the fans around him. He was outraged and declared that, "Them Cubs, they ain't gonna win no more." That was thought to mean that another World Series game would not be won at Wrigley Field, and it has not.

Still we die-hard fans always believe that maybe *this* could be the year. My favorite song from the Broadway play and movie about the Cleveland Indians, *Damn Yankees,* is "(You've Gotta Have) Heart." I know all of the lyrics and sometimes sing them in the shower.

Bill Stevens could easily retire on his book royalties. But he continues to prowl the streets of Chicago with a reporter's notebook in his hip pocket. He says that this keeps him at the top of his game as a crime novelist.

Given the rapidly declining state of the print newspaper business, it's fortunate that Bill has a second career. So many of his colleagues have been laid off, or taken buyouts, he said, that you could fire a cannon in the *Trib's* newsroom without fear of hitting a member of the Newspaper Guild. Every day unemployed reporters and editors could be found at the Billy Goat Tavern eating burgers, drinking draft Goose Island, and commiserating about the good old days of Chicago newspapering, back when Mike Royko was writing his column for the *Chicago Daily News* and reporters covering a big fire or triple murder would grab a pay phone, dial the city desk, and yell "Get me rewrite!"

Bill has offered to work for a dollar a year so that a colleague can keep his or her job. But apparently that's too complex a concept for upper management to deal with. So instead he makes generous contributions to the Guild's Health and Welfare Fund, and helps reporters down on their luck in other ways as well.

I went to my bedroom, took the manuscript of *Stoney's Last Stand* and a pen downstairs and out to the backyard table, and began to read from where I'd left off:

Stoney saw Marcus Lamont standing in the middle of the room, buck naked, his shotgun aimed high, expecting whoever the fuck it was out there to stroll in standing up, apparently.

Not the first time Lamont had guessed wrong in his sorry life.

Stoney, still on the floor, assumed the prone position and put three hollow-point .357 Magnum rounds into Lamont's chest. Lamont dropped the shotgun as the force of the volley threw him backward, ending up with his back against a wall. He looked down at his chest as if surprised at the blooming crimson stain and then slumped to the floor.

Stoney got to his feet, walked over to Lamont, the S&W still trained on him, and kicked away the shotgun, a Benelli Super Black Eagle.

That was unnecessary because Marcus Lamont wasn't a badass anymore; he was a lump of lifeless meat.

Just as I said: Stoney survived unharmed. Which is convenient, because Bill is already at work on the next Stoney novel.

I underlined the name of Marcus Lamont's shotgun, a Benelli Super Black Eagle. That's a fine example of a semiautomatic shotgun, maybe the best of the breed, along with the Beretta, Franchi, and Mossberg. I'd once fired a Benelli when I was invited to a private pheasant hunting preserve in northern Illinois owned by a former Loyola classmate of mine who went into commodity trading instead of police work. Apparently a knowledge of the pork belly futures market is very lucrative.

In my opinion, a scumbag like Lamont wouldn't have a Benelli. So I made a note in the margin that Bill should change it to a Remington Model 870 Pump Action, which would do the job just as well at one-tenth the price, unless Lamont stole the Benelli from someone, in which case Bill should mention that. Otherwise Bill might get a letter from some rod-and-gun club member in Louisville or Latvia.

I continued reading:

The detective noted with professional interest that his shots were not grouped on the recently deceased's chest as tightly as he would have liked, but hey, this wasn't the police pistol range. And any gunfight you walked away from was a good one.

Stoney's ears cleared from the gunfire noise and he became aware of screaming in the room. He turned to see a woman on the bed, clutching a sheet to her chin.

She was young and very pretty.

He swung the S&W toward her, walked over to the bed, and pulled down the sheet.

Not only was she unarmed, she was also unclothed, and almost certainly underage. She had a body that, properly managed, could have taken her a lot further in life than to this crime scene formerly known as her bedroom.

She stopped screaming and was shaking and looking at Stoney with teary, terrified eyes.

He lowered his gun and said, "Chicago police, ma'am. Please get dressed and wait with me for the officers to arrive."

"I just wanna leave, mister," she said. "Please let me go. I didn't do nothin' wrong . . ."

"Can't do that," Stoney told her.

She hadn't pulled the sheet back up over her naked body and Stoney didn't suggest it.

"You're a witness to a shooting," he told her. "You'll need to give a statement."

He took his cell phone from his pants pocket and called it in. Uniforms would arrive first to secure the scene, and then detectives would come to inquire about how the guy on the floor had come to be there. After that the assholes from Internal Affairs would look into whether or not this was a righteous shooting.

Detective Jack Stoney had been through that drill before. He hoped the girl would tell the truth about how it went down. He had a rep in the department as a gunslinger and he just did not need another reprimand on his record.

I LEANED back and smiled. Bill Stevens based that last part on my encounter with a jamoke named Demarius Little when, for the first and last time, I did not immediately call for backup.

Fortunately for my career, the girl did tell the truth.

12.

A Flatware Conundrum

In my experience, a dinner party for "a few friends" involves grilling burgers and drinking beer in the backyard. Ash's version resembled a state dinner at the White House, or how I imagined one to be.

A group of about thirty men and women were standing around chatting and sipping drinks under a big white tent on the back lawn. A string quartet from the Naples symphony was set up near the bar.

It was a black-tie event. I was wearing one of Sir Reginald's tuxedoes. I thought I looked rather dashing in it, something of a James Bond-ish figure of a man, although I didn't have Bond's Walther PPK in a shoulder holster under my jacket. I'd thought about wearing my little Glock 26, aka the Baby Glock, in an ankle holster, but decided against it. It seemed unlikely that I'd have to shoot it out with a KGB agent at the dinner party. If trouble developed, I'd have to go hand-to-hand using a butter knife.

Ash looked stunning in a full-length purple silk evening gown with a side slit that went from Maine to Florida, revealing a very shapely leg. I told her she looked very nice. She replied by saying, "You look so handsome tonight that the only thing preventing me from jumping your bones is that I might break my hip."

She was shepherding me around the tent, introducing me to her friends, when she got distracted by something amiss with the catering and walked away to make it right. I was left alone with a beautiful young woman named Jennifer who was wearing a red dress that looked like it was spray-painted on by an Earl Scheib shop.

I took her to be in her late teens or early twenties and at first assumed she was someone's granddaughter. But Ash had introduced her to me as Mrs. Jennifer Lemaire and pointed out a man in his seventies standing by the bar. The man, Ash said, was Peter Lemaire, the managing partner of a private equity firm in New York, and Jennifer's husband.

So, trophy wife. Certainly not a rarity in a town like Naples. In my opinion, there is nothing wrong with some elderly gent dating or marrying a young lady as long as she is of legal age and has not been sold to him by human traffickers.

"So, Frank, how do you like Naples so far?" Jennifer asked as we stood sipping our drinks. Hers was a martini. Mine was not. "I understand you're looking for a place of your own in town."

"What's not to like?" I said. "I find Palm Beach too showy, don't you agree? Naples is so much more understated."

Did I really say that? No, Frank Chance did.

"We've got a home here and one in Palm Beach, too," Jennifer said.

Oops.

"But I agree with you," she added. "Peter and I spend more time here than in Palm. We keep the boat there, and our polo ponies, but Naples is where we come to relax from that high-octane social whirl."

I decided not to tell her that I keep my houseboat in Fort Myers Beach and come to Naples to chase murderers. I noticed that her hubby was walking toward us. She squeezed my bicep and said, "Peter travels a lot looking for companies to buy, leaving me with a lot of free time."

Petey boy arrived before I could respond. I'm loyal to Marisa, but Jennifer wasn't talking to me, she was talking to Frank Chance. Who knew how Frank would handle an offer like that?

We were all seated in Ash's dining room. Not since Marine Corps mess halls have I been at a table that could seat so many people—and here, no one said, "Pass the fucking salt."

When I was growing up, our family's Thanksgiving dinners always involved supplementing seating with card tables and folding chairs; it was always a big deal to be promoted from the "kids' table" to the main one.

This definitely was the main table. Each place setting had multiple forks and spoons in all shapes and sizes. Before the guests arrived, Ash and I sat at the table and she, with great amusement, gave me instructions on which utensils to use when, but I'd forgotten, so I dealt with this dilemma by using the same fork and spoon for everything. Maybe I'd be the subject of catty comments by my fellow diners on their way home: "Did you *see* that horrible fellow, Clarence? Using his sorbet spoon for the soup? I thought I'd simply regurgitate."

I was seated next to a woman named Marcie something whom I'd met at the country club lunch; I forgot who her husband used to be. On my other side was a distinguished-looking gentleman named Vasily Petrovich. He spoke with what sounded like an Eastern European accent, and was in his mid to late sixties, of medium height, with slicked-back dark hair flecked with grey, and a matching Van Dyke beard. He was wearing a white dinner jacket with a row of medals pinned on the left breast pocket over a starched white shirt with a red bow tie and tuxedo pants. All he lacked was a sash and a sword.

Marcie had introduced herself pleasantly and then conversed with a woman on her left all during dinner. But Vasily was quite talkative. He spoke about art, antiques, and the global financial markets, while I listened, nodding my head sagely and wondering how the Blackhawks were doing against the Islanders that night.

As a dessert that was on fire was being served, Vasily said, "I've enjoyed speaking with you, Frank. I do hope we can continue the conversation another time."

"Sure, that'd be nice," I told him, realizing that he'd learned quite a bit about Frank Chance's life (I was glad I'd practiced the details) but that I'd learned very little about his, other than that he had lived in London and New York before moving to Naples and was in the investment management business.

Later, when all the guests had departed, I asked Ash if she'd like me to help with the cleanup. Ha ha. After a backyard cookout with my family, I was in charge of scrubbing the grill and throwing away the paper plates and plastic cups. Instead, Ash and I sat in the library she with a snifter of brandy (it was very olde) while Martin and Suzette took care of the housekeeping.

"I noticed you chatted with Vasily all through dinner," Ash said.

"He seems to be an interesting guy."

"He is. His full name is *Count* Vasily Petrovich. He's descended from Russian nobility, I hear. He's not married, or at least no wife is in the picture now. He mostly dates younger women."

Like so many of the old geezers in town, as I've noted. I wondered what the minimum net worth was in order for a cheerleader to notice you.

"Who did he used to be?" I asked her.

"He still is. He runs an investment firm of some sort. Reggie put money into one of his funds. I think I still have money in it. That's up to my financial advisors. I don't pay much attention to that kind of stuff. I think some of the people at the dinner are in that fund too. The Atocha Fund, I think it's called. It's very exclusive, apparently. The buzz is that Vasily is very selective about taking on a client. He has to know and like you, I'm told."

Just like Bernie Madoff.

THE NEXT morning, I was up at six thirty, did one hundred push-ups and sit-ups, and went for a run along the beach before having breakfast on the patio. Ash had an appointment so did not join me.

During my run, I passed a tai chi class on the sand where ancient Caucasians were performing flowing and graceful ancient Chinese movements, poetry in motion led by a young female instructor wearing a pink leotard that almost caused me to stumble on a rock and fall down.

The workout allowed me to pig out on another one of Suzette's sumptuous breakfasts without guilt. All alone, I pretended I was in China and enjoyed a nice after-meal burp.

I'd asked Ash if she'd mind having an extra guest at the house and told her whom I had in mind. She said sure, she'd be delighted. So after breakfast, I borrowed the Shelby Cobra and drove back to Fort Myers Beach to pick up Joe. I knew I'd be staying in Naples for a while, and I missed him.

Ash sent Martin to PetSmart to stock up on cat supplies because I hadn't thought to pack Joe's gear, including a bed, which I knew Joe would never use, a litter box, food and water dish, and a supply of the brand of cat food I specified, to be supplemented by whatever Ash and I ate.

Before I went to Marisa's house for Joe, I stopped by the Fort Myers Beach police station to visit Cubby Cullen. I found him in the parking lot behind the building, standing beside a tan military Humvee with a .50-caliber machine gun mounted on the top.

"Spring break gets wilder every year," I said.

Cubby grinned and patted the fender of the vehicle as you would a horse. "Courtesy of the federal government. Can't say I've ever felt the need for one of these bad boys, but why turn down a gift from Uncle Sugar?"

The militarization of police departments via surplus government armaments had become a national controversy. There were days toward the end of my time on the job in Chicago when I could have used one of those Humvees to answer calls on the South and West Sides. That is not profiling or prejudice, it is just a fact. That's where the shooting was, and I wasn't at all eager to get hit again.

"I just stopped by to tell you I took that consulting job in Naples," I told Cubby.

"So I heard. How's it going?"

"It's turning out to be something more than consulting, Cubby."

"Wade told me that. You can borrow the Humvee whenever you want. Just pay for any bullets you use, and make sure to top off the gas tank when you return it."

"I might take you up on that before I'm done."

"Let me show you something," he said.

I followed him to the rear of the Humvee. It had a name freshly painted in white on the bumper: MYRNA.

"After my mother," Cubby said. "She could really kick ass too."

On the drive back to Naples, Joe stood on the front seat with his paws up on the dashboard, enjoying the scenery while the wind ruffled his fur.

I explained to him what was going on with my detective job. I was pretending to be Ash's nephew, I told him, and he would be undercover, too, posing as Frank Chance's cat. He took this exciting news by curling up on the seat and going to sleep.

13.
The Funeral Home King Of Iowa

When Joe and I arrived at Ash's house, I carried him inside through the front door. Ash met us in the foyer, scratched Joe behind his ears, and said, "It's nice to meet you, Joe. What a handsome kitty you are."

He looked at her and meowed.

"I think he just said that I have good taste in felines," Ash told me with a laugh.

She said that a messenger had delivered a large envelope for me while I was gone, and Martin had left it in my bedroom. I put Joe down, and he followed me upstairs.

I found the envelope on the dresser. It contained two manila file folders with the additional background on the deceased Eileen Stephenson and Lester Gandolf that I'd asked Chief Hansen to pull together. I decided that I'd take the folders out to the backyard table to read. Joe hopped onto the bed for a nap, the nap during the drive here having apparently worn him out.

I sat at the table and began reading. Martin appeared with a pitcher of iced tea, a tall glass, a container filled with ice, and a small plate with lemon slices. He put the iced tea and accompaniments on the table and went back into the house without saying a word. Apparently, butlers should be seen and not heard. Which is fine with me, as long as they deliver something to eat.

The background included more detailed information about Eileen and Charles than the case files I'd read. I made notes on the yellow legal pad I'd asked Martin to bring. Eileen and Charles's lives did intersect in a number of places. They both attended the First Episcopal Church. They both belonged to the Olde Naples Country Club and to the Collier Yacht Club, and they served on the boards of several of the same charities. They had different financial advisors, but they both were invested in Vasily Petrovich's Atocha Fund. I assumed that Mayor Beaumont had connections allowing him access to their financial records without obtaining a subpoena.

Hmmm. Was this finally a clue? Money is one of the main motivations for murder, and a hedge fund is all about building wealth. Maybe The Atocha Fund had a substantial penalty for early withdrawal. I made a note to look into Vasily's background too.

Just as I finished reading the files, Martin reappeared, followed by Wade Hansen. Hansen took a seat at the table and waited for Martin to depart. He looked upset. He rubbed his eyes, sighed, and said, "There's been another one. Another suspicious death. Jesus, Jack, this thing is getting completely out of control . . ."

"Tell me."

"It's a guy named Bob Appleby. He and his wife, Janet, are from Cedar Rapids. They have a home on a canal in Port Royal. He owns a chain of funeral homes. Yesterday morning, he apparently decided to take a cruise on his boat, a big Carver motor yacht moored at a dock behind his house. It looks like he started the engines and the boat blew sky high, scattering parts of him and debris all over the neighborhood. We're still trying to figure out exactly what happened. We haven't ruled out a bomb."

"Sometimes boats blow up," I said. "Gas fumes build up in the engine compartment, or there's a leak in the fuel line, or the battery sparks and sets off a fire. Mostly with older boats."

One more reason to keep *Phoenix* at the dock.

"That's right," Hansen said. "But this boat was brand new, just delivered a few weeks ago. One of my detectives talked to the dealer. It passed a sea trial just before delivery. Sure, it *could* have been an accident. But now we have a third death that looks suspicious."

"Who's examining the wreckage?"

"The Coast Guard will go over it, just like the FAA does after an airplane crash. I know the chief petty officer who'll supervise it. He owes me a favor for going easy on two of his men after a bar fight. So he'll keep the results under wraps for as long as he can."

"Was the wife on the boat too?"

"Nope. Janet Appleby was back in Cedar Rapids doing something or other. But we did find the body of a young woman. Or at least parts of her. Appleby's girlfriend, I'm guessing. We haven't ID'd her yet."

"I'll need a background check on him."

"Already in the works. But I can tell you that, although he'd made a lot of money planting customers six feet under in the Great Plains, he didn't exactly fit in here."

"Meaning?"

"People considered him . . . well, boorish, I'm told. Loud, and rather obnoxious. Not someone who was welcomed into the inner circle. His nickname was The Funeral Home King of Iowa, and he apparently was proud of it. Maybe even coined it himself, from what I hear. I don't think he had much in common with the likes of Eileen Stephenson and Lester Gandolf."

He smiled.

"What?"

"Ironically, we didn't find enough of the Funeral Home King to bury."

14.

Bloodthirsty Killer Loose In Paradise

Frank Chance and I spent the next few days enjoying the life of a member of the ruling class while I waited for the Coast Guard report and for the background check on Bob Appleby.

I mentioned that I was living the cop dream by owning a bar and living on a boat. But my life as Frank Chance was so over the top that no cop could even dare to dream it.

I attended a charity auction with Ash during which one bidder paid more for a bottle of vino than the cost of a car. Someone bought an Alaskan cruise for two for the price of the ship. We went to seafood night at Olde Naples Country Club featuring ice sculptures and all-you-can-eat lobster. I learned that I could eat three. It would have been more if I hadn't also grazed on the stone crab claws, shrimp, oysters, and assorted other stuff from the land and the sea, plus desserts. I learned I could eat two slices of key lime pie and still have room for a turtle sundae. If I kept chowing down like that, I'd soon be too big for Uncle Reggie's clothes, and mine.

Ash brought home some poached salmon for Joe. When she put it in his dish, he rubbed against her leg before digging in.

"You're welcome," she told him.

It took the Coast Guard team two days to thoroughly examine the wreckage of Bob Appleby's boat, which was named *Condolences*. That name seemed perfect for a vessel owned by the Funeral Home King of Iowa.

I was washing my car in the driveway at Ash's house when a messenger delivered a copy of the Coast Guard report, along with the background on Bob Appleby. I finished with the car, then took the reports and a cup of coffee I got from the kitchen to the outside table.

Martin came into the kitchen as I was pouring the coffee from a pot on the counter. He seemed flustered that he hadn't been there to meet my every need. I asked him if I could pour a cup for him, too, and when he seemed about to faint from the inappropriateness of it all, I smiled and said, "Just messin' with ya, Marty my man."

To which he replied, "Very well, sir," and backed out of the room.

You can take the butler out of Boodle's but . . .

From the Coast Guard report, I learned that there was no bomb. The boat's fuel lines and blower motor had been tampered with. This allowed a build-up of gas fumes in the engine compartment that exploded when the engines were started.

That confirmed that Bob Appleby and his girlfriend, who'd been identified as a twenty-four-year-old waitress at the Port Royal Club named Tess Johannsen, were murdered. If Eileen Stephenson and Lester Gandolf had been, too, that brought the total to four.

And if they were all offed by the same person, he could now, according to the standard law enforcement definition, be officially classified as a serial killer, the minimum body count being three.

If that news ever became public, Sir Reginald's newspapers would be in tabloid heaven. I could envision a headline in the *Tattler*: BLOODTHIRSTY KILLER LOOSE IN PARADISE. That would be bigger news than Vladimir Putin's sexual proclivities and the countless stories about the Air Force's Area 51 facility in the Nevada desert being UFO Central.

According to his background report, Bob Appleby had nothing in common with Eileen and Lester except that he, too, was invested in The Atocha Fund. Maybe Count Vasily Petrovich's hedge fund wasn't so exclusive after all. I made a note of it and underlined my earlier note about looking into Vasily's background.

Without any solid evidence of wrongdoing by Vasily, or even compelling circumstantial evidence, no judge would sign an order allowing me access to The Atocha Fund's records. Unless Mayor Beaumont's connections could get that kind of information, I'd need to find another way to pursue this lead.

The investigation was finally heating up. Not only did I have a solid clue, I also had a lead, which, according to the *Detective's Handbook*, is one step up from a clue.

I looked up from the reports and saw that Joe was sitting beside the table looking at me. That usually meant he wanted something. I checked my watch and saw it was lunchtime. Martin appeared with the handset to a cordless phone. He had a way of suddenly appearing, which can creep you out until you get used to it. It must be something they teach in butler school.

"A call for you, Mr. Chance," he said, handing me the phone. Joe followed him into the house, in search of lunch, I assumed.

"Frank, this is Vasily Petrovich," the voice on the phone said. "You may recall that we met at Lady Ashley's dinner party."

"Yes, of course," I said, not adding that I'd just been thinking about how to find out if he'd murdered three of his customers and one bystander. If I were sweating him in an interrogation room back in Chicago, I would have just asked him that. Some of my fellow detectives might have hit him in the head with a phone book first, just to get his attention. But, in this circumstance, I didn't think the straight-out accusation would have been effective.

"I enjoyed our discussion and wondered if we might continue it over lunch," he told me.

Bingo.

"Sure, that sounds good."

"If you are free tomorrow, perhaps we can meet at my office and then go somewhere from there."

It seemed unusual to meet at his office first instead of at a restaurant. Maybe Vasily wanted to deliver a sales pitch for The Atocha Fund. Frank Chance was, after all, extremely wealthy.

I wondered if I should bring along my S&W and wear a Kevlar vest under my navy blue blazer just in case he became grouchy if I said no to the investment.

"Let me check my calendar and get back to you," I said, making a mental note to go to Office Max and buy an appointment calendar so I could check it. We ended the call. I was again startled to find Martin standing beside me. Maybe butlers should wear bells.

"Lady Ashley is away, Mr. Chance," he said. "Would you care to take your lunch out here? Cook has prepared a nice salad with seared ahi tuna steak on top."

"Yes, that'd be fine," I answered, guessing that Joe was in the kitchen enjoying the same thing, minus the salad.

After lunch, I went to the library, sat at an antique desk with a red leather top, and went back to work on Bill Stevens's book manuscript. My deadline for editing it was approaching.

That rascal Jack Stoney was up to his ass in alligators once again. This time, he'd ended up in bed with a mob boss's wife, not knowing who she was. That was truly fiction, because every time I was in bed with a woman I knew her identity, or at least the one she gave me.

The difficulty for Jack Stoney was that the FBI had planted bugs in the mob boss's Gold Coast estate home, including one in the bedroom. The boss was away and his wife, in the throes of passion, had yelled out, "Fuck me, Detective Jack Stoney!"

Talk about bad luck. At least she didn't give his badge number. Maybe she was a cop groupie. Or maybe she was a confidential informant for the feds. Or maybe just an orgasmic blabbermouth. Whichever, Stoney had yet another appointment with Internal Affairs.

In the manuscript, that IA meeting went like this:

> *Stoney and two IA guys sat in a conference room at precinct headquarters. The two guys were wearing identical cheap grey suits, Stoney noted, as he walked into the room, purposely fifteen minutes late. Maybe that was the IA unit's new uniform, purchased at a bulk rate from Men's Wearhouse.*
>
> *The IA guys were seated opposite one another at one end of the table. Instead of taking the chair at the head of the table between them, as they obviously intended, Stoney went to the other end.*
>
> *Let the pissing contest begin.*

One of the IA guys was a lieutenant Stoney knew named Stan Caldwell, an African American. He was in his late fifties—a stocky bear of a man whose career had stalled for some reason Stoney didn't know about, so he'd been sentenced to a term in IA.

The other was Terry Thornton, a tall, thin man in his late twenties who was either prematurely bald or who'd shaved his head as a fashion statement. He was one of those cops who saw IA as a stepping-stone to advancement in the department, which sometimes it was, if you didn't make an enemy of the wrong people along the way. He was a sergeant.

Caldwell cleared his throat, appearing uncomfortable with the proceeding, which he probably was, because he didn't like his job, and thought that Stoney was an effective, if unorthodox, cop.

He began: "So, Jack, you know why we're here. We'll be recording this session, unless you have an objection, in which case the meeting is over and we'll need to involve your union rep, or your lawyer."

"Let's get it done," Stoney told him.

The "asshole" at the end of that sentence was unspoken, but mutually understood. Stoney didn't really think that Caldwell was an asshole, he was basically an okay guy, but anyone working in IA was put into that category for the duration of the assignment.

Caldwell stood and placed a small voice recorder in the middle of the table because of the distance between them, and turned it on.

"For the record, Detective Jack Stoney, you've chosen not to have your union representative or an attorney present, isn't that correct?" Thornton asked.

"Yes, that's correct," Stoney answered.

Caldwell stood, turned off the recorder, and said, "I think that's unwise, Jack."

I made a note in the margin here telling Bill that an initial IA interview like this one would not be recorded. No cop would be dumb enough to allow that, especially without a union rep or lawyer present. Only an official deposition, if things went that far, would be recorded.

I continued reading:

Stoney looked at Caldwell and said, "What's unwise is wasting my time with bullshit like this while the real bad guys are taking over the streets of the City of Chicago."

I always had a union rep or a union lawyer, or sometimes both, present when called on the carpet by Internal Affairs, and I knew enough not to wise off like that. But I liked the way Stoney was handling it, so I left that part alone. He could afford to push it because, as I've noted, he wasn't real and could never be fired, unless Bill decided he should be. Detective fiction is like that.

With the help of a police union lawyer, I could have fought my forced retirement, and maybe won. But I was offered three-quarter pension payments for life. If there ever was a time to begin the second act in the Jack Starkey story, that was it.

It turned out that the joke was on the taxpayers of the City of Chicago. I returned to the gym as soon as I could after my injury, and now my shoulder works as good as ever. I don't feel guilty about taking the money, however. If I left it in the city kitty, the pols would squander it or steal it. That's how it works in my hometown. Four of the last seven Illinois governors were sent to prison, with two serving at the same time when I left.

Gotta love a state like that.

15.

Claire, Jenny, Harold, Alice, and Joe

As I was reading the manuscript, my cell phone rang. I had to stand to get it out of the pocket of my jeans, which had become tighter since this highly caloric assignment began.

"Hello, Jack, how are you?" a familiar voice said. It was Claire, my ex-wife. Her call was even more surprising to me than Vasily's. We talked every now and then, but I always initiated the calls.

"I'm fine, Claire. What's up?"

I wished that I could tell her how great I really was doing as Frank Chance. I think she would have liked Frank, as long as he never lapsed into Jack Starkey-like behavior.

"Jack, I wanted to tell you that Jenny was engaged and . . ."

I interrupted her, stunned and saddened that our daughter had developed such a close relationship with a man I knew nothing about.

"Engaged? To who?"

"To whom. You don't know him. He's an assistant US attorney in Chicago."

"As long as he isn't a cop. *Was* engaged? So they broke it off?"

"In a manner of speaking. They got married."

Now I was beyond stunned. I was gobsmacked. "When?"

"Last Saturday," Claire said in a soft voice. "It was very nice. The ceremony was at Saint Stephen's and the reception was at the Ritz-Carlton."

"I guess my invitation got lost in the mail."

"Jack, I'm sorry. Truly. Jenny and I had a long talk about inviting you. I thought her father should be there to give her away. But she still has a lot of anger about . . ."

"It's okay. I don't blame her."

"I know it hurts."

"No more than a triple bypass without anesthesia."

"Jack—"

"It's not her fault, Claire. It's mine. I take full responsibility for our relationship. Do you like him?"

"He's very sweet and they're very much in love."

I wanted to say that we were like that once. But she knew it.

"It's not forever," Claire said. "You can still rebuild your relationship with Jenny. I know, deep down, she wants that too."

"I'm working on a case," I said. "When I'm done with it, I'll come there for a visit."

Claire was silent. I knew I'd blown it again with my family. I was working on a case, and that came first. She didn't ask what the case was or if I'd become a cop again. I guess she didn't care.

"Thanks for telling me," I said. "I will visit."

"We'll get together when you do," she said. "It'll be good to see you."

"You too. Bye."

Although my relationship with my daughter was still on the rocks, my ex-wife said it would be good to see me. I didn't know if, given the chance, I'd want to get back together with Claire. Or if I wanted my relationship with Marisa to become more than it was. But it's bad karma to have someone on the planet hating you, so it would be good if Claire and Jenny could someday forgive me my sins of omission and commission. According to Brother Timothy, God could. But could they?

As I sat there after the call, I thought about my former life in Chicago. My father, Harold Starkey, was a Chicago fireman. He and my mother, Alice, denied themselves many luxuries in order to afford the steep tuition at Saint Leo's high school and Loyola University for me, and for my older brother, Joe.

The Jesuits at both institutions made certain that Joe and I got first-rate educations, despite the fact that I was more interested in sports and girls than schoolwork. I played basketball for the Loyola Ramblers. Joe was a three-sport athlete and a more serious student.

I once asked Brother Timothy why I had to learn "all this kind of arcane stuff" I'd never use "in real life."

He replied, "Because, first of all, Mr. Starkey, we are teaching you how to *think*, not necessarily how to remember 'all this kind of arcane stuff,' and second, I still work the heavy bag in the gym, and I'll explain to you in the ring why you should diligently apply yourself to your studies."

He added, "But you do get points for using the word arcane, so consider your ass safe for today."

I found that to be an extremely persuasive argument for doing my homework, and not cutting classes.

After graduating from Loyola, I did a tour as an officer in the Marine Corps, and then became a cop. The marines taught me to shoot; where else but the police force could I use that skill legally and get paid for it?

Joe followed dad into the fire department, although our parents wanted him to go to law school. He did enroll in Loyola's evening law program so he could work and pay for his own tuition. He died when the roof of a burning South Side tenement collapsed on him as he was attempting to rescue a little boy's golden retriever puppy, which my Uncle Tommy was able to save.

I met Claire Nordquist when I was a rookie patrolman, riding in a squad car with a partner named Jim Lorenzo. Claire grew up in Lake Geneva, Wisconsin, and was working as an art director at a Chicago advertising agency. She was coming out of a restaurant in Old (not Olde) Town with two girlfriends as Jim and I were cruising along North Wells Street. A guy wearing a black hoodie came up behind the girls, grabbed Claire's purse, and ran.

Jim was driving. He stopped the car; I jumped out and ran after the thief. It took two blocks for me to catch up and tackle him. I cuffed him and walked him back to the scene of the crime. Before driving the perp to the station house, I asked Claire if I could call her sometime. She said thanks, but no, she was involved in a relationship. I called her anyway, using the number she gave on the police report. She agreed to lunch, maybe only because she was grateful for the return of her purse.

Claire's boyfriend at the time was a dentist. Perhaps, when our lunches eventually turned to dinners, she liked my blue uniform more than the dentist's white tunic. Maybe she found my charms irresistible. Maybe it was because I kept saying, "Rinse, please," evoking a dentist's spit sink and making her laugh. We were married a year after we met.

Jenny was born two years after that. By then, I was a detective sergeant assigned to the homicide division. Because of the stress of the job, or just using that as an excuse, I began stopping at the Baby Doll Polka Lounge on the way home after my shifts. A lot of cops did that, and some became alcoholics and were eventually served with divorce papers.

I knew that Claire didn't bad-mouth me to our daughter. She didn't have to. When you miss enough family dinners, birthday parties, school plays, and soccer games, it becomes obvious that you are falling short in the parenting department. By the time Jenny was in high school, she seemed to have given up on me. And Claire clearly had too.

At Claire's request, I moved out of our townhouse in Rogers Park and into an apartment in Wrigleyville. Not long after that, living alone, it occurred to me that this was not the life I wanted. I started going to AA meetings in church basements, where we sat in folding chairs and told our sad stories to fellow drunks. But it was too late to save my marriage, or my relationship with my daughter.

I really did intend to go to Chicago to see Claire and Jenny as soon as I could. Making amends to people you've hurt is the ninth of the Alcoholics Anonymous twelve-step program. It was time for me to take that step.

I should have taken a break from the case and flown to O'Hare that day. In Bill Stevens's novel *Stoney's Escape*, my alter ego was successful in reclaiming a relationship with his ex-wife and daughter. But, as I said, Jack Stoney is a better man than I.

Claire got an MBA from Northwestern after our divorce. She is a senior vice president with Wells Fargo Bank and lives in a row house in the Gold Coast. Her situation has improved considerably since she was Mrs. Jack Starkey, and not just financially.

I'd heard from friends that Claire is seeing an orthopedic surgeon, a step up from a dentist—and several steps up from a detective. I'd heard that from friends because I regularly called to ask them about her. That news made me jealous and, at the same time, pleased that she was doing just fine after dumping her inattentive, alcoholic cop husband.

Our divorce was what was termed "amicable." I suppose that meant she didn't mind talking to me on the phone occasionally, and wouldn't consider it particularly good news if I were found floating facedown in the Gulf of Mexico.

Claire had not asked for alimony. I insisted on paying Jenny's college and law school expenses. Claire said we could share them, but agreed to let me handle it because, I was certain, she understood that I needed to do that for our daughter.

That night, still upset about the news that Jenny had married without inviting me, and thinking about how Mr. Jack Daniel's might comfort me, I drove back to Fort Myers Beach and went to an AA meeting at Saint Paul's Episcopal Church, my first meeting in six months. I figured that Brother Timothy wouldn't mind the Protestant venue as long as I was working on mending my eternal soul.

I moved away from my hometown because I decided that I needed to change my game if I was ever to reconnect with my family. At minimum, I wanted Claire to know that I regretted our break up, that I took full responsibility for the problems we had, and that I wished her all the happiness she deserved, with or without me.

Jenny is now an attorney with a big corporate law firm in Chicago. She took her mother's side in the divorce—as did I. After I moved to Florida, I called her every holiday and on her birthday, and regularly invited her to visit me in Fort Myers Beach. She was always too busy. She could have mentioned her engagement and wedding in those calls, but didn't.

It's said that one definition of insanity is to keep doing the same thing over and over and expecting a different result. I left Chicago, a city I loved but where all my bad habits had developed, and moved to Fort Myers Beach to start over.

My first stop before leaving Chicago was the Baby Doll. I went there to say good-bye to old friends. They surprised me with a noon-time going-away party. We always went to the Baby Doll after the funerals of fellow policemen killed in the line of duty. My party, nice as it was, felt kind of like that.

Tommy Boyle, my partner during my final years as a homicide detective, was also there. He was a third-generation cop, a big man with the ruined blood vessels in his cheeks and nose of someone not unfamiliar with strong drink. Tommy had saved my life once by hearing a guy we couldn't see jack a shell into his pistol. I'd saved his career more than once by being loose with the facts when interviewed by Internal Affairs about things he'd done.

Tommy and I promised to stay in touch. But that hadn't happened. They say that a partnership on the police force is like a marriage. That's an overstatement, but there is one similarity: When it's done, it's done.

After leaving the Baby Doll, I walked over to Graceland Cemetery to say good-bye to my family. Graceland, on North Clark Street, is a sylvan glade within the city; it bills itself as "an oasis of art, architecture, and horticulture since 1860." There is a lake, an ivy-covered stone chapel, and 119 acres of manicured parkland.

The cemetery's literature notes that many prominent people are buried there, including architects, musicians, artists, writers, and business leaders. Al Capone and John Dillinger are buried elsewhere. But for me, Graceland is the place where my mother, father, and brother lie at eternal rest. My will stipulates that I join them there when my time comes.

We can, ultimately, go home again.

I walked through the open front iron gates and down a winding path leading to the Starkey family gravesite, beneath an ancient oak tree. I read the headstones, even though I knew what they said by heart:

Harold Gilbert Starkey
1927 – 1999
Beloved husband of Grace and father of Joe and Jack
Deputy Chief City of Chicago Fire Department
At Rest After a Lifetime of Service

Alice Greenleaf Starkey
1931 – 2001
Beloved wife of Harold and mother of Joe and Jack
The Angels Weep at Such a Passing

Joseph Harold Starkey
1959 – 2002
Beloved son of Harold and Alice and brother of Jack
Firefighter, City of Chicago Fire Department
Taken From Us Too Soon

I looked at the empty plot beside Joe that was waiting for me, and wondered what the epitaph on my headstone would say, and who would compose it. My ex-wife, Claire? Our daughter, Jenny? Or maybe Bill Stevens? Maybe I should put the wording in my will: Jack Gilbert Starkey, He Did the Best He Could.

But had I really? When you think about your life being summed up by a single phrase carved in marble for all eternity, it is reason enough to do all you can to be a better man while there is still time.

I think it's going well so far. I haven't had a drink, shot anyone, or been shot since quitting the job and moving to Florida. I'd call that real progress.

16.
The Atocha Fund

Atocha Securities occupies the top floor of a six-story building that held an Italian restaurant, a clothing boutique, and a women's shoe store, which Marisa liked. As I mentioned, Fifth Avenue South is the premiere address for financial institutions, shops, and restaurants catering to the carriage trade. Vasily obviously wants his customers to feel comfortable when they visit their money.

Approaching the building, I wondered if Vasily had penetrated my false identity, and an ex-Red Army sniper with a Dragunov was tracking me though his scope from a nearby rooftop. Or if I'd find, behind the reception desk in his offices, some no-neck goon with a shaved head, jagged knife scar on his cheek, and an AK-47 at hand. I didn't know at that point if Vasily was the perp in my case, but paranoia has saved many a cop's life.

I was wearing a short-sleeved, cream-colored linen shirt, tan slacks, and brown loafers—with socks, because I was packing my Baby Glock in an ankle holster.

In terms of firearms, Florida is like Dodge City in Wild West times. The state is more than generous with issuing concealed carry permits, so a very large percentage of the population, and not just the bad guys, is armed.

State firearms laws create the presumption that a citizen, if he or she feels even mildly threatened, has the right to throw a flurry of hot lead at the alleged offender. In most states, you can only do that if someone breaks into your home or workplace.

But not in the Sunshine State. Here it's unwise to honk your horn at someone who cuts you off in traffic, even if the other driver is a little old lady. Once, while visiting a gun shop in Fort Myers, I saw an elderly woman trying out handguns to see how they fit into her purse, and asking if any came with a pink grip, which some do. Florida's senior citizens are scary enough behind the wheel of a car; knowing that some of them are armed can make you consider wearing a Kevlar vest on your way to the grocery store.

I walked into the building's lobby, took the elevator to the top floor, and entered the Atocha Securities offices through floor-to-ceiling glass doors. I found a large, elaborately furnished reception area with oil paintings on the walls and an Oriental rug over a hardwood floor. Oriental rugs over hardwood floors are apparently as common in the best circles as are no socks with loafers. There was furniture that looked more expensive than comfortable. But the most impressive feature was the stunning young blonde sitting behind the reception desk.

She smiled at me and said, "Mr. Chance?"

"In the flesh."

As was she.

"Please have a seat. Mr. Petrovich will be with you shortly. Would you like tea, or coffee, or water while you wait?"

"Water would be good," I told her. She stood and went through the door to the inner offices, reappearing after a moment with a bottle of Evian and a glass with ice in it. She was wearing a white satin tee shirt and a short black leather skirt that showed more curves than a Grand Prix racetrack, plus red stiletto heels that—well, you get the idea. I wasn't a dirty old man, at least not yet, but forgive me, Brother Timothy, for my impure thoughts.

The young lady handed the water bottle and glass to me and said, "It will be just a moment longer. Mr. Petrovich is on a call."

I took a drink straight from the bottle. It always seemed odd to me that you would pay three bucks for a bottle of fancy bottled water and then dilute it with ice cubes made from the tap. I walked over to a glass display case that contained a model of an old-fashioned sailing ship. A brass plaque identified it as a replica of a Spanish treasure galleon named the *Nuestra Señora de Atocha*.

As I was looking at the ship, the receptionist said, "Mr. Petrovich will see you now, Mr. Chance. Please follow me."

She led me through the door, down a corridor, and into Vasily's large corner office. On the way, we passed a number of other offices with open doors. They were unoccupied. Maybe it was time for staff marksmanship training at a shooting range.

As I entered his office, Vasily was sitting at a desk that looked like Louis XIV might have used to dash off his correspondence. He stood and came around it to greet me. There were oil paintings on the walls, as well as stuffed game fish and the heads of wild animals. I felt that a cape buffalo was staring at me, wanting me to arrest his killer. Maybe I'd get to that later.

"Ah, Frank, I'm so glad you could come," Vasily said as he gave me a firm handshake.

He was wearing a white linen suit with an open-collared pale blue shirt and a paisley ascot. I was glad that I was wearing Sir Reginald's clothes and not my own. Dressed in my usual garb, I might look like I could qualify for a reverse mortgage, at best, and not an investment in a high-flying hedge fund.

Vasily directed me to a red leather sofa and sat in a matching club chair beside it. At the last moment, I noticed that I was about to sit on a little mound of white fluff. It raised its head and revealed itself to be a dog of some sort. Without moving, the doggie growled at me.

"That's Sasha, my Maltese," Vasily said. "She's really quite friendly."

Unless you are going to sit on her, apparently.

Vasily picked her up and held her on his lap, stroking her fur. Ernst Stavro Blofeld, the villain in one of the James Bond movies, had a dog like that and petted it as he planned the destruction of the world.

"I'm happy we could get together again, Count Petrovich," I said.

"Please, call me Vasily."

"And please call me Frank."

He smiled and added, "In America, the only true aristocracy is based upon money, and not royal bloodlines, don't your agree?"

I did agree. Legit or not, Vasily's kingdom was one of supercomputer flash trades, global currency hedging, shell companies, and offshore bank accounts. I guessed that Atocha Securities was incorporated in the Cayman Islands, or in some other offshore nation where the smart money hides and a customer can get in some snorkeling while there.

"Tell me about the model in your lobby," I said.

Vasily grinned. "Her name is Lena. She is from Vladivostok. She is very . . . efficient."

"I meant the ship model," I said. I was going to get to Lena next.

"Yes, of course, the ship model," he chuckled. "That is a replica of a Spanish galleon that sank in a hurricane off the Florida Keys in 1622 while carrying a cargo of gold bullion and other fabulous treasures. Maybe you recall that the ship was found by that famous treasure hunter, Mel Fisher, thirty years ago, and the treasure recovered."

In fact, I did remember that but I hadn't connected the name of Vasily's firm with that lost ship.

He stood, walked over to a mahogany cabinet built into a wall, and pushed a brass button. I noticed that he walked with a slight limp. From a bullet wound during the Russian occupation of Afghanistan? From falling off his horse during a cavalry charge somewhere in the Balkans? Who knew at that point what secrets Vasily's past held. Or maybe he just had arthritis of the hip.

The front panel of the cabinet slid upward like a garage door, revealing a fully stocked bar.

"May I offer you some refreshment?" he asked as he selected a bottle from one of the shelves. "Perhaps a single malt scotch? This is Talisker, which I'm especially fond of. It was bottled ten years before Lena was born."

What to do? I couldn't admit that I was a recovering alcoholic and ask if he had root beer. After all, Frank Chance was a player, not a pussy.

"Thanks, but I'll have to pass," I said. "I must have eaten something that didn't agree with me last night. My stomach is a bit queasy."

Actually Ash and I shared an anchovy and mushroom pizza as we watched the Bulls playing the Pistons on TV last night and my stomach liked it just fine. Even the final score of the game didn't upset it.

Vasily nodded, took a short glass from the cabinet, poured in two fingers of the scotch, and returned to his chair. He sipped his drink and said, "If I may, Frank, I'd like to tell you just a bit about Atocha Securities before we go to lunch. I apologize if this seems rude, as if you've been roped in by a time-share salesman with an offer of a free meal."

"Not at all." I was there to learn about Atocha Securities. The free meal was a bonus.

"Excellent. I only invite a select few people to invest with us. The fact that you are related to Lady Ashley, a woman of the finest reputation, provides your bona fides."

He took another sip of scotch, rolling it around in his mouth before swallowing, and continued: "My grandparents, Count and Countess Petrovich, were members of the Russian aristocracy, a group known for, shall we say, an excessive lifestyle, the kind among the Russian nobility that led to the revolution of 1917. My grandparents escaped to London, where my grandfather took up a career in finance. He founded an investment firm that my father joined. I attended Oxford, and then the London School of Economics. After a few years with the family firm, I decided I wanted to make my own mark in the business world, so I moved to New York, took a job with an investment-banking firm, and eventually opened my own shop. I called it Petrovich Securities. The firm did well by our clients. During the height of the Cold War, I decided that a change of name would be prudent. The Russian thing, you know. Right at that time, a client gave me a coffee table book about the *Atocha* treasures, and from that fortuitous event the name Atocha Securities was born. As was the name of my hedge fund, The Atocha Fund. The implication being that I would create great wealth for my clients."

Vasily moved to a glass display case near the window, opened the top, picked up a gold coin, walked over, and handed it to me. "This coin was minted in Seville," he said. "It is called a doubloon, with a denomination of two escudos. It might have been in the pocket of a wealthy passenger aboard *Atocha*, in that no gold coins were minted in the New World in 1622 or earlier. I bought it, along with some silver coins, gold and silver bars, and jewelry, at a Christie's auction of *Atocha* treasures in New York."

I took the coin. It had an irregular shape, with a cross on one side and a coat of arms on the other. As I held it, I imagined the scene aboard the *Atocha* as it foundered in a hurricane four centuries ago: listing badly, taking on water, masts snapped by the ferocious winds, the passengers huddled below decks surely knowing their fate, perhaps a priest holding up a cross while reciting a prayer for help that his God, busy with more important matters, would not answer.

I thought about slipping the coin into my pocket as a joke. But maybe Vasily wouldn't find that funny and call for a bodyguard named Igor, the hit man who dealt with clients wanting to withdraw their funds.

I handed the coin back to him. He returned it to the display case, took the chair near the sofa, smiled, spread his hands, and said, "For today, I just want you to know that you are welcome to hear more about our investment philosophy and results, if and whenever you wish. Or not. Believe me, we have many more people who want to become clients than we are able to accommodate, so feel completely free to pass on this opportunity. My feelings will not be hurt. In any case, that's the end of my little sales pitch."

He stood, picked up Sasha, and said, "Now we shall eat. I hope you have time for more than a quick bite."

Was I just imagining it, or did his killer Maltese seem to perk up when he said "quick bite"?

17.

Aboard The *Treasure Hunter*

It was a fifteen-minute drive from Vasily's office to the Palm Harbor Yacht Club. We made the trip in a black Maybach limousine piloted by a young man who Vasily introduced as Stefan. The backseat was as comfy and luxurious as a den in one of the city's mansions, complete with leather, mahogany, a bar, and a television. My seat had a footrest that I powered up and down a few times, just for fun.

The chauffeur had a thick neck, wide shoulders, and a flat, Slavic face. He wore an expensive-looking black suit with a white shirt and black tie. Hatless, his blond hair was cropped short, military style. He gripped the wheel with hands the size of HoneyBaked hams. Sasha sat on the front passenger seat while Vasily and I rode in back.

As our Maybach approached the big iron gates of the yacht club entrance, Stefan held up a white plastic card and the gates swung slowly open. We drove through them and along a winding road, passing a very large concrete building.

"That's where they keep the smaller boats," Vasily said.

I could see inside through the open end of the building. The boats, stored in racks going up to a high ceiling, looked plenty big to me.

"We're dining on my boat," Vasily said as Stefan parked in front of a one-story building with grey shingles. As we were getting out of the car, a long golf-cart-type vehicle pulled up. The driver, a man in his seventies wearing a tee shirt with the name of the yacht club on it, said, "Welcome back, Count Petrovich."

Vasily took Sasha from the car and carried her. We got into the cart which drove along a wooden bridge with a mangrove swamp on the left and boat docks in a harbor on the right. More picturesque than Salty Sam's, and with higher rents. The boats moored at the docks clearly would not fit into the storage building. We stopped at a two-story grey wooden structure that was obviously the clubhouse. People were dining at tables on a second-floor deck. I followed Vasily along one of the floating docks that ran out into the harbor.

It was a perfect day for a boat ride, the sun glowing yellow in a cloudless, azure sky and a light breeze blowing in from the water. To the west, the harbor ended in a bay that fed through a pass leading to the Gulf of Mexico. Boats of all sizes came and went at idle speed through a channel marked with red and green buoys.

"Red Right Returning" was the boater's navigational mantra: Keep the red buoys on your right when returning from open water to port. Or maybe it was "Green Right Returning." I'd have to get that straight if I ever piloted more than a fishing skiff in the backwaters.

We stopped beside a motor yacht with a powder blue hull and a flying bridge. It was, I estimated, somewhere between sixty and seventy feet long. A big mother. A nameplate on the side near the bow said Azimut, which I recognized from boating magazines as a premier boat builder in Italy.

The name of Vasily's boat, painted on the stern, was *Treasure Hunter.* From the size of the boat, it was clear that its owner already had found the treasure.

"We'll cruise north along the coast toward Sanibel while we eat," Vasily said as he led me across the gangplank and onto the deck. "That's about two hours round-trip, if you've got that much time."

"Fine by me," I said. The only other thing on my agenda for the afternoon was catching a serial killer. On a boat like the *Treasure Hunter,* cruising to Australia would have been just fine too.

A young woman with short blonde hair, wearing a white tee shirt that said *Treasure Hunter* in gold script, white shorts, and blue canvas boat shoes (no socks), was waiting on the deck at the end of the gangplank. She smiled at me, probably thinking, "Not on your best day, gramps."

Standing near the ladder leading up to the flying bridge was a man in his thirties with a shaved head and muscles bulging beneath his *Treasure Hunter* tee shirt.

"Inform the captain we are ready to get under way, Serge," Vasily said to the man. He handed Sasha to the young woman. "She'll have her lunch and then a nap, Elena," he told her.

Frankly I'd have preferred to have lunch with Elena, and then a nap, if she was drowsy too. Another impure thought, as Brother Timothy would have said. But he taught me that we couldn't control our thoughts, only our actions. Because of my relationship with Marisa, I had no intention of taking any action with Elena, even if it were possible. But sometimes, impure thoughts are a lot of fun.

So now I'd met Vasily's staff: Stefan, Serge, Lena, and Elena. Maybe he used a Moscow employment agency that specialized in hard-ass special ops types and drop-dead gorgeous blonde Lolitas.

"This way, Frank," Vasily said. "I'll give you a tour of my boat, and then we'll have lunch."

THE WIND came up, causing a moderate chop on the gulf, no problem for the *Treasure Hunter,* as we made way for Sanibel, a barrier island to the north, just off the coast of Fort Myers.

Sanibel is twelve miles long and four miles wide. It is best known for shelling on its sugar-sand beaches and for the heavy traffic on Periwinkle Way, the main artery. I always wondered what families from Saint Cloud, Minnesota, or Hammond, Indiana, did with all those shells when they got home.

Elena served lunch as we sat at a teak table under a blue canvas awning on the upper deck. We ate grilled spiny lobsters with rémoulade and key lime pie. Vasily sipped an icy mug of Bass Pale Ale and I had freshly made lemonade. He made light conversation about sports and politics and climate change before getting down to business during the pie course.

"Allow me to explain why I invited you to hear about The Atocha Fund," he said, pushing back from the table and offering me a cigar, which I declined. He snipped off the end with a sterling silver cutter, fired up the stogie with a matching lighter, and continued:

"There is, as I've said, a waiting list of people with considerable assets wanting to invest with me. I limit our client list to fifty so I can give everyone personal attention. Frankly the only way to get in is to be at the top of the waiting list when one of my clients dies. In this, we are not unlike the Olde Naples Country Club."

He smiled at this analogy, took a puff of the cigar, and went on: "In fact, sadly, three of our valued clients have gone to the great beyond recently."

Eileen Stephenson, Lester Gandolf, and Bob Appleby.

"Only Mr. Gandolf's widow has elected to cash out of the fund. I've decided that, as openings occur, it would be good to offer them to younger people. All of our clients are in the fund for the long run. It would be advantageous to fill the openings with people who have a longer term, so to speak. When I met you at Lady Ashley's dinner party, I thought you would be a perfect candidate the next time there was an opening."

Only in a place like Naples would a man my age be considered young. Marisa told me that an old saying is, "I thought I was old and rich until I moved to Naples."

"Makes sense," I said, even though it didn't, to me. Money was money, and even when a client croaked, and the heirs wanted to withdraw the funds, there was that waiting list. Vasily must have a different agenda in offering me a spot. I'd have to let it play out.

"I'm glad you agree. You would not regret your decision to invest with me."

Fish on! Vasily had swallowed the bait: me. Assuming that he would make such an offer, I had decided I would hit up my employers for my investment in The Atocha Fund. Then, after a while, I would find a reason to ask for it back, and be ready for an unannounced visit from one of Vasily's employees. If Vasily was not legit. If he was, Marisa would have to come up with a Plan B.

The nighttime visitor would most likely be Stefan the driver or Serge the first mate. Or maybe Lena the receptionist or Elena the second mate had been to assassin school in Mother Russia too. That would be a smart play, because I would hesitate to pull the trigger on one of those lovely ladies, and as they say, he who hesitates is lost.

We finished lunch as the *Treasure Hunter* made a sweeping turn, heading south, back toward the yacht club. It was warmer now because the wind was at our backs. We moved down a deck and sat in canvas chairs, sipping Cuban coffees. It was a pleasant moment, out there on the blue water in an amazing boat, feeling content from a good lunch and the rich, dark coffee. Maybe Vasily had a barista on the crew. It would have been even more pleasant if my host weren't a suspected serial killer. I hadn't told anyone about the boat ride. If I didn't return, no one would know what happened to me.

"I would like to invest in your fund," I told Vasily.

He smiled at this. "Excellent, Frank. You can come to my office at your earliest convenience to do the paperwork."

He pointed out a pair of manatees floating off the port bow. The captain was turning right to avoid hitting them. Vasily said, nonchalantly, "Did I mention that our minimum investment is $10 million?"

The *minimum* investment? Fortunately I wasn't swallowing coffee at the moment or I might have choked on it and blown my cover. I recovered and winked at him. "As my father always said, go big or go home. I'll start with one unit, and we'll see how it goes from there."

What my father really said was: "People who pretend to be someone they're not always get knocked down a peg."

Or shot.

18.

Show Me The Money

I had a friend in the Chicago PD who was an undercover narc. He once got approval to use ten K of the city's money for a drug buy. The buy went south, as did the dealer, with the cash and the drugs, all the way to Mexico. You want to take a limo from downtown to O'Hare or Midway airport, you can call my friend to drive you.

If I sold The Drunken Parrot, the *Phoenix*, my 'Vette, emptied my bank account, and put everything else I owned up for sale on eBay, I could maybe get into the mid six-figure range, nowhere near the mountain of zeros Vasily required. It was possible that Bill Stevens had that kind of dough from his book sales. But that wasn't the plan.

When I got back to Ash's house, I called Wade Hansen and explained the situation. Maybe his department had some counterfeit currency stashed away from arrests over the years that was good enough to pass Vasily's scrutiny. Or maybe the city could float a bond issue.

Hansen said he'd arrange a meeting with Mayor Beaumont and call back with the time and place.

The time was eight the next morning, and the place was the Naples City Dock at the end of Twelfth Avenue South. We were to go out on a charter fishing boat owned by a man Hansen knew. The man had been a Naples PD patrol sergeant whose wife had inherited some money, allowing him to live his own version of the cop dream.

The boat was a thirty-seven-foot Grady-White named *Eloise*; the captain was a guy named Jimmy Burke. Eloise was Jimmy's wife.

It turned out that we were actually going to fish. Maybe my employers wanted to keep our meetings secret from then on, and didn't want anyone to see me going into the Naples city hall now that I was pursuing an actual "person of interest," as the feds say. Or maybe they just wanted a morning on the water.

We were twenty miles out, trolling for bluefin tuna, when Beaumont informed me that he'd come up with the $10 million for Vasily Petrovich's Atocha Fund. He made it clear that he'd like very much to get it back, and that he'd keep the source of the funds to himself.

Did a city like Naples really have that much in the mayoral slush fund? Even if it didn't, it wasn't impossible to imagine that, in order to keep the city safe from scandal, there were individuals willing to front the dough without asking why on the mayor's assurance that it was for something important. All of which was completely unreal to a kid from Wrigleyville, but what about this whole undertaking wasn't?

"A TD Ameritrade account will be opened in the name of Frank Chance," Beaumont said as we sat in deck chairs on the stern, watching the lures trailing behind the boat. "The $10 million will be wired into the account a few days from now. I'll let you know when it's available."

"Fish on!" Captain Jimmy shouted as one of the poles bent down and line began running out, the reel emitting a high-pitched whine.

The mayor was the ranking member on the boat, so the honor of fighting the first fish went to him. He moved to the chair holding the rod with the strike and did well for a man his age, the cords on his neck popping, and sweating and breathing so heavily I thought he might have a heart attack or stroke. But he shook off an offer from Captain Jimmy to relieve him.

Macho man, all the way to the cemetery.

After what seemed like a few weeks—fishing is boring when you're just watching it—the mayor finally brought the tuna alongside the boat. Captain Jimmy hooked it with a gaff and horsed it onto the deck, where it flopped around until the captain gave it a whack on the head with an aluminum baseball bat.

This time the catch was a tasty game fish and not a Russian count. If Vasily really was a count. Hansen was doing a background check on him and his firm. He told me this was taking longer than usual because it had been discovered that Atocha Securities is, in fact, registered in the Cayman Islands, as I'd guessed, where corporate and financial information is difficult to obtain.

Difficult, but not impossible, Hansen said. Maybe, with the connections the mayor had, he could order the waterboarding of the president of the Cayman National Bank, if necessary, until he gave up the info.

"Let's take a private jet to Paris for dinner," I said to Marisa when I called her on my way back to Ash's house after the fishing trip. I was driving the Bugatti this time.

"Huh?"

"Actually, we can do that a few days from now," I said, "when a certain wire transfer arrives in my investment account."

"I didn't know you had an investment account," Marisa commented.

"I don't, but Frank Chance does. We'll go to the fanciest restaurants, stay at the most expensive hotel, and go shop till we drop. I'll explain everything over dinner tonight at Captain Mack's Clam Shack."

"Captain Mack's? So tonight I'm dining with Jack Starkey and not Frank Chance."

"That would be correct. Disappointed?"

"I'll get back to you on that. Money isn't everything, but it does paper over a lot of flaws."

Later that afternoon, I sat with Ash at a pine table in the kitchen where, I assumed, Martin and Suzette took their meals. Ash didn't quiz me on the details of my developing investigation, but I could tell this took all of her willpower.

Afterward I found Joe sleeping on a footstool in the living room. The stool was near a window that was in the sun at that time of day. Clearly he was comfortable in his new digs. I sat down beside him, scratched his head, and gave him an update on the case. I assumed that briefing my cat did not violate my confidentiality agreement, especially when he was asleep.

19.

Bad, Bad Leroy Brown

Captain Mack's Clam Shack is just over the causeway from the mainland on Sanibel Island. It is a favorite of mine because most menu items were battered and deep-fat fried. Marisa always has some sort of broiled fish and a salad. In my opinion, you could batter and fry an old shoe, and it'd taste great with tartar sauce.

Marisa listened to my explanation of this stage of the plan, with me investing in the hedge fund and then asking for a withdrawal, making me a possible target to test the theory that Vasily was behind the murders. When I was finished, she said, "If that fake count hurts you, I'll hunt him down and cut off his balls just to get his attention, and then we'll get into some really nasty stuff."

She was a very refined lady. That was her hot Latin blood talking. I found it to be erotic, but I found everything about her to be erotic.

I put my fork into a fried clam, dipped it in tartar sauce, chewed, and swallowed it, and said, "It's good to know you've got my back."

"And your front and your sides, big guy," she responded with a wink.

After dinner, we drove to Salty Sam's so I could check on *Phoenix*. Because I was the real me tonight, I was driving my Corvette.

My boat was as shipshape as it ever got. Sam checked on it periodically to make certain it wasn't overrun by wharf rats. I thought about suggesting a roll in the hay to Marisa, but I didn't want her to think that's all I ever had on my mind, even though it mostly was.

Then we went to The Drunken Parrot. I was pleased to find a good-sized crowd. We took seats at the bar. Without asking, Sam served a glass of chardonnay to Marisa and a chilled mug of root beer to me.

"Looks like you've got things well in hand," I told Sam.

"I do. And when you're not here, I find it easier to skim from the cash register."

Sam was completely trustworthy, and would never do anything like that. In addition, he didn't need the money because he was a Seminole and got a share of the tribe's substantial profits from its five Florida casinos. I don't know how much that is, but he once told me that if I ever want to sell the bar, I should ask him first. I promised that I would.

I heard raised voices. At the other end of the bar, two men were apparently staking a claim to the same woman.

Jim Croce's song "Bad, Bad Leroy Brown" covered the same situation in Chicago. One of the men was of medium height, portly and bearded, wearing a wife-beater tee shirt, camo cargo shorts, and cowboy boots. It was not a good look for him. The other guy was tall and wiry, wearing jeans and a black tee shirt with white lettering that said, "Fuck Off." Apparently he wasn't into making new friends.

Both men appeared to be in their thirties. The woman, who was apparently trying to choose between Dumb and Dumber, had long red hair and was wearing a tight blue tee shirt and Daisy Duke denim shorts. She was older than the men, maybe in her late forties, but she had a body worth fighting over, at least in a dim bar if you'd had enough to drink.

I noticed that Sam was on full alert, watching for a line to be crossed. There was a shotgun under the bar, but Sam never used it if a troublemaker didn't appear to have a weapon. I knew from experience that there were two kinds of men in this world: talkers and fighters. Talkers face off, belly-to-belly, trade threats and insults, and declare that, as soon as the other guy throws the first punch, there'd be hell to pay. Generally you could leave them alone; they'd talk themselves out and the confrontation would eventually dissipate. Fighters didn't talk at all. If provoked, they'd move in on you and end the confrontation as quickly as the strike of a cobra. SEAL Team Six didn't tell Osama to fire the first shot.

These two guys were clearly talkers, but the talk was getting loud enough to bother the other customers, so Sam walked down to their end of the bar and said, "How about if you gentlemen take it outside?"

The men stopped arguing and looked at Sam. The woman said, "And why don't you mind your own damn fucking business, chief."

To which Sam replied, "Tell you what, ma'am. Why don't you pick one of these two crackers and leave with him. The loser will get the next drink on the house."

She thought about that, looking at each man in turn, said, "I pick neither one," and walked out of the bar.

The men watched her go, then looked at one another as if uncertain about what the rules of macho behavior required of them in a situation like that.

"So it's two drinks on the house," Sam told them, skillfully diffusing the situation. "What'll it be?"

"An Early Times with a draft Bud back," the portly guy said.

"Same for me," the thin guy said, which could be the basis for a fast friendship.

Marisa and I finished our drinks. After I greeted some of the regulars, we left. As we did, the two guys were chatting amiably.

"I'd say all three of them are better off, and that Sam has a future as a marriage counselor," Marisa told me as we got in my car.

"A marriage counselor with a shotgun can be very persuasive," I said.

20.

The Eagle Has Landed

I returned from my morning run on the beach and was heading upstairs for a shower when Ash found me and said, "Wade Hansen called and told me to give you a message: The eagle has landed. Whatever that means."

More specifically, ten million eagles had landed in Frank Chance's TD Ameritrade account. Funny how that amount of wealth can change a person's outlook on life, even if it's fake wealth for a fake identity. I thought about Margie Lewin, the girl who'd broken my heart in junior high school. If only Margie could see me now.

As I showered, I thought about my next move. I'd call Vasily and tell him I was ready to make my initial investment in The Atocha Fund. My account statement, if I was in the fund long enough to get one, would surely show substantial investment gains, which would probably not be real.

But I wouldn't be in The Atocha Fund long enough to get an account statement. I'd let my money ride for a few weeks, and then call Vasily and say that, because of changing circumstances of some kind, I needed to withdraw my $10 million. If I was right about him, he'd send one of his soldiers instead of a wire transfer. While I was waiting for the assassin, Ash would go on a trip to be out of harm's way, and Joe would be at Marisa's house so he wouldn't get caught in the line of fire. Of course all of this would be a fool's errand if Vasily was running an honest business. If he was, the investigation was back to square one.

In sting operations conducted by the Chicago Police Department, an effort is made to plan for every contingency. The undercover officer wears a wire so that the transaction can be monitored. SWAT teams are waiting in vans, and snipers are watching from rooftops.

I'd have to go it alone. If things went my way, I'd subdue the assassin and hold him for Chief Hansen and his troops. He'd be arrested, and an effort would be made to get him to rat out his employer in return for a reduced sentence. Or I'd kill him but maybe his tie to Vasily would be enough to get a judge to issue a warrant to delve into Vasily's finances. If things didn't go my way the City of Chicago would have one less police pension and disability payment to make.

Or, if no assassin showed up, I could order a pizza delivery and watch whatever sporting event was on TV—anything but soccer, which was actually *more* boring than watching paint dry.

I called Vasily the next morning and told him I was ready to do the paperwork. He said he'd clear his schedule to meet with me whenever I wanted. I'd clear my schedule, too, for an appointment with $10 million. I said that I was free that afternoon at three o'clock.

LENA GREETED me when I walked into the office by saying, "It's so nice to see you again, Mr. Chance."

"Please, call me Frank," I told her. "Or call me Czar Nicholas, if you prefer."

I'd read an article in *Men's Journal* about the traits women find most attractive in a man. The article had men guess what they were. The majority of answers involved high net worth, good looks, and a big Glock. Those would have been my answers too. But for the women, a sense of humor was at the top of the list, followed by intelligence, and "sensitivity to a woman's needs"—which were, presumably, high net worth, good looks, and a big Glock. I guess Lena had not read the article, because she didn't laugh at my clever quip. "Mr. Petrovich said you should go right to his office when you arrive," she said.

I bet Lena called him Vasily, and not Mr. Petrovich, when they were alone. Or maybe Count Honey Bunny.

"So, Frank, we have some business to transact," Vasily said, rising from his desk and indicating that I join him at a small round table. We both sat, and he withdrew some papers from a manila file folder he'd taken from his desktop.

"Unless you have changed your mind about investing with me, there are just a few documents for you to sign," he said. "Of course if you would prefer to have your attorney review them first, that would be fine."

"That won't be necessary. I'll look them over right now." As if reviewing complex financial agreements was just another day at the beach for me.

He handed one of the documents to me. "This one is required by the Securities and Exchange Commission. It states that The Atocha Fund is a high-risk investment, and that the past performance is no guarantee of future profits. If it's acceptable, please sign at the bottom."

I looked it over as if understanding it and almost signed my real name, but caught myself.

"And this one is our client agreement," he said, handing me a second form. "It gives me the authority to invest your funds as I see fit, in return for a management fee of 2 percent of the account total, plus 20 percent of the annual profits from your portfolio. It explains that we will provide you with quarterly reports, an annual report, and a form 1099 at the end of the year for income tax purposes."

The only investment terms I was familiar with were for my checking and savings accounts at First Chicago Bank. When I opened them, they gave me a choice between a stadium blanket and a toaster. I took the toaster because it would be better than my old one for making Pop-Tarts due to the wider slots. If I wrote a check with insufficient funds, they could repossess my car, or something like that. When I opened an account at Sunshine Bank and Trust in Fort Myers Beach, the highflying days of consumer banking had ended and there was no gift. Sunshine's attitude seemed to be that I should consider myself fortunate that the bank would serve such a small fry.

I pretended to read the complex legalese, and signed as Frank Chance. Vasily handed me the third document.

"Finally, this certifies that you are a qualified investor, meaning that you have a net worth of at least $1 million, or an annual income of at least $200,000. As you know, the government requires this because it indicates you have a sufficient degree of financial sophistication to judge the appropriateness of a high-risk investment."

"Of course," I said.

In fact, my total financial sophistication came from browsing through *Investing For Dummies,* which I bought upon retiring from the police force, and flipped through before dozing off. I recall that "buy low, sell high," is something an investor should do. I didn't pick up how to do that.

"Very good," Vasily said when I'd signed the last form. He returned them to the file folder, then moved to his desk and took another piece of paper from a desk drawer.

"Assuming that you wish to wire your funds to us, here are the instructions," he told me. He winked. "We also take cash, checks, and credit cards, except for American Express."

Just a little humor among us sophisticated investors. I took the wire transfer instructions and said, "I'm not carrying that much cash today. I'll have my people wire the funds ASAP."

I figured that a guy like Frank Chance had people to take care of things like that.

THE $10 million was wired into The Atocha Fund's account at the Grand Cayman International Bank the next day. My people (actually, the mayor's people) were very efficient.

Hansen called and asked me to meet him for lunch at a Hooters restaurant on Pine Ridge Road, next to the Harley-Davidson dealership.

Boobs and bikes. Excellent marketing concept. I'd once been in a Hooters in Chicago for a bachelor party for one of the guys on the force. This was during my drinking days; I remember being mildly titillated by the waitresses, and leaving a very large tip, which was obviously the point of the skimpy outfits.

Apparently the Hooters corporate marketing strategy had been refocused, because there were some motorcycle guys drinking and dining there, but most of the customers were families eating chicken wings and burgers. Maybe Disney had acquired the chain. I found Hansen sitting in a booth and joined him.

"Let's order," he said. "Then I'll give you some interesting information about our Russian count."

We both ordered bacon cheeseburgers with fries. Our waitress, who was a nice lady in her fifties, seemed a bit uncomfortable to be dressed like a Hooters babe. While we waited for our food, Hansen said, "We got the FBI report on Vasily. Turns out he's really from Brighton Beach, which is a big Russian neighborhood in Brooklyn. His father was a top boss in the Russian Mafia. Vasily graduated from City College of New York with a degree in finance. His name is Boris Ivanovich. He worked on Wall Street for a penny stock brokerage firm that the SEC shut down for fraud. The owners went to prison, and young Boris lost his brokerage license. He has an elaborate set of identity papers in the name of Vasily Petrovich, no doubt supplied by his mob connections. Passport, driver's license, the works, including the SEC and state licenses required to operate his investment firm."

"So the man's an impostor," I said. "And Boris Ivanovich from Brighton Beach now has somebody's $10 million, along with his other investors' money."

Hansen nodded. "We haven't been able to penetrate his Cayman Islands bank account. They're very serious about confidentiality. We can assume that The Atocha Fund is as phony as his identity. We can't prove that yet, and we can't connect him to the deaths of his three clients, plus Bob Appleby's girlfriend. But what we do have, using a false identity to operate an investment business, is enough to arrest him. That is, if I wanted to, which I don't, yet."

I understood what he meant. Murder trumps financial fraud every day of the week. So I was still in the detective business.

21.

Who's On First?

Bill Stevens flew in from Chicago for one of his periodic visits. I met him at the Fort Myers airport in my Corvette. It would be way too complicated to explain why I was driving one of Sir Reggie's Hot Wheels; maybe he'd think I was skimming from our bar's cash register.

I'd told Hansen I needed to spend a few days at home, taking care of business, and to call me if anything new happened. Joe was with me, curled up on the passenger seat. Bill, along with Marisa, was on the short list of people Joe liked.

Bill spotted me waiting at the curb outside baggage claim, waved, and came over carrying a duffel bag slung over his shoulder. He was wearing his usual tropical attire: Ray-Bans, a Cubs hat, a loud Hawaiian shirt, baggy Bulls basketball shorts, and flip-flops.

"Welcome to paradise," I told him. "You, as always, are a study in sartorial splendor."

"Back atcha," he said. "And I mean it."

I hadn't thought to change out of Sir Reginald's clothes. I handed Bill the keys so he could put his duffel bag into the trunk. He did, and then noticed Joe on the seat. Joe looked at him and meowed, which might have meant, "You're no Hemingway, but you're all we've got." I lifted Joe onto my lap and Bill got in.

"So, who's on first?" he said as we drove away.

"Yes," I answered.

"I mean the fellow's name."

"Who."

"The guy on first."

"Who."

"The first baseman."

And as we tooled along the highway toward Fort Myers Beach, we went though the classic Abbott and Costello baseball routine, "Who's On First?" word for word, as we had many times before.

Old friends are best friends.

THE NEXT morning, our aluminum fishing skiff was drifting in the current in the backwaters of Estero Bay as Bill and I were casting flies for bonefish. I'd borrowed the boat from Salty Sam's.

Bill and I hung out at The Drunken Parrot last night. I invited Marisa to join us, but she said she'd heard all our stories before and wanted to be home to watch HGTV. Go figure.

Bill was staying at the Shipwreck Motel on Estero Boulevard, where he always did when in town. I didn't know how much he actually slept, because a very attractive young woman who was majoring in English literature at Florida Gulf Coast University was in the bar with friends. Bill spotted her in the crowd, walked over, and handed her a copy of *Stoney's Revenge*, flipped to the back cover showing his photo. In the photo, taken by a *Chicago Tribune* photographer, he was wearing jeans and a leather bomber jacket and was leaning against a lamppost on Michigan Avenue. His ironic yet lady-killer smile was something he practiced in the mirror.

The young lady seemed thrilled to meet a famous author. Bill, in turn, seemed thrilled to be met. Before long, they left the bar together for a private autograph session.

Bill noticed a fish rising to the surface near a mangrove island and dropped his Black Gnat Red-Tail lure right on it. In a glint of sunlight on the water, the fish nosed the fly, then languidly swam away in search of breakfast without a hook. Bonefish are smart. Once they've been caught (and released, they are a game fish and not good eating), they're not likely to be fooled again.

We'd been at it for nearly two hours, starting at seven. We'd each had a few nibbles, but had put nothing in the boat. It was time to open the cooler Marisa packed for us that morning before leaving the *Phoenix* for work. In it, we found two of the best breakfast burritos money couldn't buy, some fresh fruit, and OJ she'd squeezed by hand because I didn't own one of the fancy machines she had at home.

Bill took a bite of burrito, looked out across the water at a shrimp boat that had been beached and abandoned because Asian frozen shrimp had killed the domestic fishery, and said, "If this ain't living, then I'm not missing anything by not."

"Good thing you write better than you speak," I said. "But I know what you mean."

"That's what counts."

"I'm almost done going through the manuscript of *Stoney's Last Stand*," I told him. "Are you into the next one yet?"

"I am. The working title is *Stoney's Dick Is Bigger Than Yours*, but I expect the publisher will change it."

"Pity."

"Last night at the bar, Sam briefed you on the business," Bill said. "Why?"

"I've been doing some consulting work for the City of Naples, so I haven't been around much for the last few weeks."

"Doing what?"

"I'm working with the police chief on a case I can't discuss."

"That's the best kind," Bill said. "I wish I'd brought my notebook."

"No, really, I can't. Maybe someday. Hell of a thing is happening there . . ."

"And they're able to keep a lid on it?"

"So far."

"If I used the story for a novel, it wouldn't come out for a year or more."

"I need to see this thing through, and then maybe I can get permission to tell you about it."

"Not a problem," Bill said.

A school of bonefish were sunning themselves just off that mangrove island. They must have known we were on a breakfast break. My cell phone rang and the fish bolted. I found it at the bottom of my canvas boat bag. The caller ID said it was Wade Hansen.

"I've got to take this," I told Bill.

"Are you going to finish your burrito?" Bill responded.

I answered and Hansen said, "Am I interrupting anything?"

"No, a friend and I are busy not catching fish. What's up?"

"It's Ashley Howe," he said.

"Is she all right?" I asked him.

"No, she's not all right. She's dead."

A homicide detective gets hardened to murders. If you get too personally involved, you can't do your job properly. Emotion gets in the way of deductive thinking. But this news shocked me to the core. I wanted to hang Vasily upside down and use a bullwhip to get the truth out of him. If it turned out he was innocent, I'd say sorry about that and offer to buy him dinner.

We ended the call and I told Bill I had to attend to some business that couldn't wait.

"Your case," he said. "Knowing you, that means someone's dead."

"I can't confirm or deny that."

"Meaning it's true. This isn't my first rodeo, partner."

I powered up the skiff, returned to Salty Sam's, and drove Bill back to his hotel. He was staying for three more days and said he could amuse himself for the rest of his visit. I wondered if that English lit major had classes that day.

"WHAT DO they know?" Marisa asked when I called her. "About what happened to Ash?"

"Her butler found her in bed this morning when he delivered coffee to her room, as he does every morning," I told her. "An empty prescription bottle was on the bedside table. When he couldn't awaken her, he checked for a pulse and called 9-1-1. Hansen said they haven't been able to contact any of her family yet, but there will be an autopsy because a crime might have been involved. Of course if she was murdered, the autopsy report will have to be kept quiet."

"So what happens now?" Marisa asked.

"The first thing is to look for any connections between Ash and the three other victims. I know one thing for certain. They were all investors in Vasily Petrovich's hedge fund."

"And now you are too."

"And now I am too."

When I turned into the driveway at Ash's house, everything appeared completely normal. No crime scene tape, no police vehicles, no news crews. It wasn't officially a crime scene, but to me it was. I had told Marisa I'd keep her informed. She had told me to "Be safe." I assured her that I would be.

Martin met me at the front door. He looked stricken. I told him that I was sorry for his loss, as if he was a relative, which is how Ash seemed to treat him. He thanked me and led me to the patio, where Charles Beaumont and Wade Hansen were waiting at the table. I took a chair and asked, "So what've you got?"

Hansen pulled a notepad from his pocket, flipped to a page, looked at it, and said, "Ashley's prescription was for a drug called estazolam. Her doc said that this is one of a class of sleep medications called benzodiazepines, or however the fuck you pronounce it. He said that taking a whole bottle of the stuff can cause death by impairing breathing and stopping the heart. The bottle was empty, but until the autopsy we don't know how much she took, if any."

"Any sign of forcible entry?" I asked.

"None," Hansen answered.

"Any sign of a struggle?"

"No."

Beaumont spoke for the first time, anger in his voice. "No matter how Ash died, we've got a freakin' serial killer running loose in our town. It's a goddamned disaster. Maybe it's time to bring in the FBI."

Hansen said, "I don't know that we can keep a lid on it if we call in the feds, but we've got to put a stop to this, and fast."

"I think we should pursue the lead on the Russian," I told them.

They both looked at me. "A lead?" Beaumont asked.

“The Russian,” I said. “Vasily Petrovich. Who we now know is really someone else.”

“When we got the report about him, I assumed he was just another scam artist,” Beaumont said. “We get a lot of them here.”

“All of the victims were invested in Vasily’s—or Boris’s—hedge fund,” I told him. “I don’t believe in coincidences like that.”

“Christ, I’ve got a shitload of money in that fund,” Beaumont said. “I was about to pull a portion of it out and buy some investment real estate, now that the market’s strong again.”

“I’d hold off on that,” I told him.

After all, if the mayor was dead, who would sign my checks?

22.

Going Home

The report of Ash's autopsy showed a nontoxic level of estazolam in her blood. It also showed she had an undiagnosed obstruction of the two major coronary arteries. She'd died of a heart attack. I decided I had to get control of my eating habits.

Her will, which I found in Sir Reggie's desk, stated that she wanted to be buried in her family's plot in a cemetery in her hometown of Mount Clemens, Michigan, a small city near Detroit. She left generous sums to Martin, her butler, and Suzette, her cook, and the rest of her estate to the various charities she and Sir Reggie had supported over the years. Those included the Mount Clemens and the Naples Centers For Abused Children, as well as the animal shelters in both cities. Those bequests made more sense when Mayor Beaumont told me about Ash's earlier life. He said she had confided in him but that he no longer felt obligated to keep her secrets from her friends.

Her maiden name was Ashley St. Claire. She was sexually abused by a stepfather and ran away from home when she was thirteen. Obviously, as evidenced by her will, she felt great sympathy for other abused children, and for abused animals as well. She supported herself with different jobs and got her high school equivalency diploma. She had a sister named Irene who drowned in a pond at age nine. Ash suspectred that Irene had been abused by their stepfather too, although they never talked about it, and that Irene, who knew how to swim, may have drowned herself as a result. How very sad all of that was.

Ash was working as a model, attending a community college, when she met Sir Reggie. His family disliked her. They saw her as a fortune hunter. He had a son and some nieces and nephews. When they found out they weren't in her will, Beaumont told me, they wouldn't attend her funeral.

SAINT STEPHEN's Church, which I knew she had attended, was packed to overflowing for Ash's memorial service. Beaumont and a long list of her other friends spoke about what a fine and generous lady she was. Frank Chance said a few kind words too. Lady Ashley Howe, aka Ashley St. Claire, had played the bad hand she was dealt as well as anyone could.

A large contingent of her Naples friends, including the mayor, flew to Michigan aboard the plane that carried her coffin to be at her funeral. Ash was buried in a family plot near her mother and sister. Beaumont made certain that Ash had a nice headstone and he personally gave the cemetery an amount of money to make certain that all of the St. Claire family graves were properly maintained, and flowers put on Ash's grave on her birthday. Despite all the unpleasantness of her youth, the pull to return home at the end was obviously very strong for her.

When the mayor returned, he told me that Ash had named him as executor of her estate and, as such, he'd like Marisa to supervise an inventory of her possessions so they could be sold and the proceeds distributed according to her will, and to sell her house. He said I could remain living in it until my assignment was completed.

IT WAS time for me to tell Vasily that, because of my aunt's death, I'd decided to leave Naples, and that I wanted to withdraw all of my money from The Atocha Fund and have it managed in New York, where I'd decided to live. Then I would wait, like a chunk of raw, bloody beef on a hook, dangling in the water, for Vasily's shark to come for me. By then, I was all but certain he was behind the crimes, in part because no other suspects had turned up, and in part because of The Atocha Fund connection to the victims.

Once again, I didn't have to call Vasily, because the next day he called me. Martin found me standing in the library, admiring Sir Reggie's collection of rare books. There were also popular fiction titles on the shelves, which I assumed belonged to Ash. Martin handed me the phone and withdrew. Does anyone but a butler withdraw from a room, as opposed to just leaving it?

"Frank, this is Vasily Petrovich," he said. "I want to again express my deepest sympathy over the passing of your aunt. Ashley was a friend and a fine lady. She will be missed."

"I was going to call you," I said. "Now that my aunt is gone, Naples has lost its appeal for me. I've decided to go back to New York. I have a financial advisor there and I want him to handle all of my money."

"I understand completely," Vasily said, sounding sincere. "As soon as you give me the instructions, the funds will immediately be wired to your account."

He's good, I thought. But maybe he meant that the funds would be wired to me posthumously.

23.

Killing Monet

It happened at three the next morning. That's the hour when a pro does a home invasion and law enforcement officers choose to take down a sleeping perp, because that is the time of deepest REM (rapid eye movement) sleep. By the time the target is fully awake, it's too late, Elvis has left the building.

I didn't actually hear a noise, but Joe must have, because he jumped up onto the bed and batted my cheek with his paw. He'd never done that before. I woke up and started to say something to him, but stopped, because then I did hear something. Nearly imperceptible, it was a sound that the big old house had never made on its own since I'd been there. It was not breaking glass, or a door lock being picked, or the tread of a foot on a stairway, or a doorknob being slowly turned.

I'd have to say that it really was not a noise at all. Rather, it was a feeling that something was not right, of a presence in your space that should not be there. Bad karma was in the air. We know that animals have the ability to sense something like that. Marines develop it too, when in harm's way, and learn to trust it.

I slipped out of bed, looked at Joe, and put my finger on my lips to indicate that he should be quiet. I'd never done that before, and had no idea if he knew what I meant, but he did not meow.

I found my boxer shorts on the floor (another item on Claire's list of things about me that annoyed her), took my Glock out of the drawer.

In a situation like that, you've got two choices: wait for trouble to come to you, or go to meet it head-on. Depending upon the circumstances, there are advantages to both responses. But I was never good at waiting, so I moved toward the closed bedroom door. As I did, I recalled a scene in one of Bill's books, where Jack Stoney hears a noise in the night and heads toward the trouble; a guy with a gun was coming for him, and the guy, of course, didn't have a chance. I pushed that out of my mind because that was fiction. If Bill didn't like the way a scene turned out, he could do a rewrite. But this was real, and there were no do-overs.

I eased the door open, waited a moment, listening, then went into the hallway, just like you see in the movies: crouched low, gun extended in both hands, swiveling from side to side.

Clear.

Rather than trying to check all of the bedrooms on the second floor, I decided to go downstairs to look for a point of entry. I thought about Joe and hoped he was hiding under the bed. I hadn't been in a gunfight in many years. Maybe I should have been under the bed too.

I kept my back along the wall as I made my way down the staircase. Bright moonlight through the windows illuminated the scene. As I reached the bottom of the stairs, I heard two noises simultaneously: a gunshot, and a meow. If Joe was trying to tell me to duck, he was just a fraction of a second too late.

The bullet hit the wall a few inches high and to the right of my head, probably because I'd just stepped down from the stairway. Although it was a tactical mistake, I looked back up behind me and saw Joe standing there, looking down at me from the top of the staircase. He had my back.

I heard the sound of running footsteps and found the door to the patio open and one of the chairs at the table turned over. A pane of glass in one of the french doors was broken.

I went outside and stopped to scan the backyard. Nothing. I heard the sound of a boat motor starting and ran toward the dock. By the time I got close to the beach, a small black rubber inflatable boat, called a Zodiac, the kind commandos use, was speeding out into the gulf, too far away for a pistol shot.

I went back inside and to the stairway. The bullet intended for me had hit the Monet painting. The insurance company wouldn't like that.

24.

Try Again, Over Dinner

It was 3:10 A.M. I decided not to awaken Hansen from his REM sleep. No way I could nod off after being shot at, so I read the book I'd selected from the downstairs library. It was a crime novel. Even though I didn't usually read them, except for the ones by Bill Stevens, who paid me to, I wasn't in the mood for *The Decline and Fall of the Roman Empire.*

The book was *Hard Stop,* written by a guy named Chris Knopf. The main character, Sam Acquillo, was a former corporate tech specialist who became a carpenter in the Hamptons, a wealthy resort area of Long Island not unlike Naples. Sam thought he'd signed up for a serene existence, but gets drawn into an investigation of a crime that threatens his life. It's one of a series. I liked the book, because I identified with Sam's situation.

Joe went back to sleep in his favorite bedroom chair, confident that I had the watch and he'd be safe.

At seven A.M., I heard a commotion downstairs and knew that Martin and Suzette had reported for duty. I decided that I'd go down for some breakfast before calling Hansen to tell him about my night visitor. Remembering Ash's coronary arteries, I had coffee, oatmeal, and some fruit. Then I used my cell phone to call Hansen.

"I had a bite last night, but the fish got away," I told him when he answered on the first ring.

"Where?"

"At Ash's house."

"Anyone hurt?"

"Just Claude Monet."

I told him what had happened and that I was certain Vasily had sent someone to kill me.

"It would be nice to actually have some proof of that," Hansen said, with a touch of sarcasm in his voice.

I'd been at this awhile, and proof was in short supply.

"Wait there, I'm coming over with a crime scene tech," he said. "And don't touch anything."

As I was having a second cup of coffee while waiting for him, Martin came out of the house with the phone, handed it to me and said, "Mr. Petrovich for you, sir."

Which was, as we say in the detective trade, an unexpected development. Maybe Vasily was checking to see if his man's bullet had hit me, not Claude.

"I hope I'm not calling too early," he said.

"No, I've been up for a while," I told him. Since three A.M., to be precise.

"Good, good. Let me buy you dinner before you leave. How about tomorrow night at Provence? It is my favorite French restaurant in town."

Interesting. His assassin blew the assignment, so now Vasily's strategy was to kill me with cholesterol-laden french sauces. Or maybe take me out while I was on the way to the restaurant. I had to hand it to him. The man had brass testicles.

Marisa liked the Provence too. Whenever we went there together, I always began my meal with escargots. I'd remove the disgusting little snails from each hole in the round serving dish, set them aside, and sop up the garlic butter with crusty french bread. The first time I did that, Marisa just shook her head and said, "You can take the boy out of Wrigleyville . . ."

"I know the place," I told Vasily. "I'll see you there."

"Eight o'clock then. And again, I'm sorry for your loss."

Meaning, I thought, he was sorry that the loss didn't include me.

HANSEN ARRIVED ahead of the crime scene tech. I walked him through the events of that morning, beginning in my bedroom, and ending down at the dock.

We found nothing anywhere that looked like a clue, except for the broken window on one of the french doors leading out to the patio. I also filled the chief in on the details of everything that had recently occurred between Vasily and me, including the dinner invitation.

"Maybe he means to take you out on the way to the restaurant," Hansen said as we stood on the dock looking out over the tranquil gulf. "He wouldn't try it in a public place like a restaurant. Car accident, sniper, something like that."

"I've thought of that," I said. "I'm not going to give him the chance."

"Do you have another one of your plans that I shouldn't know about?"

"That would be correct," I admitted.

"Okay," he said as we walked back to the house. "For some reason, it seems Vasily's given up on trying to make the murders look accidental. Or maybe he thought shooting you last night would look like a burglary gone bad."

"If it's him," I said.

"Yeah, there's still that 'if.' "

"To go to the next step, I'll need some help," I told him.

"Such as?"

"Tonight, during hours I designate, I'll need the electrical power to a certain downtown building turned off. Can you arrange that?"

"I can do that. I know a guy in the city engineer's office. Just say where and when."

We went outside and sat at the table. Martin came out and took our drink order. "I'm going to miss having a butler," I told Hansen.

25.

Cat Burglar

Three A.M. again. Two can play the REM sleep game. I parked my car on a side street four blocks from Fifth Avenue South in downtown Naples, got out, and started walking through a residential neighborhood toward the building where Atocha Securities was located. I'd decided to break into Vasily's offices to see if I could find any incriminating evidence of fraud and murder.

I was wearing a black, long-sleeved turtleneck shirt, black nylon workout pants, and black running shoes, which I'd purchased that day for the occasion, my neon green Nikes not right for the job. I was carrying a small black canvas satchel containing burglary tools. If I ran into a member of the local constabulary, I'd have some "splainin" to do, as Ricky said to Lucy.

It was not likely that Vasily would leave any evidence of his involvement in serial murder lying around his office, but you never knew. Sometimes, in my experience, white-collar criminals were so arrogant that a search warrant of their places of business and homes yielded paper and electronic trails that led directly to the slammer.

I'd cased the joint that afternoon, pretending to be a customer, locating the stairways and other significant features. I went to the back of the building where there was a metal double-door entrance for deliveries. No one noticed me when I went out that door and put a strip of electrical tape across the lock. If someone had found and removed it, I'd pick the lock.

I went around back, opened the door, removed the tape, put it in my pocket, and went inside. I took a Maglite out of the satchel and followed the powerful beam up a stairway to the sixth floor, occupied only by Atocha Securities. It was easy to jimmy the outer door lock.

I went into the lobby and down the hallway to Vasily's office, went in, and looked around for a place to start. Moonlight through the open blinds illuminated the room, so I switched off the Maglite and put it on the desk.

I assumed that Vasily had a hidden safe somewhere. Guys like him always had hidden safes containing diamonds, gold bars, bundles of cash, and false identity papers. Maybe his also contained a video of him making a full confession of all of his crimes. Or maybe there was nothing but a handwritten note saying, "The joke's on you, Jackie Boy."

There was a laptop computer on his desk and a wooden filing cabinet along one wall. I didn't have the skills to hack my way into his password-protected computer, so I moved to the filing cabinet. The drawers were locked. I put my satchel on the floor, opened it, and took out a small universal key to see if it fit in the lock. I could have easily pried open the drawers, but then Vasily would know someone had been there.

I inserted the key into one of the drawer locks, fiddled with it, and the lock popped open. I rolled out the top drawer and found a line of hanging files with labels stating their contents. There were no files marked "Murder Victims" or "Ponzi Scheme." Nor was there one saying it contained "Nude Photos Of Lena And Elena." Maybe those were on his iPhone.

I was thinking about whether or not to spend time going through files marked with benign titles such as "Charity Wine Auction," "Boat Insurance," and "Naples Ferrari Club." Not worth it. His business files must be in another drawer. I put my key into the lock of the second drawer. Before I could open it, I heard what every burglar dreads: a noise behind me.

I turned to see Stefan, Vasily's chauffeur, standing in the doorway. He was wearing only a very large handgun that was pointed at my chest. It was a Desert Eagle Mark XIX, available in .357 Magnum, .44 Magnum or .50 Action Express.

That revolver is a big mother, appropriate for hunting elephants or tanks. In the semidarkness, I couldn't tell the caliber of that particular model, but at a range of ten feet it hardly mattered. The .357 and .44 would throw my body against the wall; the .50-caliber would blast me into tiny pieces. Either way, you're dead meat, Pete.

It amused me to wonder where Stefan concealed the Desert Eagle when he walked around, buck-naked like that. I'd carry something in a smaller caliber. I noticed that Lena the receptionist was standing behind him, also naked. If you are about to die, you might as well be looking at something pleasant like the lovely Lena, so I focused upon her and not the Desert Eagle. I noticed she had a mole on her left breast, which only added to her allure. Small flaws can enhance beauty.

Come on, Jack. Concentrate on the situation at hand. So I swung my attention back to Stefan, the man with the gun.

His other weapon was also oversized. Lucky Lena. He had the lean, muscular physique of a fighter, not a talker. There was a small white star-shaped scar on his right chest, a gunshot wound, and a tattoo on his left bicep, hard to tell exactly what it was; the designation of some commando unit was my guess.

Stefan smiled and said something in Russian, perhaps, "I just got fucked but you are even more fucked, Amerikanski pig." He glanced down at my right ankle, where I was wearing my S&W .38. He must have seen the bulge under my pant leg. In a contest between the two firearms, always bet on the Desert Eagle. So I left the .38 where it was, nodded at Lena, winked, and said to Stefan, "I won't tell if you won't." Worth a try.

Stefan stepped inside the office, and Lena followed him. If I were naked, too, they would have known how happy I was to see Lena like that.

Stefan took my flashlight from where I'd left it on Vasily's desk, turned it on, and gestured with it for me to walk out into the hallway as he and Lena followed. He pushed me into one of the other offices, where I saw a tan leather sofa, and two piles of clothes on the floor.

Lena dressed and then held the gun on me as Stefan did the same. He gestured for me to turn around, with my back to him. I did, and that's when Stefan, not the Naples city engineer, turned off my lights.

WHEN I regained consciousness, I was lying on my back on the couch with my hands tied behind my back and my ankles bound together with the kind of plastic restraints police use. I guessed that guys like Stefan always had a supply of them at hand, even if Jack Stoney didn't.

I had the mother of all headaches. Obviously Stefan had used the butt of the Eagle on the back of my head and the Eagle won.

The lights were on. A clock on the wall said five A.M. By then, I'd planned to be at Ash's house, asleep. As my vision cleared, I saw that Vasily was sitting behind a desk, sipping a drink. Lena was gone.

Vasily said something in Russian to Stefan, who took out a combat knife from a leather case on his belt. Had he told Stefan to gut me like a sturgeon? Stefan used the knife to cut the plastic ties from my wrists and ankles. I sat up on the sofa. My pistol was not in its holster.

Vasily looked at me and spread his hands. "We have some important things to discuss," he said. "First of all, I am not your enemy. The evidence of that is you are alive."

"Go on," I said.

"Not here. Not like this. Over dinner tomorrow night is best, if you are still free."

Now that Stefan had cut the restraints, I was free as a man can be with a Russian commando packing a Desert Eagle in the room.

"It's a date," I told Vasily.

26.

Hello, Jack. Hello, Boris.

Provence restaurant occupies a one-story, white clapboard building with black shutters and a green awning over the entrance and is located near the city dock on Naples Bay. Flower boxes and vines climbing on trellises add to the look of a country inn transplanted from the south of France to the tropics.

Advil way beyond the recommended dosage had eased the throbbing pain in my head. On the way home from the Atocha Securities offices, I'd stopped at the Naples Community Hospital's ER and gotten twelve stitches on the back of my head, the shaved area now covered with a bandage.

The doc, an earnest young man not old enough to shave, or so he seemed to me, asked how I got the wound. I told him that a naked Russian commando had hit me with his gun after I'd broken into the offices of his boss, a Russian Mafia don. The doc laughed, probably thinking that I was either confused from the blow or too embarrassed to tell him I'd slipped in the shower.

I gave my Corvette to the valet, wondering if valet parking would boost business at The Drunken Parrot, went inside the restaurant, and told the young woman at the hostess stand that I was joining Mr. Petrovich.

"Yes, sir, Count Petrovich has already arrived," she said in a mellifluous French accent. She picked up a menu from the hostess stand and said, "I will show you to his table."

I wondered if her accent was real, or if she was from Iowa or Wyoming and had acquired it via a Rosetta Stone language course in order to get the job. She was tall and tanned and young and lovely, like the girl from Ipanema, and had long dark hair. She was wearing a white cotton peasant blouse embroidered with flowers and had a white orchid tucked behind her left ear.

I seem to focus in on the specifics of firearms and women's attire. The former is a vocation and the latter an avocation. I had the sexist thought that I'd never seen an ugly restaurant hostess. Young and pretty must be in the job description. I was old enough to remember when the same was true of airline stewardesses, back when it was fun to fly.

I followed the young lady through the crowded restaurant to a rear courtyard, trying to not trip over the tables as I watched her cute little derriere move beneath her tight black skirt, like a sack full of cats on the way to the river.

Vasily was seated alone at a table in a corner of the courtyard, under a white wooden pergola and beside a white brick wall covered in climbing trumpet vines with purple flowers. The other tables, candlelit, were full of diners eating and chatting under the starry sky. It was all very pleasant, and reminded me how especially nice it is to be alive on a night like this, or on any night, for that matter.

As the hostess and I reached his table, Vasily stood and said, smiling, "Hello, Jack." My real name. I was thrown only momentarily as the hostess held out my chair, handed me the menu, and departed. I sat, and then responded, "Hello, Boris."

So the cards were on the table before the breadbasket.

Boris smiled. "So, Jack, we have both done our homework."

The waiter appeared; he was an older man with a bald head and bushy white mustache, wearing a white shirt and dark pants with a starched white apron folded and tied around his waist. Another staffer right out of Central Casting.

"What may I get you and your guest to drink, Count Petrovich?" the waiter asked. His accent was Eastern European. Maybe by way of Gary, Indiana. Was anyone who they seemed in this town?

Obviously the waiter had not done his homework about Boris's true identity. Or maybe he had, but believed that a count would be a better tipper than a mobster from Brighton Beach.

"I believe I still have some pinot noir in my private stock, Henri," Boris said.

"I checked when I learned you were dining with us tonight," he answered. "You only have four bottles of the Louis Jadot Gevery-Chambertin, so I ordered three more cases." Sam Longtree does the same for me with my root beer supply.

Henri looked at me with raised eyebrows. "And for you, sir?"

There were many wise guy remarks I could have made, such as inquiring about my private stock of root beer, but this was not the time for it, so I asked for a Virgin Mary, extra hot.

When Henri departed, Boris gave me a serious look and said, "I'm glad you came, given our recent encounter. How is your head?"

"It always feels better when someone doesn't hit it with a gun."

"That was most unfortunate," he said with a shrug. "If Stefan had called me first—"

Henri arrived with our drinks and left. Boris sipped his wine and said, "I invited you to dinner because I want to ask your help with an important matter."

"You want me to commit suicide to save you the trouble of making another run at me?"

I said that a bit too loudly, and a young woman at the next table gave me a quick glance. She was with an older couple, probably her mom and dad. Maybe she was hoping for some excitement, right then and there, to relieve the boredom of dining with her parents.

"Another run at you?" Vasily asked. "What do you mean?"

"Someone broke into Ash's house and took a shot at me."

"Believe me, I know nothing about that."

"Why should I believe you, Boris?"

"Because the men I would have sent would not have missed."

Serge and Stefan. He had a point. "Who, then?"

"Over the last six months, there have been a number of burglaries in town by people from Miami, I suspect, where there are gangs that prey upon wealthy communities. They take only jewelry and cash. Maybe you surprised such a burglar."

"Why haven't I heard anything about that?"

"Because this is Naples. Chief Hansen has persuaded the homeowners to deal only with the police and their insurance companies, but not make it public. Property values, you understand."

"And how do you know about that?"

He smiled and said nothing, which I took to mean that he knows things about the city others don't.

"What do you know about me?" I asked him.

He smiled again, like the Cheshire Cat. "I know that you are a retired homicide detective from Chicago. I assume that you have been hired by Mayor Beaumont and Chief Hansen to investigate some suspicious deaths. Deaths that they, and I, believe to be murders."

"Bingo," I said. "You've qualified for the bonus round."

He continued: "I also assume that I am the primary suspect, given that you know my true identity, and that the victims were all my clients."

"Also correct. You win the Sub-Zero refrigerator," I said, imitating Alex Trebek, host of the TV game show *Jeopardy!*

"In your place, I'd think the same thing. But I assure you I am not the killer. I propose that we join forces to find out who is murdering my clients."

"Continue."

"To state the obvious, as I told you, if it was me, you would be swimming with the fishes rather than dining on them tonight. The fish is very good here, by the way. Further, I assume that because you have been focusing your investigation on me, you have no other suspects."

"That is also correct," I admitted. "I'm curious about something. What blew my cover? Was it my table manners at the dinner at Ash's house?"

"Not at all. Although I did notice that you used the same fork and spoon all evening. I do a background check on all of my prospective clients. You know my family connections. We have considerable resources. Your false identity was not difficult to penetrate. And I am not surprised that you did a background check on me as soon as you made me a suspect."

He took a sip of wine and added, "By the way, I really did invite you to invest in my fund because I am seeking some younger clients."

I considered that information to be in the good news-bad news category. My table manners had mostly passed muster. But the Russian Mafia knew who I was and where I lived.

Henri arrived and told us that the specials that night included vichyssoise, a warm goat cheese and fig salad, beef bourguignon, and branzino, which, he explained to me, and not to Vasily, was a Mediterranean sea bass.

I'll admit that I don't know a branzino from a doorknob. My favorite fish is the fried perch you can get at the Baby Doll during the annual spring perch run in Lake Michigan.

"I think the vichy, a Caesar salad with anchovies, the duck a l'orange, and I'll preorder a Grand Marnier soufflé," Vasily told Henri.

Here was another opportunity to reveal the real me by asking for a double bacon cheeseburger with fries but that wasn't on the menu. I ordered the french onion soup, goat cheese salad, and the branzino, just to show Henri that I, Frank Chance, was a player in the world of haute cuisine. I added a preorder of a chocolate soufflé, to seal the deal.

That business finished, Boris said, "I ask that you relay my offer of assistance in the investigation to Mayor Beaumont and Chief Hansen. Tell them that we share a common interest. We all have a stake in finding the real murderer and in keeping the whole affair confidential."

At that point, I was beginning to believe him. I was, after all, alive. "And that common interest is?" I asked him.

"The City of Naples needs to protect its image. I wish to do the same for my business. If it became public knowledge that investing with me could be fatal—" He shrugged. "You see what I mean."

"So that your fraud can continue? That's not likely, now that we know who you are and that you're running a Ponzi scheme."

"The Atocha Fund is *not* a Ponzi scheme," Vasily asserted, sounding sincere. "True, that was the original idea. But I found out that I was, in fact, highly skilled at the hedge fund business. I was making such good returns that I did not need to defraud my investors. As you know, a Ponzi scheme eventually collapses upon itself. But a hedge fund, if successful, can go on for a very long time. My family was very enthusiastic about being involved in a legitimate business that is making money."

"Your family being the Russian Mafia out of Brighton Beach."

"Russkaya Mafiya has become an outdated term," Boris said as our soup arrived. The bowls came with big spoons, so no problem there. "True, there still are various organizations which can be said to come under that umbrella. But they are far outclassed by the oligarchs who hold most of the wealth and power in Russia today. For those in organized crime, such as my family, there has been a great incentive to convert from crime to capitalism, where the risk is less and the returns can, if successful, be far superior. Given that we can't own a piece of Russia, we want to own a piece of America."

I'd expected a confrontation with an assassin, and instead I was getting a lesson in the politics and economy of modern Russia. All of this was getting curiouser and curiouser, as Alice said in Wonderland. Naples certainly is its own Wonderland to me.

"So how can you help me with the investigation?" I asked as the salads arrived.

"I have a theory about what is going on," Vasily said. "But I will need assurances that, if we are successful in finding the real killer, I, in return, will be left alone to run my legitimate business."

During my law enforcement career, I'd been part of joint task forces with the FBI, the Illinois State Police, and the Cook County Sheriff's Office. Here was the chance to add the Russkaya Mafiya to that list. I wondered if I could request that Lena or Elena be my liaison.

"I'll pass on your offer to my employers," I told him.

"That's all I ask, Detective Starkey," Boris said.

He gave me an impish grin. "By the way, I'm a fan of the novels. I hope you don't mind me saying that, if Detective Jack Stoney was on the case, he'd have solved it by now."

Ouch.

We enjoyed the rest of our dinners, with me randomly switching forks and spoons, while discussing such topics as the problem of inflation in the Chinese economy, which he knew all about, and the National League Central Division pennant race, about which I possessed the expertise. Just two worldly gentlemen, breaking bread at the best French restaurant in Naples, Florida, a town that was the playground of the American Oligarchy.

When we were finished, Boris said, "One more thing. Because we are both undercover, I suggest you continue to call me Vasily Petrovich and I will call you Frank Chance. After all, there *is* a murderer out there who may be watching us."

"Right," I agreed. If Boris/Vasily wasn't the doer, we'd need to keep our heads down.

He insisted on paying the check. As we were about to leave, he said, "Of course, I will return your $10 million investment to whoever owns it. But I can provide audited reports showing that my fund is beating the market averages by a considerable margin, and that it ranks near the top of all hedge funds in America. Perhaps the person will wish to leave the funds with me."

In summary: A fake count who is the scion of a Russian Mafia family in Brighton Beach is alleging that he is an investment genius and legitimate businessman who can help me catch a serial killer.

I felt that I had now joined Alice, all the way down the rabbit hole.

27.

Quid Pro Quo

The next morning, I went to Naples city hall to present Vasily's unusual and perhaps off-the-wall offer to Mayor Beaumont and Chief Hansen.

Kathi smiled pleasantly when I walked in. Manning the reception desk back at my old Chicago PD station house on South Wentworth Avenue was a sergeant named Jablonsky, who everyone called Tiny because, in a culture where irony was highly valued, he was anything but. Kathi is a definite upgrade, as receptionists go.

Beaumont was seated behind his desk. Hansen was in one of the club chairs beside the couch. I sat in the other chair. Without preamble, Hansen began: "Bishop, that's the crime scene tech, dug the bullet intended for you out of the wall at Ashley Howe's house. It's a nine-millimeter. Because none of our vics were shot, that tells us zip. Tell me *you've* got something."

"I might," I said, and gave them a report on my early morning visit to the Atocha Securities offices, and my dinner with Boris, aka Vasily, at Provence restaurant.

When I was finished, Beaumont leaned back in his chair, rubbed his forehead, and said, "I want to believe him because that would mean he really is earning an average return of 28 percent on my money."

Hansen drummed his fingers on the desktop and asked, "So what's this plan of his?"

"He didn't lay it out for me," I answered. "Before he does, he wants a promise that, if he helps us, he'll be allowed to continue with his investment business as Vasily Petrovich. He says he'll open his books for an audit to prove that Atocha Securities is legit."

Hansen considered this, then said, "So we've paid you to recommend that we partner with a Russian mobster to hunt down a serial killer who, for all we know, may be him?"

"It doesn't sound so good when you put it that way," I answered.

"Put it any way you want. It's fucking nuts."

"If Vasily really is the killer, he knows he's our prime suspect, so he'll stop," I said. "If he's not, and we work with him, maybe he can help. I don't see a downside."

"How about this for a downside," Hansen said, with stress and annoyance in his voice. "The Count From Montefucksto isn't the bad guy, he helps us catch the real one, and then he owns us by threatening to hold a press conference if we don't give him anything he wants, now and forever."

"I think it would be a case of what was called in the Cold War mutually assured destruction," I said. "We want these crimes quietly solved, and Vasily wants to keep on turning borscht into gold. Nobody wants a press conference."

Hansen looked at Beaumont, who said, "All right. If Vasily's plan sounds at all feasible, we make a deal with the Devil."

28.

The Gang Of Three

I was the last to show up for the meeting. I'd been up late showing Marisa how much I appreciated our relationship. I hadn't seen her for a few days, and I didn't want her to think I was neglecting her for the investigation. Been there, done that, with my family.

When I arrived at city hall, Beaumont was seated at the head of the conference table with Hansen to his right and Vasily to his left. Vasily and Beaumont were looking at an oversized sheet of paper that contained a bar chart done in multiple colors. Later, Hansen told me they were reviewing the performance of the mayor's investment in The Atocha Fund. We were after a serial killer, but first things first.

Coffee, juice, and doughnuts were on a sideboard along the wall. No one had taken any. Maybe the goodies were made of wax for display purposes only. Just to satisfy my curiosity, I walked over and picked up a plain doughnut. It was real. No one would want a doughnut I touched, so I took it with me on a napkin and sat beside Hansen.

"Vasily says he has a theory of the case, but we waited for you," Hansen told me. He looked at Vasily and said, "Okay, let's hear it."

Vasily folded the chart, put it into his briefcase, looked at the mayor, and said, "Have your ever heard of The Gang Of Three, Charles?"

I'd heard of The Gang Of Four. They were men who, for a time, controlled the Communist government of China during the Cultural Revolution of the sixties and seventies.

Beaumont said, "Sure, I've heard of them. That's a Naples urban legend. They don't exist."

"Maybe, maybe not," Vasily responded. He looked at me. "The rumor, if it is a rumor, is that three men, bored with retirement, formed a triumvirate a couple of years ago. They amuse themselves by seeking to control certain events in town by bribing public officials, forming shell companies to buy land and get the zoning changed to allow development and make a profit, and spreading gossip, real or false, about people they dislike."

"There's never been any evidence," Beaumont said.

"True," Vasily admitted. "I always took it for a myth, as well. But several years ago, I decided I wanted to be on the board of the Naples symphony. I enjoyed the orchestra and wished to support it. I began making large donations, which is how you get asked to be on the board. My donations were more than enough to qualify me for consideration. But, after two years, I still had not been approached. I felt some invisible hand at work, blocking me. I was, in effect, being blackballed."

"Not every donor gets asked to serve on a board," Beaumont told him.

"True," Vasily answered. "But I am, by nature, curious. And I was annoyed. So I invited Lauren Davidson, who is a friend, and the symphony board chairperson, to lunch. I asked her about the situation. She was hesitant at first, but then admitted that, when my name was mentioned, a board member who is one of the organization's largest benefactors suggested to a number of board members, not herself, that he might have to reconsider his generosity if I became a member of the board. Lauren refused to reveal the identity of this man for fear of losing his support. I looked at the donor list, which is printed in the symphony's programs. One of the annual million-dollar givers is a man who wanted to invest in my fund. I had to tell him that we were fully subscribed at that moment. I could tell he was upset."

"And who was that man?" Hansen wanted to know.

"Arthur Bradenton," Vasily said.

"The retired chairman of Bradenton Industries," Beaumont told me. "That's a big company that makes everything from communications satellites to oil and gas pipelines and drones for the military."

Another one of the town's prominent used-to-bes.

Beaumont drew in a long breath, as if pondering all that. That gave me an opening to get another doughnut. All of them were plain. I'd have to speak with Kathi about that lack of variety.

Then Beaumont said, "You know, awhile ago a member of the city council changed his vote, allowing a big marina development to move forward. I thought that was odd at the time, because that councilman had been one of the project's biggest opponents. It was to be adjacent to a nature preserve, and his wife was president of the local Audubon Society."

"Who benefitted from that vote?" I asked.

"Christopher Knowland was behind the marina project," Vasily said. "He founded Knowland Homes, one of the country's largest homebuilders. His son runs it now."

Gangster number two.

"And who do you think is the third member of this group?" Beaumont asked.

"I have an idea, but I'd rather not name him until I'm more certain," Vasily answered.

"Let's say you're right about all this," Hansen said. "Bradenton did keep you off the symphony board because you wouldn't take him on as a client. And Knowland bribed a councilman to get his marina project through. Let's even say that they made an unholy alliance with a third guy and formed a club to exert power and influence behind the scenes. It's a very big leap from that to serial murder."

"It is indeed," Vasily acknowledged.

I noticed that, even though we all knew his real identity, Vasily remained in character as a member of the Russian aristocracy. I imagined that, in Brighton Beach, they said things like, "Sure as shit," and not, "It is indeed."

"So what now?" Beaumont asked.

It was time for me to contribute something more than decreasing the doughnut population of the room.

“I need to get on their radar screen,” I said. “Find some way to annoy Bradenton or Knowland and see what happens, while Vasily does more research about the third guy.”

Annoy them enough to get them to try to put me into the Starkey family plot in Graceland Cemetery.

29.

The Horsey Set

Lena from Vasily's office called to say that her boss was inviting me to attend a polo match in three days. She said that I'd have the opportunity to meet one of his friends there, a Mr. Arthur Bradenton.

So he was the first gangsta on the agenda.

"Do they sell hot dogs and peanuts at polo matches?" I asked Lena. "Like at a baseball game?"

She hesitated. "I'm sorry but I really don't know. I've never been."

"I suppose I could pack a lunch."

By this time, Lena either thought I was a pretty funny guy or that I was off my meds.

"I don't think bringing a lunch would be a problem, Mr. Chance," she said uncertainly.

"In that case, count me in."

I attended a polo match once, about two years ago, near Immokalee, an agricultural town northwest of Naples where migrant workers harvest oranges, melons, tomatoes, potatoes, and other crops. The players were mounted on ATVs; the field was a mud patch also used for swamp buggy races, which is a very big sport in Florida among what I would call "normal" people: those who don't live in mansions and belong to fancy country clubs. The players used aluminum softball bats to strike a soccer ball. A spectator's enjoyment of the match was in direct proportion to the amount of beer he drank. I was sober, so a large part of the enjoyment of the event was lost on me. I guessed that the match at the Naples Polo Club would be organized differently.

I told Hansen about the invitation. On Friday, a uniformed police officer delivered a package to me at Ash's house. It contained background on Arthur Bradenton. I learned that he and his wife, Paige, were from Minneapolis, where they still spent summers. In Naples, they lived on a twenty-acre estate outside the city limits, in horse country.

Bradenton's passion was the breeding of thoroughbreds, the background said. Bradenton Farm horses regularly ran in major races around the country, including the Triple Crown, consisting of the Kentucky Derby, the Preakness Stakes, and the Belmont Stakes. His steeds had never won any of the Big Three, or even placed. But Bradenton, the man and the farm, had high hopes for a three-year-old named Maiden's Breath.

I doubted that this horsey's breath really was like that of a maiden, unless the maiden ate oats. I did once date a maiden who was quite fond of garlic; the relationship lasted for only a few meals. I like garlic, too, but not secondhand.

My opinion of cutesy horse names is the same as it is of stupid boat names. Back in the day, I was a regular at Arlington Park, a racetrack in the Chicago suburb of Arlington Heights. One time, all I had to do to hit a big Trifecta was for a pony named Chili Dog to show. Instead, the nag decided that running one entire mile on the turf was too much effort so he stopped on the backstretch while leading the pack by a half length and strolled the rest of the way home, ignoring his jockey's whip and my shouted disapproval.

Bradenton was seventy-eight years old, the background told me. Paige Bradenton was heiress of a Texas oil company fortune. Maybe Art was working in the oil patch when they met, and began laying pipe in Paige's bedroom.

One way to get Arthur Bradenton's attention was to steal Maiden's Breath. I was certain that, if I traced the Starkey family tree back far enough, I'd find a horse thief or two. I could sneak into the barn at night, saddle her up, and ride away, shooting my Glock and yelling yippee-ki-yay so that Bradenton would wake up, look out his bedroom window, and see who had purloined his prize mare.

But maybe that was too heavy-handed. Instead of sending his hit man for me, he'd probably just call the cops. If he called the Collier County Sheriff's Office and not the Naples PD, I'd be up to my neck in horse manure. I needed a Plan B that didn't involve jail time.

THE NAPLES Polo Club is located on a large tract of land adjacent to Bradenton Farm. Vasily told me that Arthur Bradenton had donated the land, and was one of the organizers of the club.

I arrived at ten A.M., wearing a pink Lacoste shirt, white flannel pleated slacks, and black Gucci loafers with their trademark gold horse bits. When in Rome. No socks, of course. Topping off my outfit was a tan straw Panama hat, set at a jaunty angle. Before I left the house, I had Martin take a photo of me using my cell phone camera. Maybe I'd make an eight-by-ten print, frame it, and give it to Marisa, or hang it in my bar: Jack Starkey, bona fide member of the horsey set.

I was driving Uncle Reggie's Mercedes Gullwing coupe. I turned into the club entrance at the end of a long, winding road and drove though a gate in a white wooden fence that surrounded the club property.

I followed the road to the clubhouse and handed over the Mercedes to a uniformed parking attendant. As the young man slid into the driver's seat, I patted the car's fender and said to him, "Take good care of my mount. Her name's Thunder Road."

He drove away without comment. At least I didn't tell him to wait until my car cooled down before putting her in the barn, as you would a racehorse.

The clubhouse is a rambling, one-story, red wooden structure designed to look like an upscale horse barn, surrounded by flowerbeds and palm trees. I went inside and followed the hubbub of many voices conversing to a large clubroom and bar. The clubroom was paneled in knotty pine. On the walls were crossed polo mallets and photos of uniformed polo players swinging mallets at a small white ball while riding horses at full gallop as well as individual shots of men in ties and jackets, and women in stylish summer dresses and big hats. Small brass plaques at the bottoms of the picture frames identified the men in the photos as past or present officers of the club. Apparently the women in the photos were there as arm candy. Maybe this was the place to hang that photo of me.

A long mahogany bar with a polished brass rail occupied one side of the room. On the opposite side was a large glass case containing shelves holding fancy silver trophies. Waiters in white jackets, bearing silver trays with champagne flutes and hors d'oeuvres, passed among the crowd of elegantly dressed people.

As I stood in the clubroom doorway taking in this elegant scene, I noticed Vasily walking through the crowd toward me. He was wearing a white linen suit, an open-necked white shirt with a paisley ascot, and white suede shoes, which I hadn't seen since Elvis's early years.

"I'm glad you could make it, Frank," he said. "I'm a social member here, meaning I drink and dine, but don't ride. In my view, a man of my age has no business in the saddle, unless it involves a dinner date."

You can take the boy out of Brighton Beach, but . . .

Vasily led me around the room with his hand on my elbow, like a horse by the reins, introducing me to various club members. They all wore what Marisa would describe as "smart casual" attire. She termed my personal knockabout outfits as "dumb casual."

We went outside to a bar and dining area behind the building and stopped at a group of two men and two women who were chatting and sipping champagne.

"I'd like everyone to meet a friend of mine," Vasily said to them. "Frank Chance, this is Alex and Dedria Cruden and Arthur and Paige Bradenton."

I saw no indication that Arthur knew who I was, or that Vasily had ID'd him as the man who vetoed his Naples symphony board membership. Maybe Art studied at the Actors Studio in New York, or maybe that break-in at Ash's house was really just a burglary.

We shook hands all around as I assured them that I was delighted to make their acquaintances. They were delighted to meet me too. Delightfulness was in the air.

Bradenton was tall, maybe six three, with an aquiline nose, dark hair greying at the temples, and the fleshy physique of a man who might have been in shape during the Eisenhower Administration. He was wearing sunglasses with green lenses and tortoise-shell frames. His wife was slim and pretty, with brown hair to her shoulders; she was wearing a green blouse and tan slacks.

"Frank is the late Ashley Howe's nephew," Vasily told them. "He was visiting her when she passed away."

"My condolences," Bradenton said, looking like he meant it. The Actors Studio had taught him well.

"How long will you be staying in Naples?" Alex Cruden asked me.

"Just long enough to help put Aunt Ashley's affairs in order," I answered.

"I knew her," Dedria Cruden told me, touching my arm. "She was a fine lady." Then she squeezed my bicep. Maybe Alex traveled a lot on business, just like Peter Lemaire, Jennifer's husband, from Ash's dinner party.

A waiter passed among us, hitting a set of chimes he was holding with a rubber-tipped mallet.

"The match is about to begin," Vasily told me.

I'd hoped that also meant that lunch was about to be served. Along with everyone else, we walked to a large, canvas tent like the one at Ash's dinner party, set up on the edge of the polo field at what would have been called the fifty-yard line at Soldier Field. Valet parking and circus tents seemed to be *de rigueur* among the upper crust.

A long buffet table held an array of food. There were mounds of shrimp, oysters, and stone crab claws on ice; trays of sushi; and a carving station where a chef wearing a white toque and starched white jacket (his name was Frank, just like mine wasn't) stood at the ready, holding a knife with a long, serrated blade, ready to serve us slices of ham, turkey, pork tenderloin, and beef fillet. A dessert table held all manner of sweets—including doughnuts! There was also a bar where the bartender was making drinks in a whirring blender. Maybe he could make a milk shake.

On the field, eight riders, four on a team judging by the color of their shirts, were maneuvering their mounts into position. There was also a rider wearing a black-and-white striped shirt, obviously the referee.

Vasily told me that the green team was from the home club and that the men in red shirts were from the Palm Beach Polo Club. What looked like oversized hockey nets were placed in each end zone.

"How long does a match last?" I asked Vasily. We were each holding plates of food.

"About an hour and a half, with six chukkers of seven minutes each plus a halftime break," he told me.

"I always wondered how long a chukker lasted," I said. How had I survived this long without that knowledge?

Bradenton was at the bar in the tent, chatting with a man sipping a mint julep. That man was short, stocky, and bald, with a florid complexion. Was that one of the other coconspirators? To find out, should I walk over, order a drink, and throw it in his face in order to provoke him? Did the club employ security people with Mace and stun guns?

During the first couple of chukkers, the red team was kicking the greenies' asses, scoring three goals to zip. Then the green riders had a reversal of fortune, tying the match. All riders were highly skilled as they jockeyed for position and swung their mallets in graceful arcs at the white plastic ball, every now and then slamming it into the net with the accuracy and speed of a Bobby Hull slap shot. No one seemed to be rooting for one team or the other, which must have been considered gauche. Everyone applauded all goals. Not at all like when the Bears play the Packers.

A curious thing happened during halftime, when the riders headed for a large red wooden barn, which I took to be a horse locker room. Everyone walked onto the field and began stepping on divots kicked up by the horses' hooves, like golfers repairing divots on a course. So as not to be judged a gluttonous lout, I tore myself away from the buffet table and joined them. I almost stomped on the dainty foot of a woman going for the same divot. I begged her pardon and, just for something to say, remarked, "These horses sure can mess up a field."

She was a handsome woman with blonde hair tied into a bun and a dark suntan. Her age suggested that she was someone's first, and not second or third, wife. A keeper.

"They're called ponies," she informed me with a smile.

"When I was a kid, a man came around our neighborhood taking pictures of children mounted on his Shetland pony for five bucks," I said. "These animals look much bigger."

"These are mostly Arabians and quarter horses," she told me as we walked together from divot to divot, taking turns stepping on them. "Originally no horse bigger than thirteen hands and two inches was allowed to participate in a polo match. That restriction has been removed, but, by tradition, all the horses are still called ponies."

I didn't think I'd ever use my growing knowledge about polo, but, as Brother Timothy used to say, knowledge is an end unto itself.

The match resumed. When the final buzzer sounded, the scoreboard said that the visiting team had bested the homies, eight to seven. As far as I could tell, Palm Beach seemed to have the better riders, or better-trained ponies, but maybe it would have been considered ungentlemanly for them to run up the score. That was not an issue in the Chicago PD slow-pitch softball league. My team once beat a team from another precinct, twenty-two to zip. We would have happily scored more, but it got dark.

Everyone went back into the clubhouse for more drinks. Vasily found me and said, "That was Roland Cox with Arthur Bradenton over by the bar when we first went into the tent. I suspect that he is the third member of The Gang Of Three. They play golf together, go quail hunting, and recently went fishing for salmon in Alaska."

"Who did Cox used to be?"

"He was the managing partner of the largest law firm in Washington, DC. The first President Bush appointed him ambassador to France."

Remembering my divorce, I said, "It wouldn't surprise me if a lawyer is one of the men behind all this."

30.

What Would Jack Stoney Do?

Marisa and I were strolling along the beach in front of Ash's house. There was a moderate wind; the waves were washing up around our bare feet as sandpipers skittered about in the frothy surf. It was late afternoon, and the sun was a red-orange disc low on the horizon, getting ready for its plunge into the gulf. This daily event always attracted tourists to the beach with folding chairs, bottles of wine, and cameras. Sunsets are very picturesque in this part of the country, but my attitude is, you've seen one, you've seen 'em all.

However, there is one bit of scenery that can always attract me to the beach: Marisa, wearing a diaphanous white cover-up over her black bikini, accessorized by a big floppy hat, and Dior sunglasses.

I was attired in a tan Tommy Hilfiger tee shirt and a green Ralph Lauren boxer-style bathing suit (the polo player logo now seemed most appropriate), both birthday gifts from Marisa. I hoped no one would notice that my designers didn't match. Marisa was trying to wean me off my usual beachwear consisting of . . . Never mind, you know me well enough by now to figure that out. Hint: Chicago sports teams are involved.

An older man with a hairy chest and a protruding belly that blocked his view of his feet was walking toward us. He was wearing a tiny red Speedo-type bathing suit that showed more of his family jewels than anyone other than his urologist should ever have to see.

"European tourist," Marisa commented. "Maybe you should get a suit like that."

"If I did, you'd be the envy of all the ladies on the beach."

She giggled. "Got that right."

"But enough about my superior anatomy," I told her. I briefed her on the latest developments in the investigation, including the polo match.

Then we came abreast, and I do mean abreast, of a young woman wearing a bikini seemingly made of strands of dental floss.

"Have you heard that a world-record tarpon was caught in Boca Grande Pass?" I asked Marisa, just in case my staring was too obvious.

"That diversionary attempt would be more convincing if you weren't drooling."

"Anyway," I continued, "I need to find a way to provoke at least one member of The Gang Of Three, if that's who they really are, into ordering a hit on me."

"A hit? You mean, like, a contract killer?"

"No way those old guys could murder someone themselves. They wouldn't have the guts, or the ability to cover up the killings as skillfully as was done. Unless one of them was a Navy SEAL, they're paying someone to handle their wet work."

Marisa stopped walking and gave me a serious look. "Please don't go up against a professional assassin, Jack. I don't want to have to reenter the singles scene."

"Not to worry, hon," I said. "I'm a pro too."

Or used to be.

INSTEAD OF art imitating life, I decided to see what would happen in the reverse. When I returned to Ash's house after our beach walk, and Marisa went back to Fort Myers Beach for a house showing, I called Bill Stevens at the *Tribune.* I needed help so I decided to violate my confidentiality agreement and tell him about the situation in Naples on the condition that he not use it in a book or in a newspaper story without my permission. Then, because the real detective wasn't doing so well, I asked him to imagine how Detective Lieutenant Jack Stoney would handle my case.

Telling Bill was the second time I'd violated my confidentiality agreement with the City of Naples. I'd gotten a pass from my bosses for telling Marisa because of her valuable contribution, and her nice smile. I'd have a harder time explaining why I'd blabbed to a writer.

"You're asking a fictional character to assist in your investigation?" Bill asked, with great amusement in his voice.

"Correct," I told him. "I'm not saying I'll follow his lead, but, at minimum, I'll be informed by it."

"You're on, with one condition of my own."

"Which is?"

"When the smoke clears, you'll ask your handlers if I can use the story for a future book, cleverly disguising the people and places, of course."

"I can do that."

"All right. I'll e-mail you some pages in a few days. Try not to get shot before then."

"I always try not to get shot," I said. "With mixed results."

Bill must have really gotten into it because, late the following afternoon, I had his e-mail with a Word doc attached. I went into Sir Reggie's office and printed the attachment. The title of the novel fragment was *Jack Stoney: Undercover In Paradise*. It began:

> *Jack Stoney and Maryanne, his realtor girlfriend, had passionate sex under the soft glow of moonlight on the beach in front of the palatial Palm Beach oceanfront estate . . .*

A good beginning. I can do that.

> *. . . where he was living undercover as the nephew of the home's owner, Lady Jane Ashcroft, widow of the late Sir John Ashcroft, who'd made his fortune in the Australian sheep business.*
>
> *When they were fully satiated and lying on their backs, looking up at the twinkling starlight of the constellation Ursa Major,*

Maryanne said, "Don't you ever die. You've spoiled me. No other man could come close to taking your place."

I FELT a wave of jealousy. Marisa had never said anything quite that definitive about my sexual performance. She'd never complained, but she'd never indicated that, if I croaked, she'd enter a nunnery. Once again, Jack Stoney had bested me. I read on:

Stoney drove Maryanne back to her house in Boca Raton, and then stopped by to check on his own home, a forty-two-foot sailboat named The Busted Flush, *which was moored at a marina in West Palm Beach. The boat was fine; he got back into Sir John's silver Bugatti Veyron 16.4 Grand Sport Vitesse and drove over the causeway, back to Lady Jane's digs.*

Gag me with a spoon. Jack Stoney lived on a forty-two-foot yacht named for the boat that was the residence of John D. MacDonald's fictional detective, Travis McGee. His ride was a $2.4 million supercar with a top speed of 258 mph. Even Uncle Reggie didn't have a car like that. I continued to read:

The plan was for Stoney, in his undercover identity as a rich trust-fund slacker, to lure Benson Hurst into that most heady and lucrative of all business deals in the Sunshine State: a real estate development project. To lure him in with the promise of easy money, and then to have him "accidentally" discover that his investment had disappeared into a secret account in an offshore bank, and not into real estate at all.

Because the venture was . . .

A Ponzi scheme! Brilliant!

The story went on for a few more pages, with Jack Stoney kicking ass and taking names, but I had what I needed. Frank Chance would set up the same kind of scam I had suspected Vasily of running—and maybe still did.

Christopher Knowland, the homebuilder from Canton, Ohio, would be my target because he'd be especially angered at being taken in by a fraudulent real estate deal. When the scheme was revealed (on purpose), I'd have to be punished. And who better to help me set up this sting than Boris Ivanovich, the ex-Brighton Beach financial wiz? Surely there was a Ponzi scheme or two in his past.

Bill included a note at the bottom of the last page saying, "You can take it from there, Sherlock. If it doesn't work out, I'll take good care of our bar and your Corvette."

I guess he understood that Marisa could take care of herself.

31.

Ponzi Scheme

I called Vasily on his cell phone that afternoon to tell him I had an idea involving Christopher Knowland. He said he was in New York, returning to Naples late that night. Maybe there was a family wedding or birthday in Brighton Beach, or a retirement party; what do you get after thirty years service to a Mafia family, a gold semi-automatic revolver?

Vasily invited me to come to his house the next morning for breakfast. His house is on Keewaydin Island, a private barrier island just off the Naples coast, he told me. He instructed me to go to the south end of Gordon Drive and park near a boathouse at seven thirty, where a launch would be waiting.

When I arrived at the boathouse, Elena from Vasily's boat crew was at the helm of a classic mahogany Chris-Craft speedboat moored at a small wooden dock. A lovely sight. And so was the boat.

The name *Osetra* was painted on the stern. A kind of Russian caviar, I knew, because Marisa liked the stuff. In my opinion, fish eggs are only good for making baby fish.

Elena smiled. "Do you remember me, Mr. Chance?" she asked. "I am Elena. We met aboard Count Petrovich's yacht."

It would have been easier to forget the Sears Tower. She was wearing a blue denim work shirt with the sleeves rolled up and the shirttails knotted above her navel, tan shorts, and pink canvas boat shoes. Apparently the shirt was missing its top buttons. How careless to not get that fixed.

"Yes, of course I remember you," I assured her.

"Come aboard please. It is just a fifteen-minute ride to the island."

"Do you have enough gas to make it to Cuba?" I inquired.

"How well can you swim?" she asked, with a grin. Finally, a young lady who appreciated my sense of humor. It was something we could build on.

She cast off the bowline. I took care of the stern and pushed the boat away from the dock. She took the captain's chair, eased the throttle forward, and we were off—toward Keewaydin, not Cuba.

It was another perfect Southwest Florida day, with a bright yellow sun hung in an azure sky. Elena went to full throttle and a pair of dolphins began to frolic in our bow waves.

Detective work does have its moments, as I may have mentioned. When you're not getting shot at or hit on the head, it can be downright enjoyable.

As advertised, we arrived at Keewaydin in fifteen minutes. Elena eased the boat alongside a wooden dock. Stefan, Vasily's chauffeur, handled the mooring lines and then drove Elena and me in a golf cart along a brick path leading up a hill to Vasily's house.

The word "house" didn't do justice to the structure. I wanted to take a cell phone photo of it to show Marisa, but I didn't want to look like a tourist. It resembled one of those Victorian bed-and-breakfasts on steroids. It was maybe 30,000 square feet of gables and spires and porches, painted in bright rainbow colors. So Vasily had a fun side.

As Elena went off somewhere, maybe to pose in an itsy bitsy bikini for the annual *Sports Illustrated* swimsuit edition, Stefan led me up the stairs and through the front door of the house into the foyer. It was tricked out with oil paintings, a large grandfather clock, Oriental rugs over a hardwood floor (of course), and a sweeping wooden stairway, down which came Vasily, making a grand entrance. He was carrying Sasha, the killer Maltese.

"Welcome to my home," he said. "We'll have breakfast by the pool."

I followed him through the kitchen and outside to the backyard where there was a pool that could host a summer Olympics swimming event. We sat at a table beneath a green-and-white striped canvas awning. Sasha reclined on a lounge chair near the cabana. After a few minutes a woman pushing a cart served us breakfast. She also put a small bowl in front of Sasha, probably filled with caviar.

"Thank you, Viola," Vasily told her.

She was short and stocky, with grey hair, and was wearing a white apron over a housedress, the kind of woman Russians call a babushka. For the important staff position of cook, Vasily apparently chose function over form. We had coffee, orange juice, eggs Benedict, sweet rolls, and cheese blintzes. Joe and I both would have to go to a health spa when I was finished with this case.

As we ate, I told Vasily about Bill Stevens's Ponzi scheme idea, without revealing its source. I didn't want to admit that I'd told a newspaper reporter about our investigation or that I was following the lead of a fictional detective.

Vasily pondered this, then exclaimed: "Perfect! A Ponzi scheme! There it was, right under my nose, and I didn't see it. And you're right. Christopher Knowland is the best of the three men to approach. As a real estate professional, he'll be furious over being scammed. Perhaps murderously so, my friend."

"All I have is the basic idea," I said, taking a bite of a cheese blintz that was to die for (not literally). "I'll rely on you to flesh out the details and set it up so Knowland will be fooled."

Vasily was about to say something when Elena came out of the house. She shrugged off a white terry-cloth robe, dove into the pool, and began swimming laps, sleek as the dolphins on the voyage here.

"She swims to stay in shape," Vasily said.

"It works," I said, watching Elena do a flip turn with the skill of Mark Spitz, but easier on the eyes. As we ate, Vasily began talking through how our real estate investment project could be set up. He was a quick study. I didn't understand most of it. What I did get was that he would assemble a small group of friends who would pose as investors in case Knowland wanted to do his due diligence by speaking with them. The project would involve development of a high-end, mixed-use shopping center complex consisting of boutique shops, restaurants, a movie theater, and condominiums. It would be located on a prime parcel of land south of downtown Naples that was for sale.

Because he came up with the particulars so quickly, and with such instantaneous specificity, I wondered if he had such a project in mind for himself, legit or otherwise. I would approach Knowland, Vasily explained, and tell him that our partnership had an opening for one more investor. I'd say that I'd learned of his real estate development background, which would be of great value to our project. It was still a secret because I had not yet acquired the land. If the scope of the project were public knowledge, the price would skyrocket.

"So, Frank, what do you think?" Vasily asked.

"I think it'll work," I told him.

"I have a good way to get Christopher Knowland's attention," Vasily said as he led me to the driveway, where Stefan was waiting with the golf cart. "I will tell a few people in strictest confidence that you have decided to stay in Naples following your aunt's death because you think this is a good town for a real estate project, and that you have completed successful projects in such places as New York, Hong Kong, and Dubai. That news will spread in the right circles and reach Christopher by cocktail hour tomorrow. Then I'll figure out a way for you to be together with him."

"You da man," I said.

I hopped aboard the golf cart, rode back to the dock, and stepped aboard the Chris-Craft. Elena returned me to the Gordon Drive boathouse. Cuba would have to wait.

32.

Pop-Up Dinner Party

Back at Ash's house, I changed into a Chicago Blackhawks tee shirt, shorts, and running shoes, and did five miles on the streets of Port Royal in an attempt to stay under 300 pounds during this high-calorie investigation.

It was one more unusual thing about Naples. All of those stately, expensive homes, street after street of them, and you hardly ever saw any of the residents, just their lawn crews, or housekeepers, coming and going. Many of the owners had residences in other cities and countries, and only used their Naples mansions now and then, Marisa told me.

As in: Larry and Penny Networth are having breakfast in their Park Avenue townhouse in New York one morning. They decide it would be nice to have lunch by the pool at their Port Royal home. Larry makes a call to order the flight crew to spool up the Gulfstream. After a pleasant lunch in Naples, Penny says it might be nice to have a few friends over for a dinner party at their ski lodge in Aspen . . . Having such lavish homes mostly vacant seemed like a waste. Maybe the federal government would propose a program to house the nation's homeless in properties like those. I'd vote for that.

Back home, I showered and called Marisa. "Are you free for dinner Thursday?" I asked.

"Let me think," she said. "I'm scheduled to have dinner with George Clooney at his place on Lake Como in Italy . . ."

Marisa would fit right in as a neighbor of the Networths.

"Wouldn't want to spoil that opportunity," I told her.

"Make me a counteroffer."

"Okay. Have you heard of pop-up dinner parties?"

"Sure," she said. "A chef prepares an elaborate meal in some unusual venue that you don't learn about until the day before. They're all the rage."

"I happen to know from a source that there will be one Thursday in the Robb & Miller furniture store, and we have a reservation."

"I love that store. Sounds yummy. I'll cancel George. So what's the deal with the pop-up?"

"Vasily set it up for us. It'll be a working dinner. He knows the chef, got the guest list, and discovered, as he suspected, that Christopher Knowland and his wife, Lucille, were on it. He thought maybe the other two gangsters were on it too, but it was just the Knowlands."

I told Marisa about the Ponzi scheme and that Vasily had arranged for us to be seated at the Knowlands' table.

"Should I wear a Kevlar vest beneath my dress?" Marisa asked.

"That won't be necessary. If a gunfight breaks out, I'll cover you with my body."

"Let's hope for a gunfight then."

I SPENT the time until Thursday doing my homework about the real estate development biz. When I was done, I had a master's degree in the subject from Google University. I was at least reasonably conversant in the language of the game, including terms like triple net lease, ROI, agglomeration economies, income capitalization approach, and weighted average cost of capital. I imagined saying things to Christopher Knowland at dinner like, "Please pass the ketchup and, by the way, Chris my man, how's your sales price point of indifference?"

THURSDAY CAME. The pop-up dinner began at eight. I picked up Marisa at her house at seven. She looked ravishing in a simple black cocktail dress and black heels, sans Kevlar vest.

On the way to the furniture store where the dinner would happen, we stopped at a liquor store for wine because the dinner was BYOB. Assuming that the menu would include fish, fowl, and various meats, Marisa selected a bottle of her favorite red, a Jordan Cabernet Sauvignon, and a white, a Lynmar Estate Russian River Valley Chardonnay.

Robb & Miller was located on US Route 41, aka the Tamiami Trail, named when the road was the main artery between Tampa and Miami. I pulled into the driveway and gave the Shelby Cobra I was driving to the valet—by then, I knew that rich people never parked their own cars—and we went inside.

A man in his thirties wearing a starched white chef's tunic and toque was greeting arriving guests at the front door. The chef offered his hand to Marisa, and then to me, saying, "Welcome. I'm Gilbert Merchant. You'll find our dining area right through the Henredon gallery, between the Oriental rugs and the bedroom furniture."

This must be the place where everyone bought their Oriental rugs to spread over their hardwood floors. Gilbert Merchant, I knew from Vasily, was one of the nation's hot young chefs. He moved to Naples from San Francisco a few years ago to open a restaurant. I guess he thought the tips would be better here. These pop-up dinners were an adjunct to his catering business.

We followed the chef's directions and made our way through the furniture store to a candlelit dining room set up with eight tables with seating for six people each. Along the way, Marisa paused frequently to inspect the furniture, saying she needed a new breakfront, whatever that is. I asked if she had room for a Barcalounger, preferably with the massage option, for when I came over to watch sports on TV. She handled that question by ignoring it.

The charge for the dinner was $325 a head, plus tip for the wait staff and valet, with Vasily picking up our tab. He told me that the profits were donated to the Boys and Girls Club of Collier County, a worthy cause, but not so worthy that I'd spend that much of my own money on the feed, no matter how tasty the tasting menu was.

We were the first to arrive at our table. As promised, the place cards indicated that Vasily had arranged for Christopher and Lucille Knowland to be seated next to us, arranged boy-girl, boy-girl.

Marisa sat next to me while we perused the menu left at each seat. I imagined that feasts like this were one of the prime causes of the decline and fall of the Roman Empire, as well as of the French and Russian revolutions. Somehow the British monarchy still survived, but then, the food on the island—overcooked prime rib with Yorkshire pudding with a heaping helping of bone marrow (yuk)—was apparently not as inflammatory to the peasantry.

But this night's menu clearly would, if made public, bring the masses to the furniture store bearing torches and pitchforks. It began:

Passed Hors d'oeuvres
Buffalo Mozzarella Spheres
Tomato Water, Basil Oil, Aged Balsamic Caviar

Smoked Duck, Candied Apple & Butternut Squash Tartlettes
Toasted Pecans, Brown Butter, Fried Sage

First Course Duet
Porcini "Egg" Custard
Lemon Sabayon, Caviar, Micro Chive
Lobster Salad Cones
Avocado Lime Mousse, Mango Cloud, Tarragon Pearls

Second Course
Heirloom Golden and Red Beet Salad
Organic Frisée, Goat Cheese Semi Freda, Compressed Apples,
Blood Orange Vinaigrette, Pistachio Crisp

Third Course
Black Truffle Vichyssoise
Brioche Cloud, Crispy Purple Potato, Chervil,
White Balsamic Drops

Fourth Course
Burled Figs & Foe
Balsamic
Cherries, Foie Gras Mousse, Melted Camembert
Port Wine Gelée, Hazelnut-Lavender Thyme Ice Cream

It went on for eight more courses. "Jesus, Mary, and Joseph," I exclaimed. "A person could gain twenty pounds just by reading this menu."

"I'm sure they'll be small portions," Marisa said. "But still, it does seem a bit over the top."

"I'll have to pass on the port wine gelée, the vodka shooter, and the bourbon jus. I don't want to go back into rehab."

"I've never been to one of these pop-up dinners," Marisa told me. "This is a real treat. Thanks for inviting me."

"I took an ancient civilization course at college," I said. "The Roman nobility was able to eat and drink for days at a time during their bacchanals because they would take vomit breaks."

"Thus was born bulimia."

The Knowlands and the other couple at our table arrived together. Marisa and I stood as introductions were made all around. Then we took our seats, with Lucille Knowland to my right and a woman named Janet Crombie to my left.

Lucille was an attractive woman with shoulder-length auburn hair and green eyes who appeared to be about her husband's age. Janet was in that age range, too; she had short silver hair, smooth skin, and a warm smile. Marisa was seated between Christopher Knowland and a man who looked to be in his eighties. The courses came and went; Chef Merchant gave an informative little chat about each one, after which I still didn't know a Tarragon Pearl from a Tomato-Horseradish Granita. By watching my tablemates, I mostly got the flatware thing right.

I listened carefully when the chef got to an offering called "Forest Mushroom Dirt." It didn't sound promising. The sauce was something involving olive oil and shredded black truffles, which did resemble dirt but apparently was not. I bowed to peer pressure and took a bite. Quite tasty, actually.

When we first added a fried orange roughy sandwich to the menu at The Drunken Parrot, the wholesaler told me that the fish's original name was "slimehead." Maybe the Slimehead Fishermen's Association hired an advertising agency to rebrand the product. Imagine a waiter saying, "And our fish special this evening is slimehead with a nice lemon butter sauce."

Sell much?

Eventually it was eleven P.M. and our three-hour excursion through the Land of Culinary Excess was complete. As Marisa had predicted, the courses were small, but they did add up to gluttony, with a raging case of gout not out of the question. Chef Merchant got a standing ovation from those of us who could still stand, and we all agreed that we'd had a marvelous time.

Because of the seating arrangement, I hadn't been able to interact with Christopher Knowland beyond our initial introduction, but that was okay. The purpose of the evening was to meet him in a proper venue, not to begin outlining my real estate deal with a Sharpie on my linen napkin. That would come later.

As Marisa and I waited for the valet to bring back the Cobra, we turned on our cell phones. We both had voice mails.

Hers was from a client who'd decided to make an offer on a house. Mine was from Naples Police Chief Wade Hansen informing me that someone else was dead.

33.

The Perpetual Par Three

Corpse number five was none other than Naples Mayor Charles Beaumont. A shocking development, and I'm hard to shock. It was up close and personal now.

His wife, Helen, found him while Marisa and I were pigging out at the pop-up dinner party in the furniture store. Hizzoner was lying on the floor of the garage of their home in Royal Harbor. The garage door was closed and the engine of his 1953 MG TD was running. Charles told Helen he was going into the garage to do some work on the car, which was his baby.

Helen told the two uniformed officers who responded to her 9-1-1 call that her husband would never kill himself, and she repeated that to a detective. He was looking forward to playing in the member-guest tournament at the Olde Naples Country Club that very weekend, she said. He and his former Yale roommate had won last year. Apparently that proved her point: Any true golfer would wait until *after* the tournament to do himself in, especially if he was the defending champ.

Friday morning, I met with Hansen in his office at police headquarters. There didn't seem to be a reason anymore to stay away from the building, now that we weren't trying to hide my identity from Vasily. I'd not gotten the idea that he and Charles Beaumont were good friends, but he was clearly shaken. The murders had gotten too close for comfort and indicated that the bad guys had become bolder. Hansen told me that a man named Henry Thurgood, the deputy mayor and retired chairman of a Des Moines bank, would be acting mayor until the next election.

Thurgood, who was in his late seventies, would be told that Mayor Beaumont had died of natural causes, and, of course, nothing about our murder investigation. He had accepted the deputy mayor's job with the understanding that he'd have no official duties whatsoever. He obviously had no idea that events would place him in the mayor's chair, and he was panicked by the thought that he'd actually have to show up every day and make decisions on issues he knew nothing about. Hansen told me he'd assured the new mayor not to worry because he could just rubber-stamp city council decisions and let department heads do the heavy lifting.

Hansen would invent a reason that the police department needed funding for confidential projects from the mayor's discretionary budget. Perhaps the police department had an antiterrorism task force, secret so as not to frighten the citizenry, and the late Charles Beaumont had signed off on the funding, he'd tell the new hizzoner. Something like that.

After the meeting with Hansen, I called Vasily with the news. He, too, was shocked. Then he updated me about our real estate project.

"My people are preparing all the documents needed to set up our venture," Vasily said.

"Who are your people?"

"For this sort of business, I use a law and accounting firm in Brighton Beach. They will create false government filings and anything else we'll need."

Great. I'd been on the right side of the law as a consultant to the former mayor and the police chief, but now I was about to become a party to an investment fraud using documents created by the Russian Mafia and its minions.

That would only be an issue if we failed to solve the crimes, or if Christopher Knowland was not one of the murderers. If he wasn't, he'd be very upset when he discovered that my investment project was as phony as my identity. He would make every effort to have

Frank Chance put in prison for a very long time, or in the ground in perpetuity. And wherever Frank Chance went, Jack Starkey followed.

Charles Beaumont's obituary began on page one of the *Naples Daily News* Sunday edition. It reported that he was born in Indianapolis and educated at Yale and the Wharton School of Business at the University of Pennsylvania. After serving as a naval officer aboard a destroyer in the North Atlantic, he went to work for Pfizer, the pharmaceutical company, starting as a salesman and ending up as chief executive officer. He and Helen bought a vacation home in Naples forty years ago, and became full-time residents ten years ago. They had two sons, a daughter, and seven grandchildren.

Vasily and I attended Charles Beaumont's memorial service at Trinity by the Cove, a little white Episcopal Church in Port Royal. Jesus said, "It is easier for a camel to go through the eye of a needle than for a rich man to enter the kingdom of God." Every Sunday, in churches like Trinity by the Cove, wealthy parishioners gathered with the hope that Jesus was just kidding. Wouldn't a large contribution to the church building fund allow their souls to slip through the eye of that needle on their way to the Magic Kingdom in the Sky?

I entered the church, found Vasily seated in the back row, and slid in beside him. He nodded a greeting. I noticed a bulge under his suit coat indicating that he was packing heat. Maybe Serge was up in the belfry with a sniper rifle. If The Gang Of Three had ordered a hit on the mayor, maybe they knew we were after them.

Helen Beaumont sat in the front row, dressed in widow's weeds, as the minister and various family members and friends said kind words about the deceased. Kathi, his secretary, was there too. I wondered, if given a turn to speak, what Kathi would have to say about her dear departed boss. Would she talk about the good times they'd had bantering at the water cooler?

Of course, I don't know if there was anything improper about the relationship Kathi had with the late mayor; just because he was an old goat and she was a sexy young woman whom I never observed typing or filing when visiting the office didn't prove that any hanky-panky had occurred.

We should always assume the best about people, Brother Timothy instructed us. Claire had said that also, and Marisa was doing her best to help me fit into the modern world of sexual equality, but I recognized that I still had a considerable distance to travel. Fortunately you don't have to lead a perfect life to get into Heaven, the Jesuits assured me.

There was no casket in the church because the guest of honor had been cremated. One of Beaumont's sons told the assemblage that it was his father's wish for his ashes to be scattered on the tee box of the fifth hole of the Olde Naples Country Club golf course. That was a 157-yard par three, he explained, where his father had once scored a hole in one using a seven iron.

"That seems kind of creepy to me," I whispered to Vasily. "The ashes on the golf course thing."

"It's done all the time here," he responded. "The zoning laws allow it." Maybe the ghosts of deceased members roamed the golf courses of Naples at night, playing $2 Nassaus for all eternity.

The church was packed. All the members of The (still alleged, at that point) Gang Of Three were there with their wives. They were not sitting together. Christopher Knowland was with his wife, Lucille, in a middle row. Arthur Bradenton and his wife, Paige, were seated in the last row. Roland and Marcie Cox were three rows back from the front, on the left side of the sanctuary.

After the service Vasily introduced me to the Knowlands as if he didn't know we'd met at the pop-up dinner. The Coxes and Bradentons already had departed.

"Arthur, this is Frank Chance," Vasily said. "Frank is Ashley Howe's nephew."

"We've met," Knowland said. He turned to me. "Always a pleasure, Frank."

We shook hands and I gave Lucille air kisses on her cheeks, as all the right kind of people do.

Vasily said to Knowland, "Frank has an extensive background in commercial real estate. He's planning a project you might want to hear about before it's made public."

Apparently no time or place was considered inappropriate to talk about a business deal. Vasily had been spreading the word about the project around town, always telling the person he was speaking with that the information was strictly confidential. So Knowland probably already knew about it. I could almost see dollar signs flashing in his eyes.

"I'd like that," Knowland told me. He reached into the inside pocket of his suit coat, took out a silver card case, opened it, extracted a business card, and handed it to me. The card was made of cream-colored, thick paper stock, with black engraved lettering stating his name, address, and phone number. In comparison, my Chicago PD detective's business card looked like it had been photocopied.

"Give me a ring when you've got a moment," he told me.

Fish on.

34.

If, If, If . . .

I was now officially the managing partner of Gulf Development LLC, a company headquartered in the Cayman Islands. Of course there was no need to shelter profits from US taxes because there would be no profits. But I'd always wanted to visit that island nation, so maybe I'd go there for a board meeting with myself. My office wouldn't need furniture because it was a mailbox in a postal center.

At Vasily's suggestion, I rented office space in an Executive Suites complex on Fifth Avenue South in downtown Naples, with access to a kitchen, conference room, telephone line, and a shared receptionist who would answer my phone using the Gulf Development name.

I won't describe the receptionist because I've gotten into enough trouble with that kind of thing already. I'll just note that her name was Leila, she seemed very competent from our brief contact, and was a very attractive young lady.

Thanks to Vasily's "people," I had an impressive array of company materials, including stationery, high-quality business cards, documents from the Cayman Islands government incorporating my company, and a detailed description of the mixed-use development I planned, including an artist's rendition of the project on a display board.

There were also materials describing other projects I'd done: a condo tower in Manhattan, a hotel in Dubai, and a project in Hong Kong similar to the one I intended to do in Naples. There were also references from investors and bankers who were people Vasily knew and were primed to tell anyone who called what a brilliant businessman and upstanding individual Frank Chance was.

I was ready to meet with Christopher Knowland. I called him using the number on his business card.

"This is Frank Chance," I said when he answered. "I don't know if you remember me."

"Of course I do, from the dinner and the church," he said. "Wasn't that marvelous? The dinner I mean, not the funeral service."

I assured him that it was. "Do you prefer Christopher or Chris?" I asked.

"Only my mother called me Christopher, and then only when she was displeased with me. So Chris will do."

"I was wondering if you'd like to get together to talk about my development project."

"Love to," he said. "I've got a colonoscopy on Thursday, but any other day is good."

In Naples people spoke freely about their various medical procedures, assuming it was a topic of interest to others, which apparently it was. I would have just said I was busy on Thursday.

"Let's say Friday," I told him. "We can meet in my office at ten A.M., if that works for you."

My new pal Chris said that was just fine. He was much easier to hook than a bonefish. I gave him directions to the office and then called Vasily and told him about the meeting. I figured that The Gang Of Three wouldn't try to kill me as long as I was going to make money for one of them.

35.

Guacamole And Gunfire

The next morning I was back at Ash's house from a run on the beach when I got a cell phone call from my daughter. The last time Jenny had called me in recent years was never. I read her name on the caller ID and answered: "Mrs. Thornhill, I presume."

"Hi, Dad."

"Is everything okay, Jenny?" I asked her. I assumed that, for her to call me, something must not be.

"I'm really sorry about not inviting you to my wedding. That was wrong of me. It's just that—"

"I know."

"The thing is, I've got to be in Miami to take depositions Friday in a court case. I won't have time to get to Fort Myers Beach, but I wonder if you could meet me Thursday night for dinner."

If I had a conflict that would prevent me from dining with her, I'd cancel whatever it was, including a colonoscopy, or triple-bypass surgery. "That'd be great," I said.

"I'll be staying at the Loews in Miami Beach. Meet me there at seven?"

"I'll be there. How was your honeymoon?"

As soon as I asked that, I knew it was a dumb question. Two newlyweds in Paris? That's where Claire told me they were going. What's not to like about that? On my cop's salary, Claire and I had honeymooned in a bed-and-breakfast in the Apostle Islands on Lake Superior, just off the northern coast of Wisconsin. We were star-struck lovers, and for me at least, that was the best place in the world to be at that time. Paris could not have been any better.

"It was everything a honeymoon should be," she answered.

"He must be a good man if you chose him."

On the spot, I couldn't remember my son-in-law's name.

"Brad *is* a good man, Dad. You'll like him."

"I'm coming to Chicago, so I can meet him then."

"That's great. When?"

This time, I was smart enough not to say, "When I finished with a case."

"It'll be soon."

"Good. Mom will like that too."

My ex-wife and daughter would be happy to see me. I'd never won the lottery, but that must be how it felt.

"I'll be at the Loews at seven," I told Jenny. "I know a good Cuban restaurant near the hotel."

"I look forward to it. I really do, Dad. Bye."

In the shower, I sang the Louis Armstrong song, "What a Wonderful World." All I had to do was to stay alive for at least a few more days so I could eat Cuban food with my daughter.

IT WAS a two-hour drive from Naples to Miami across a stretch of I-75 known as Alligator Alley. The highway cut south and east from Naples through the Everglades, that vast inland sea of grass.

You could spot gators sunning themselves on the banks of the drainage canals along the highway, all kinds of birds rising in a feathery cloud from treetops, and white-tailed deer bounding across open fields. There were Florida panthers in there, too, but they were rarely seen. A lot of accidents happened because the drivers were checking out the wildlife.

I had the top down and the radio tuned to a Golden Oldies station. I had to struggle to keep to the speed limit because it was a nice, balmy day, I like driving the car fast, and my daughter was waiting for me at the end of the road.

At six thirty, I turned off I-75 at the Miami Beach exit and drove across the MacArthur Causeway that linked the mainland with the island of Miami Beach. A long line of cruise ships, their decks stacked high like tiers of a wedding cake, were docked across Biscayne Bay on my right.

I headed north on Collins Avenue and swung into the driveway of the Loews, pulled up to the front entrance, handed my car over to the valet (I was in danger of forgetting how to park a car myself), told the young man I'd only be a few minutes, and went inside.

Even though I was fifteen minutes early, Jenny was waiting for me in the lobby, seated on a sofa, talking on her cell phone. She spotted me, ended the call, stood, and said, "Hi, Dad. That was Brad." She gave me a hug and said, "You look great."

"Back atcha." Jenny didn't know she was complimenting a dead man's wardrobe. Jenny really was beautiful in her white cotton shirtwaist dress with a rainbow-colored canvas belt and tan leather platform sandals. With her shoulder-length blonde hair and blue eyes, she was a stunner, like her mother.

I OFFERED her my arm and we went outside, retrieved my car from the valet, pulled out of the hotel driveway, and turned right onto Collins Avenue.

"I like your ride," Jenny said. "Très cool."

"Thanks. I always wanted a classic Corvette. I got it when I moved to Florida. A bucket list kind of thing, you could say."

"You're way too young for a bucket list," Jenny said with a laugh.

I made the sign of the cross. "Bless you, my child. Even though you know not whereof you speak."

She giggled, which I had not heard her do since she was a young girl when she rode around our house on my back as we played horse and rider.

AMADOR'S CAFE Cubano is on Lincoln Road, a pedestrian mall running perpendicular to Collins Avenue. I parked on a nearby side street. As we walked toward the restaurant, I said, "I forgot to ask you if you like Cuban food."

"Love it. There's a place in West Town called Habana Libre. Brad and I go there often."

We got to the restaurant and went inside. I was glad I'd called for a reservation because the place was packed. The hostess seated us at a table near the back of the room. A handsome young man with thick black hair, wearing a white cotton shirt called a guayabera, came over with menus. He said his name was Mateo and asked for our drink orders. Jenny asked for the house white wine and I asked for a Cuban coffee.

"Tell me about your court case," I said.

"My client is the owner of a Chicago import-export company. Some of the company's goods pass through the Port of Miami. The company is suing its freight agent here, claiming breach of contract because the agent keeps raising his rates and holding the company's goods hostage in his warehouse. I'm here to take depositions from the freight agent, his accountant, and his warehouse manager."

Our drinks arrived. Mateo asked if we needed more time with the menus.

"Please order for both of us," Jenny told me. "I'm in your hands."

I told Mateo we wanted guacamole and malanga fritters to start, then shrimp ceviche and grilled baby octopus as a second course, followed by the seafood paella for two.

Mateo nodded and said, "Excellent choices." They were all dishes that Marisa liked here and sometimes cooked for us at home. I didn't mention that.

"Are you going to win your case?" I asked Jenny.

"At $200 an hour, I'd better," she answered.

She didn't smile when she said it. I could sense the kind of pressure she was under to perform, especially as a junior associate at her law firm, which was something I knew from Claire.

The guacamole and malanga fritters arrived.

"What's in the fritters?" Jenny asked. "I've never had them."

"They're a traditional Cuban appetizer made of purple taro root, garlic, and cilantro."

"You know a lot about Cuban food," she said, dipping a nacho chip into the guacamole. "Do you serve it in your bar?"

"No, the menu at The Drunken Parrot is more like Ditka's," I said. That was a Chicago sports bar named for former Bears tight end and coach Mike Ditka. I like bar food better than the gourmet feast at the pop-up dinner.

Witnesses later told police they thought the noise they heard was a car backfiring, or firecrackers. That was common. But I knew the difference between those noises and gunfire, especially when the sound was accompanied by a woman screaming.

Instinctively I grabbed Jenny's arm when the shooting started, pulled her to the floor, and covered her with my body. As the screaming continued, I reached for my Smith & Wesson .38 in its holster at the small of my back. But I'd left it in my car. A rookie mistake, especially when in Miami, a lovely city that could get very ugly very fast. And doubly dumb because I was with my daughter.

I looked toward the sound of the screaming. At a table near the front door, a young man holding a black semiautomatic pistol that appeared to be a Sig Sauer 9 mm was standing over another young man collapsed on the floor. Blood was pooling under the downed man's head. The screams were coming from a lovely young woman with long raven hair seated at the table. All three of them were Hispanic.

I guessed what was happening: A love triangle had turned violent. I'd caught a number of cases like that.

I whispered to Jenny, "Stay down. It'll be okay."

She didn't move or say a word. Now the shooter was pointing the gun at the woman. The other diners and the restaurant staff were frozen in place. Faced with imminent death, the woman stopped screaming, sighed, and said, "Oh, Miguel, please don't do this."

Miguel thought about that, turned the gun from her, put the barrel against his right temple, and fired.

Everyone had to remain at the restaurant, including the screaming woman who was now quietly crying, and the two corpses, for two hours while Miami Beach homicide detectives took our statements and crime scene techs processed the scene. The restaurant's owner, a man named Pedro Famosa, had his staff serve free drinks to the shaken patrons.

A detective named Luis Lopez sat with Jenny and me as we told him what we'd seen. Detective Lopez was a muscular man of medium height, in his forties, with a pencil mustache and a pock-marked face. He seemed very competent.

When Jenny and I were finished telling him our version of the events, he said, "So you're a policeman too, Mr. Starkey."

"Was," I answered. "In Chicago. Do I look that much like a cop?"

He smiled. "It's the way you gave your statement. Precise, and to the point. You didn't object when I had you repeat it three times, and the facts never changed. Civilians generally don't do it like that."

He took our addresses and phone numbers, told us he might be in touch again, and that we could be asked to give depositions or to testify in civil court if any lawsuits were filed against the restaurant by our fellow diners. There would be no criminal trial, only a funeral, for the shooter. Detective Lopez handed Jenny and me his business card, told us to contact him if we thought of anything else, and said we could go.

As I led Jenny by the arm toward the front door of the restaurant, the medical examiner was telling the EMS attendants that they could remove the bodies. The police already had taken the woman at the center of the violence away.

Jenny and I didn't speak as we walked to my car. I unlocked the doors, opened hers, then went around and got in the driver's side.

"Are you okay, hon?" I asked her.

She sat there for a few moments and then said, "Mom always told me she felt safe with you. Now I know what she meant."

I opened the glove compartment to make certain my S&W was still there. It was. But it's no good unless you have it with you. My Marine Corps DI would have given me a zillion push-ups and then washed me out of the program for a mistake like that. Sometimes all is right with the world, and then the tranquility is shattered by sudden, random violence. Men like me are supposed to be prepared.

Jenny saw the gun and said, "If you had that with you, you might have tried to shoot the guy, and maybe he'd have shot you first."

"It's always good to have the option."

She thought for a moment and said, "You protected me, Daddy. You're my hero."

I loved the daddy part.

"I'm not a hero, Jen," I told her. "I reacted instinctively, like any father would. Your Uncle Joe was the hero. He had time to think about how dangerous it was to run into that burning building. And he went in anyway."

She took my hand in hers and squeezed it.

"I might have to come back again for this case," she said. "We could get together again."

"That'd be great," I told her. "But maybe we'll try a different restaurant."

As I was heading back to Naples across Alligator Alley, my cell phone rang. It was Claire.

"You saved two lives tonight," she said.

"Jenny told you about the shooting."

Later to my indescribable joy, I learned she meant that I'd saved Jenny's life and that of the baby she was carrying. I guessed that Jenny meant to tell me about the baby during dinner, but decided to wait for a calmer moment.

"You know, you're still my hero, Jack," Claire said.

That was the second time that night I'd been called a hero. Coming from Claire and Jenny, that meant more to me than any decoration I'd ever gotten from the marines or the Chicago PD.

Maybe there was more of Jack Stoney in me than I thought.

36.

Strada Place

I was waiting in the conference room of the Executive Suites complex in downtown Naples when Christopher Knowland arrived.

I didn't want him to see my office, which was bare except for a wooden desk and swivel chair and a framed generic print depicting a sailboat heeled over in the wind. It was just barely above paint-by-numbers quality and I would have put it in the trashcan, but I didn't have one.

Leila, the shared receptionist, showed Knowland in and asked if we wanted coffee, water, or a soda. I declined; Knowland asked for a Diet Coke. He watched Leila walk away in her short tight skirt and winked at me. He probably wasn't thirsty. Men can be such boors.

I stood, greeted Knowland with a handshake, and said, "Thanks for coming, Chris. Have a seat and I'll tell you about my project."

He said, "I'm always interested in a good opportunity."

I opened a manila file folder, took out a document, and slid it across the table to him. "A standard confidentiality agreement."

"Of course," he said as he scanned it.

Leila arrived with his Diet Coke. He watched her come and go. I did too, but he started it.

I'd placed a yellow legal pad and pen on the table before he arrived. He took the pen and signed the agreement. I put it back into the folder.

"Our offering is almost fully subscribed with people I know from other projects," I told him. "But we have room for one more investor. I asked around town, without describing the project of course, and your name came up because you're in the real estate business."

He seemed pleased by that.

"So, Frank, what's the deal?" he asked, leaning back in his chair and lacing his fingers behind his head.

"It's an opportunity a man of your expertise will like," I told him. This seemed to please him more. Flattery is a good set-up for a scam.

I stood and walked over to the display board I'd set up on an easel showing the sketch of the development Vasily's people had prepared, and began my presentation.

"Strada Place will be a mixed-use complex on fifty-three acres located off the East Trail," I explained.

"Mixed-use complex" was one of the real estate terms I'd memorized.

"We'll have 350,000 square feet of retail space, up to twelve restaurants, a coffee shop, a midrise condominium building with ninety-two residences, a parking garage, a Whole Foods as an anchor, and one of those movie theaters with a restaurant and advance-purchase, reclining seats."

It all sounded so good I almost wanted to buy in.

I pointed out a street cutting through the middle of the buildings and said, "There will be a four-block, brick-paved main street lined with fourteen buildings, palm trees, and gaslights. Strada Place will be the first of its kind in Collier County."

"What's the projected cost?" he asked.

I took my seat at the table, ready for that key question. With the background Vasily's people had provided, it was like a slow-pitch softball coming right into the strike zone.

"We haven't dotted all the i's and crossed all the t's yet, I answered, "but we hope to bring it in at approximately $120 mill."

More business lingo. I was playing Christopher Knowland like B.B. King's Gibson, Lucille.

"Well now," Knowland said, rubbing his chin, "that's pretty aggressive. Higher than the usual per-square-foot cost around here."

Ready for that, too, thanks to Vasily's tutorial.

"It'll be higher quality than any other development in the region," I said. "We think this market will support it."

"Do you have the land?"

"Not yet. I need to get our financing in place before we make an offer. But the parcel I want has been for sale for two years. I'm confident I can buy it right."

I pushed a stack of documents and bound reports toward him. "Here's everything you need for your due diligence. The minimum investment is $500 K for one unit."

We big-time businessmen always said "mill" for million and "K" for thousand. I didn't know what we said for hundred, but then, that was chump change to guys like us.

I continued: "We have four units still unsubscribed. If you're not interested, the partners will buy them. Think it over and let me know. We'd love to have a pro like you on our team."

Just to set the hook, I added, "Time is of the essence."

In any important business transaction, time is always of the essence. If you snooze, you lose. Frank Chance, super salesman. After this, I might switch to aluminum siding or used cars, maybe win salesman of the month and get a set of steak knives. Or demo juicers at Costco.

Knowland stood, picked up the materials, and said, "I'll have my people look over these documents. I'll get back to you by next week at the latest."

It seemed that everyone had people to do their bidding except me. No, that was not entirely correct. For as long as I rented space in the Executive Suites, I had Leila. I also had Sam Longtree with his shotgun; Martin, the butler; and Suzette, the cook. And there was Joe, the cat who always had my back. Maybe I should have a staff meeting so that everyone was on the same page about my daily needs.

37.

Green Is Good

The next several days passed uneventfully. I drove to Fort Myers Beach to check on the bar and my houseboat, went for runs on the beach, washed and waxed my car, had dinner with Marisa, met with Vasily, and briefed Hansen on recent developments with the investigation.

It was time for Joe's annual exam and shots at his veterinarian's office in Fort Myers Beach. He must have heard me calling for the appointment because, when it was time to leave Ash's house, he hid. It took me twenty minutes to locate him lying on a shelf in the kitchen pantry.

I picked him up and said, "Let's go, buddy. We do this every year. We'll stop at Dairy Queen on the way home and I'll get you a vanilla cone."

He looked at me and meowed. Did that mean he wanted sprinkles on it?

Knowland called and said, "Count me in for the last four units."

He was trusting me, basically a stranger, with two million smackeroos. What a great country this is.

Then Vasily called to say that Knowland's $2 million had been wired to Gulf Development's account at Cayman Islands National Bank.

"How does it feel to be a new multimillionaire?" he asked.

"Frank Chance is one already," I reminded him.

"Ah, but this is real money, and you have access to it. Are you tempted, even a little bit?"

"I spent my career in law enforcement chasing people who yielded to temptation."

"My Uncle Vasily, I took his name for my new identity, used to say that there is no one more dangerous than an honest man. Of course, that was from his perspective as head of our family business in Brighton Beach."

"A Russian godfather."

"He loved those movies," Vasily said. "As you know, there are plenty of dishonest policemen. No offense. We had some on the payroll in New York. Still do, I suppose. I'm not in that anymore."

"I knew some cops like that in Chicago. Not many. Nothing compared to the politicians."

"My family once considered moving into Chicago to take on the Italians. In the end, we didn't because, as you said, the politicians were already stealing most everything."

"You have access to that Cayman Islands account too."

He laughed.

"We want more from Christopher Knowland than his money. We want his freedom. Or his life. With or without the criminal justice system."

You can take the boy out of the Russian Mafia but . . .

I NOW was ready to twist the screws on Christopher Knowland, who was, of course, the only investor in my Strada Place project.

As a first step, I called him to say I'd approached the owner of the land, and we'd agreed on a price I could make work and still get the ROI I needed. ROI. Return on investment. I was showing off. I said it was time for my project manager to file an application with the city zoning board for initial approval of our development. I'd keep him informed.

"I like that you're moving forward quickly," he told me. "Time is money."

I thought time was of the essence. Live and learn.

As a second step, Vasily soon instructed me to call Knowland again, this time to report that the project had hit a snag.

"One of the zoning board members has expressed a concern about the environmental impact of Strada Place," I said. "This guy seems like he'll oppose it, whether or not the project is in compliance with all the rules and regs."

"Another one of those green-is-good tree huggers," Knowland said with disgust. "I ran into them all the time in my business."

I remembered that Vasily had told me Knowland had allegedly bribed a Naples city councilman to get his marina project approved. This was a different guy who, Vasily said, was a straight arrow who could not be bribed. I would pretend to try, then tell Knowland I'd been turned down, so the project was stalled. A short time later, Vasily would make certain Knowland knew that I was running a Ponzi scheme and he'd lost his investment. Then I'd wait for the assassin.

Knowland thought for a moment, then asked, "What's the guy's name?"

As Vasily had also instructed, I said, "Gilbert Merton."

"Maybe you can reason with him," Knowland said. By which I knew he meant bribe. That part of the scam was working.

"I'll try, and let you know how it goes."

But before I could pretend to bribe Gilbert Merton, he turned up dead.

38.

Hit And Run

"You and Count Dickbrain could be charged as accessories to murder," Hansen told me when I went to his office in police headquarters to talk about the death of Gilbert Merton. I'd briefed him earlier about our bribery scheme.

Although he didn't reveal it to me, Knowland must have known that Merton was an honest man and decided that, because the zoning board member couldn't be bribed to allow our project to go forward, he needed to be dead.

Hansen was justifiably very angry. Vasily and I had cost a man his life. He was right about the possible criminal charge, but I knew he wouldn't follow up on that because everything we'd been working on together would be made public.

Merton was hit by some kind of vehicle while riding his bicycle at seven A.M. on Orange Blossom Road, near his house in a gated community. His wife said he was an avid cyclist who rode every morning at that time. The force of the impact broke his neck and multiple other bones and did severe internal damage. The driver did not stop.

Naples has many bicyclists on the roads. There aren't many bike paths, mainly narrow lanes beside some roadways, and none on others. That, combined with the many older drivers who don't see or hear well and sometimes hit the accelerator instead of the brake pedal, causes many car-bike collisions every year. And the cars always win.

Sometimes the motorists panic and don't stop, or don't even realize they've hit someone. A woman driving an SUV hit a pedestrian a year or so ago, I'd read in the newspaper, and dragged him a quarter mile without realizing it until she stopped for a red light and other drivers began honking at her and pointing beneath her car.

"Sure, it could have been an accident," Hansen told me as he sat behind his desk, clicking a cigar lighter in the shape of a pistol on and off repeatedly. At least he wasn't pointing it at me as I sat in a side chair.

"But I don't think so. He rode his bike at the same time every day on the same route. Someone watching him would know that. I'm convinced that you and Vasily set him up for murder."

"I have no excuse, chief," I told him. "I thought Knowland would go with the bribery story, and, when that didn't work, he'd come after me, not Merton."

"I think we've gotta call in the FBI," Hansen said. "This whole thing's way out of control . . ."

"You can do that. But there's not enough evidence for a conviction. There's no way these old goats are doing the hits themselves. But, with Merton, I'm now 100 percent certain that these are the bad guys. And that they've hired a pro for the wet work."

"I agree, I guess," Hansen said.

"But if FBI agents parachute in and run around town in those blue crime scene jackets with those big yellow FBI letters on the back, The Gang Of Three will simply shut down their operation. Their hit man will disappear. Give me a few more days."

Hansen stared at me, opened a bottom desk drawer, took out a bottle of Jameson and a shot glass, tossed back a drink, and said, "Okay. Then I'm calling in the feds."

As I drove back to Ash's house, I reviewed the situation. So far, the scoreboard read: bad guys 6, used-to-be homicide detective 0.

Maybe Ash could be counted as collateral damage, if the excitement of being peripherally involved in my investigation had brought on her heart attack. No way to know.

There was no time to continue with my elaborate real estate scam with Christopher Knowland, sweet as it was. No time to lounge around town as Frank Chance, waiting for the next thing to happen. No time to find out what Detective Jack Stoney would do. It was time for some old-fashioned, Chicago-style, kickass-police work.

I wasn't carrying a badge, so annoying restrictions like the Constitution of the United States and the State of Florida criminal code didn't hamper me. No evidence I gathered without following proper procedures would be admissible in court, but maybe I could get the three men to incriminate themselves in some kosher way. And, if not, maybe Vasily had his own backup plan for bringing the men to justice, Russian Mafia style. I wouldn't agree to that, but Vasily might not ask for my vote.

Vasily and I met at his house and worked out a revised plan. I called Hansen and told him we were going to take a new approach, and this time he *really* didn't want to know what it was, despite what he'd said earlier about wanting to know everything.

If the revised plan worked, he would be called in to arrest the killers, I told Hansen. If it didn't, he'd be insulated from whatever Vasily and I had done. Put that way, Hansen reluctantly agreed.

To pull it off, I needed a team of my own. Serge Chuikov, Vasily's driver, and Stefan Arsov, a member of Vasily's boat crew who had once fended off Caribbean pirates with a .50-caliber machine gun, had served together in the same Russian army unit. Serge was a sniper, and Stefan was his spotter. Targets who thought they were safe because they were 1,200 yards away found out that they were wrong. Head shots every time, according to Vasily.

After their army service, Dmitri Ivanovich, Vasily's father, recruited them as enforcers for the family business in Brighton Beach. They were hard men who'd done bad things and were fully prepared to do so again. When Vasily set himself up in Naples, they went to work for him, just in case muscle was needed.

Now they reported to me.

39.

A Long Par Four

My commando team and I were gathered poolside at Vasily's house to plan the kidnappings.

Elena had ferried the three of us to the island from the mainland. I got the feeling from their body language that Elena and Serge were very good friends, and that it would be a very bad idea for anyone to attempt to cut in on that relationship. Serge and Elena, Stefan and Lena. Colleagues with benefits, fishing from the company dock. Maybe that was part of the Atocha Securities employee benefits package. It sure would beat dental insurance.

Vasily was a member of the Olde Naples Country Club. He told me that Bradenton, Knowland, and Cox played golf there together three days a week, with an eight A.M. tee time. Various members sometimes joined them as a fourth.

Vasily booked himself into their next tee time because there was no group before or immediately after them. No witnesses. With rain threatening, the course was not crowded, but that would not deter avid golfers like our boys unless the rain became a downpour, with lightning in the area, Vasily told me. He'd never played with them before, but it would not be considered unusual to have the pro shop find a member a game. The morning of the game, just before the tee time, Vasily would call the pro shop, make an excuse, and drop out, leaving the three of them alone on the course.

The fifteenth hole was a long par four, with a stand of pine trees and flowering bushes blocking the view from the houses that lined the course. That's where they'd be taken. The par three fifth hole, where Charles Beaumont's ashes were scattered, would have been a fitting place to bring down his killers, but it was not secluded enough.

AT SEVEN fifty-five, Vasily called the pro shop to drop out. He made the call from his cabin in the Everglades, where he and I were waiting. He used the cabin for hunting and fishing.

At zero dark thirty that morning, he had picked me up at Ash's house and we had driven in his silver Range Rover to Everglades City, an hour south of Naples. His driver was otherwise engaged that morning.

Everglades City is a small fishing village eighty miles west of Miami with a colorful history. The remoteness of the city and the labyrinthine maze of mangrove swamps in the area known as the Ten Thousand Islands have always been perfect for smuggling operations between South Florida and the Caribbean and Central and South America: endangered animal species in the early 1900s, rum running during Prohibition, and a flood of drugs coming into South Florida in the 1970s and '80s, when marijuana smuggling became the mainstay of the local economy. In two raids in 1983 and '84, DEA agents arrested 80 percent of the male population of Everglades City. I learned all that from a Miami DEA agent who dated a friend of Marisa's.

Elena had been waiting for us at a small wooden dock in an airboat, which was the only way to traverse the marsh grass and open water to the small island where Vasily's cabin was located. She was perched on a raised platform in front of a large fan that powered the boat, a flat-bottomed aluminum skiff. *Fan-Tastic* would have been a good name for the boat.

When Vasily and I stepped aboard, Elena handed us headsets to cover our ears against the loud noise the fan would make. We sat in molded fiberglass chairs bolted to the deck in front of Elena's platform. She flipped a switch that powered up the fan, Vasily untied the mooring lines, pushed us away from the dock, and we were off, skimming over the surface of the vast River of Grass, as the Everglades is called.

The morning sun was burning off an early fog; as the curtain of mist rose from the landscape, all kinds of flora and fauna came into sharp focus as if I were watching the scene in a snow globe. The eyeballs of partially submerged gators watched us pass.

I'd never been on an airboat before. It was a lot of fun and almost made me forget our serious mission. After a fifteen-minute ride, Elena pulled us up to a wooden dock on Vasily's small island, which was mostly a mangrove swamp with a central mound of solid ground.

The cabin was a one-story, cedar-sided structure, with a green tin roof, mounted on tall wooden pilings. There were a number of these cabins in the Everglades, some more than 100 years old. They were grandfathered in. New construction was prohibited. From the outside, the cabin looked like a modest hunting-and-fishing retreat, but the interior was tastefully decorated and furnished in rod-and-gun-club style.

The place was so remote that it would be a perfect place to kill someone and feed the body to the gators. Had Vasily's people, on his orders, ever done that? It was not unimaginable. He was, after all, born into a family who presumably solved personnel problems that way. I wondered again whether Vasily considered that to be an option for The Gang Of Three, if our new plan didn't work out. And what if I proved to be a problem for him?

When The Gang Of Three teed off on the fifteenth hole in a light drizzle, Serge and Stefan, dressed in black tee shirts and black commando pants and boots, were waiting in the trees. Stefan gave Vasily regular reports on a cell phone throughout the operation, and Vasily told me what was happening.

When the three men were on the fairway, ready to hit their second shots, the Russians walked up to them, holding pistols at their sides. The pistols were for shock-and-awe value only. The Russians certainly didn't need weapons to handle their targets.

Serge ordered the three men to drive their carts toward the trees. He hopped onto the back of one of the carts, where the golf bags were strapped on, and Stefan got onto the other. Serge told Cox, who was driving one of the carts with Bradenton riding shotgun, and Knowland, alone in the other, to drive off the fairway and into the woods, where the carts would be hidden from view.

Stefan used his combat knife to cut the name tags off the golf bags, to delay identifying the missing golfers, and put them into his pants pocket. Serge ordered the men to get out of the carts and follow him.

I later asked Vasily what Stefan reported that the men had said as they were being abducted. Bradenton and Knowland were initially too stunned to speak, but Cox, ever the attorney, had demanded to know who they were and what the hell they were doing. That conversation ended with a hard backhand across Cox's face by Serge. Cox toppled over backward, and his friends helped him to his feet. He was bleeding from the nose and mouth. They must have thought it was a kidnapping for ransom.

The three were led through the trees and off the golf course to a white Ford Econoline van with the name of the Springtime Air Heating and Cooling Company painted on the side. Springtime Air was as real a company as was Gulf Development. The van was parked in the driveway of a house that, Vasily somehow knew, was vacant because the owners were on a cruise. Any neighbor noticing the van would think it was there on a service call.

Stefan slid open the side door of the van, which had no rear seats, and pushed the three inside. Serge got into the driver's seat as Stefan got into the rear with the men, slid the door closed, put strips of duct tape across their eyes and mouths, and bound their wrists and ankles with the tape. This was more from habit than necessity; imagine those used-to-bes taking on a pair of Russian commandos. Stefan climbed into the front passenger seat and they made the hour-long drive to Everglades City.

40.

Drowned And Confused Rats

Vasily and I were waiting at the dock when Elena's airboat arrived from the mainland. Now the sky was overhung with dark clouds, and a light drizzle had become a hard rain.

Elena was wearing a yellow rain slicker, and her long blonde hair was awash and wind blown; on her, wet and wild looked good. Her five passengers were unprotected and soaked. Vasily and I were wearing slickers like Elena's, which he had in a closet in the cabin.

He also had shown me a complete array of fishing gear, and all manner of firearms: a virtual armory of pistols and rifles in a gun safe, some meant for hunting, and some more suitable for holding off a waterborne assault. One of the long guns was a Dragunov, the superb Russian sniper rifle chambered for a 7.62 mm cartridge. With that rifle in the right hands, which were Serge's, a waterborne assault on Vasily's cabin would not reach the dock.

As Elena powered down the fan and Stefan tied up the mooring lines, Serge removed the duct tape covering the three men's eyes and mouths and gestured for them to stand up and get out of the boat. The tape already had been cut from their wrists and ankles.

Blinking in the sunlight, they stepped stiffly onto the dock, Stefan assisting them, and looked around. The term "drowned rats" came to mind. Correction: drowned and confused rats.

They spotted Vasily and me standing there. Bradenton angrily asked Vasily, "What the fuck is this all about?"

Knowland looked at me and said, "Does this mean our real estate deal is off, Frank?"

Points for grace under pressure.

Cox glared at us and said, "You're both in a world of shit. I *guaran-fucking-tee* you that."

Which might prove to be absolutely correct, depending upon what happened next.

"We'll go into my cabin, gentlemen, and all your questions will be answered," Vasily told them. "If you're smart, you'll answer ours as well."

We walked in a line from the dock to a stairway leading up to the cabin's front door and went inside. Each man was put into a separate bedroom. Before shutting them in, Vasily told them to strip off their wet clothing and to put on the tee shirts and sweatpants he'd laid out on the beds for the men when the rain began—good thing; naked was not a good look for those guys. Elena collected the wet clothing and put it in a dryer off the kitchen.

Vasily also said they could use the bathroom in the hallway, and they all did. It's axiomatic in the life of an older man: never pass up the chance for a potty break, unless you are wearing an adult diaper.

The hurricane shutters were down over the outside of the bedroom windows so that the three men couldn't try to break out. That was unnecessary, because an escape attempt was pointless; there was nowhere to go on the island, and no way to get off, because I'd seen Elena take the airboat key.

We let Arthur Bradenton, Roland Cox, and Christopher Knowland sit alone in their bedrooms for two hours. That was standard police interrogation technique. During that time, anger turned to confusion, and then to worry, and finally to despair. That was the time to begin the questioning.

While the most unlikely group of perps I'd ever come across marinated in their fear and loathing, Elena served Vasily, Serge, Stefan, and me a lunch of cold poached salmon, caviar, and a beet salad she'd brought in an Igloo cooler, and then joined us. Vasily had white wine with his lunch, and Serge and Stefan drank vodka, passing the bottle between them, as they might in a foxhole on a battlefield. Elena and I had Diet Cokes. I wondered if any other hunting and fishing cabin in the Everglades had a fully stocked wine cellar.

I thought again about the possibility that our captives had nothing to do with the murders of Eileen Stephenson, Lester Gandolf, Bob Appleby, Tess Johannsen, Charles Beaumont, and Gilbert Merton. If they were not involved, then the killer was still out there, and Vasily, Serge, Stefan, and I could be charged with kidnapping and assault. Elena could be charged as an accessory. That is, unless Vasily fed the fellows to the gators. Which, given the alternative, maybe wasn't such a bad idea.

So a lot depended upon my interrogation skills. The cop I used to be was very good at it.

Confessions obtained under these circumstances would not hold up in court. But I hoped I could get them to admit to their crimes, and that the threat of publicly exposing them for the evil bastards that they were would prompt them to do as I asked. Which was to order their hired assassin to take me out. I'd be waiting at Ash's house with my Russians. We'd attempt to take the hired gun alive. In my experience, men like that would inevitably give up their employer in return for a reduced sentence.

It was not a foolproof plan. Foolhardy was more like it. Way too many moving parts and unsubstantiated assumptions. But, at that point, it was all I had. So damn the torpedoes, full speed ahead, and hope the good guys don't get sunk.

41.

The 305 Man

I decided to start with Christopher Knowland because I knew him from our almost real estate deal. I opened his bedroom door and went in carrying a folding chair. He was sitting on the side of the bed, elbows on his knees, head in his hands. I opened the chair, placed it opposite him, and sat, waiting for him to speak first.

Suspects usually find this disconcerting and sometimes offer information that they otherwise would not. Or sometimes they just sat there in silence too. In those cases, the interrogation turns into a Zen retreat until one of us has to use the bathroom.

Knowland sat up, looked at me, and asked, "Who the fuck are you, really?"

"Your worst nightmare," I told him. That was overly melodramatic, but Jack Stoney had said it in one of the books, and it worked for him.

Then Knowland asked, "What the hell do you want from us?"

"I've already spoken with your buddies," I said. "They told me all about what you three have been up to. The Gang Of Three. Isn't that what you call yourselves?"

Standard technique for interrogating multiple suspects: Make them think their buddy or buddies have already ratted them out, so what have they got to lose by admitting their crimes?

"I don't know anything about any kind of gang," Knowland told me.

"We're way past that, Christopher," I said, trying to make him feel, by not calling him Chris, as if his mother were scolding him.

"Horse has left the barn. Train has departed the station. Flight has pushed away from the gate. Ship has sailed. Cavalry has left the fort. I've got more of those sayings, but you get the point."

"I'm not admitting anything," he said. "But if you let us go, we won't tell the police about all this. It's not too late to work something out in a businesslike way. Find a win-win, so to speak."

I stared at him long enough to make him avert his eyes. "Okay, here's the bottom line," I said. Businessmen like us always got right to that. "I know for a fact you and your pals ordered the murders of Eileen Stephenson, Lester Gandolf, Bob Appleby, Charles Beaumont, and Gilbert Merton. A young woman named Tess Johannsen was collateral damage. One more victim and you make the serial killer top-ten list. What I don't know is why, and who you hired to do the hits."

Knowland stood up and faced me. So I stood up too. Couldn't have him talking down to me.

"I told you, I have no idea what you're talking about," he said, poking me in the chest with his right index finger. I let that go; a guy I was questioning once did that and when he got the finger back, it was broken.

"I don't know what Art or Rollie might have told you, but if they said we were involved in any murders, it's not true. They were just telling you what you want to hear so you'll let us go."

Not bad. The man could think on his feet. I'll bet he was good in negotiations. He'd recovered nicely and was clearly not ready to tap my shoulder to end the match. So I brought out the big gun. I jammed my index finger into his chest, hard, which backed him up a step, and told him, "Florida carries out its executions by lethal injection. Maybe you've heard that didn't go so well the last few times. Something about a shortage of the right chemicals causing lingering, excruciating death."

Which was true, in Florida and in several other states. Clearly Knowland did know about this because he finally lost his composure; his lower lip was quivering, his breathing became rapid and shallow, and his hands were shaking badly. I thought he might be having a heart attack. If he did, I'd have to start over with one of the other guys, and the gators could have a nice lunch. And if the gators didn't get him, the Burmese pythons taking over the Everglades surely would.

He sat down on the bed and was silent. Finally he said, without looking at me, "We didn't plan to kill anyone. We really didn't."

Fish in the boat.

As I was walking out of Knowland's bedroom, I turned to him and had to ask: "Just between us, how'd I do as a Ponzi scheme real estate scam artist?"

He smiled. "You were good. I'd say you have a future as a felon."

I left Knowland and used the same technique on Art Bradenton and then on Rollie Cox. Vasily was sitting in a rocking chair on the back porch of the cabin, sipping cognac and smoking a cigar. Elena cleaned up the kitchen and then sat on the couch doing something on her iPhone. Stefan and Serge were outside somewhere. I heard the occasional report of a firearm; maybe they were honing their sniper skills by shooting endangered species, or drug smugglers.

Bradenton held out the longest, but in the end I was able to cobble together the strange story of three men who had lost their power and influence in their worlds, and, in their dotage, had discovered that the ultimate power was the power over life and death.

This is a summary of the amazing tale they told me, the truth being stranger than any fictional tale Bill Stevens ever cooked up:

About two years ago, after a round of golf, the three men were in their country club bar, having drinks and playing high-stakes gin rummy. Cox told his pals about how the Naples Department of Public Works had started trimming the banyan trees lining the street his house was on in order to prevent their branches from interfering with overhead electrical power lines.

Cox sent a letter to city officials objecting to the trimming because he believed it was damaging the trees. His request to halt the trimming was denied. He said he was angry about "being pushed around by the city."

Either Knowland or Cox, no one remembered which one, suggested that they take some action. Something not traceable to them, which would get back at the bastards. They all liked that idea. Two days later, during their next golf game, Bradenton said he'd been thinking about that and had an idea. The decision to go forward with it gained unanimous approval.

Late one night—they were rookies because it was not three A.M.—they broke in to the Naples Public Works Department garage, let the air out of all of the truck tires, used cans of spray paint to put slogans on a wall as teenagers might—NDPW Sucks! Bite Me Dickheads! Bigfoot Was Here—and broke the blades of a few of the offending tree-trimming saws.

It was, to them, nothing more than a schoolboy prank, akin to strewing toilet paper over a teacher's tree. They knew that it would do nothing to prevent the trimming of the banyan trees on Pirates Cove Drive, or anywhere else in the city. But it felt good. It was fun. More fun than they could recall having in a long time.

In their prime, they could exert power and influence. Now they were toothless old lions, and no one heeded their roars. The break-in was to them a sign that they were still alive and kicking, still players, albeit on a smaller stage. But players nonetheless. Then they forgot about it.

Four months after the Department of Public Works break-in, Cox decided he wanted to buy a vacant lot adjacent to his house so he could build a tennis court. A man named Theodore "Teddy" Lundquist, a land speculator, owned the land. He refused to sell the lot, even though Cox kept upping his offer until it was about a third more than market value. There was a real estate boom in Naples, and Lundquist apparently wanted to hold the property until its value went even higher, Cox said. Or maybe he had his own plans for the land and didn't want to sell at any price.

Cox said that he was tired of being jacked around. Recalling how good it felt to exact revenge upon the DPW, even if it was just a minor prank, they decided to hire a private detective to put Lundquist under surveillance, under the theory that everyone did something wrong sometime. In my experience, that was true.

After two weeks of surveillance, the detective reported that Lundquist, who was married, sometimes frequented a gay bar in Fort Myers. A messenger delivered an envelope to his house containing eight-by-ten color photographs of him entering and exiting the gay bar, with a neon sign in the window saying "Adonis's Cave" clearly visible.

There was an anonymous note in the envelope telling Lundquist that if he didn't immediately sell all of his vacant lots in Collier County—that way, Cox's identity was protected—copies of the photos would be given to his wife and mailed to his friends.

Over the next three months, Lundquist sold all of his properties, including the vacant lot to Rollie Cox. That was the most fun you could have with your clothes on, one of them said. It went on like that for a while, the occasional dirty trick in order to gain a result they wanted. They felt they were maybe onto something that had possibilities beyond what they'd done so far.

In their opinion, men like themselves had once ruled America, and America was a better place for it. But now, the nation was changing, *had* changed, until it was hardly recognizable, at least to them and men like them. Hispanics, blacks, Muslims, Asians, women wanting to call the shots, gays wanting to get married . . . The Great American Melting Pot had become a cesspool of groups who no longer appreciated the fact that this great nation had been built by the likes of Arthur Bradenton, Christopher Knowland, and Roland Cox.

Bradenton's granddaughter was majoring in women's studies at an elite Eastern college; there also were majors in Asian studies, Hispanic studies, and black studies. No Muslim studies, but it was being considered "by the liberal pinko administration," Bradenton told me, a look of utter disgust on his face. Of course there was no white male studies program. He said that his granddaughter had taken a course called LGBT Culture; he had to ask his wife what that meant, and was horrified when she explained it to him. His son and daughter-in-law were paying all that tuition to have their daughter brainwashed! The country was going to hell in a handbasket!

Rollie, Art, and Chris decided to organize their activities by forming a club. In a town of exclusive clubs, theirs would be the most exclusive of all. They named it The Old White Men. That was

Cox's idea. That term was usually meant pejoratively; to them, it would be a badge of honor.

Later, even though I knew it would be like talking to monkeys at the Lincoln Park Zoo, I told them that old white men weren't doing such a great job of running the country anymore, so it might be good to have some new blood in charge. None of them agreed with that, not even *in extremis*, as they were.

Now that they were an official strike force for their kind, fighting for the dignity and honor of old white men everywhere, they gained focus and confidence, and things began to escalate.

About six months before I entered the investigation, Bradenton found out that Eileen Stephenson was spreading nasty gossip about his wife, Paige. Something about Paige being "trailer trash" before she married Art. In fact, Paige came from a poor family in rural Minnesota, and the family did live in a double-wide for a time after her father lost his job at the grain silo. She met Art when they attended the University of Minnesota, she on a volleyball scholarship.

Something had to be done. It was decided that Eileen needed a good scaring. The private detective hired to trail Teddy Lundquist said he couldn't do anything like that. He could lose his license. But he gave them a telephone number in Miami.

The Old White Men never met the man who answered the phone. They never knew his name. He asked who had referred them to him, and was satisfied with the answer. He said that his fee was $50,000, plus expenses, for what he termed "a routine assignment." If "complications" or "unforeseen difficulties" developed, the fee would increase significantly.

Once an assignment had begun, the man told them, it could not be canceled. He said that if he accepted an assignment from them, and he heard that they had discussed his work, his very existence, with anyone, and he had ways of hearing, there would be "serious consequences."

The Miami man said he'd be in touch when the job was completed and would give them instructions about how to wire his fee into a numbered account at a bank in Switzerland. I guess he didn't think Cayman Islands banks were secure enough.

With all of them on a speakerphone, they described the situation with Eileen Stephenson. Maybe she could be warned by a threatening phone call in the middle of the night to stop gossiping in general. Maybe there could be a break-in at her house while she was sleeping . . .

The Miami man stopped them short by saying, "Don't tell me how to do my job." He agreed to "take care of their problem" with Eileen.

Five days later, they read Eileen's obituary in the *Naples Daily News*. It was possible that she had died of natural causes as her obit said, a heart attack or stroke, while swimming laps, before their man had the chance to do anything to her. It happened to people her age all the time.

They decided not to call their man in Miami to ask how Eileen died because it didn't really matter, and because they were better off not knowing.

"However it happened, it certainly shut her up," Knowland had commented when they got together that morning for their usual round of golf, and they all surprised themselves by laughing. It was just like the old days, they discovered. They made a phone call, and appropriate action was taken.

The day after Eileen's obituary appeared, Bradenton received a text message on his cell phone that said, "$100,000." The man had doubled his fee. They wondered what kind of complications could possibly have developed in offing an old woman like Eileen. But when you worked with a hit man, "don't ask, don't tell" was the golden rule.

Bradenton answered the text with one word, "Agreed." The money was wired to the Swiss bank account. Even if the man couldn't prove that Eileen had died because of his actions, you didn't challenge a man like that, you just paid his bill.

Time passed. The three returned to their privileged routines: golf, boating, poker, cocktail hours, dinner parties, symphony concerts, charitable work, and trying the many new restaurants that constantly opened in Naples, replacing an equal number that closed.

Paige Bradenton oversaw a complete remodeling of the kitchen in their home, which had been remodeled only one year earlier—something about her hating the backsplash, which led to a total gut job. Lucille and Chris Knowland went on the South Beach Diet; she lost ten pounds in six weeks, he lost nothing and was accused of cheating. The Coxes took a Caribbean cruise aboard a charter schooner which ran into heavy weather; they vowed that all of their future vacations would be on land.

The Eileen Stephenson matter was never again discussed. They hadn't asked the Miami guy to kill her, just to scare her. Her death wasn't on them. It was collateral damage, if that, and nothing more.

Then Cox placed a conference call to his friends, reporting that he and Lester Gandolf were vying for the one vacant seat on the Republican National Committee. It looked like Gandolf would get the seat because, as a billionaire, he'd given more money to the party and its candidates over the years, his beneficence exceeded only by the Koch brothers.

Cox had been out of politics since his term as ambassador to France ended. It would have been fun to get involved in national politics again, he said, but money talks, and Gandolf's talked louder than his.

They chatted about that for a while and then Knowland said, "Three oh five, seven seven seven, nine six eight two."

"What's that?" Cox asked.

"The phone number of our man in Miami."

They started calling the Miami guy "The 305 Man," after his Miami area code. They spoke again about Gandolf, and decided it was not a joke. And that's how Lester Gandolf came to take a header down the marble staircase of his house. The fee for that was $200,000, double the last charge. Maybe Gandolf put up a fight, or maybe the assassin was upping his fee just because he could. After all, his clients weren't about to report him to the Better Business Bureau.

A line had been crossed, the three men knew. This time, if they had not actually ordered a killing, they certainly knew that that could be the result. They were officially murderers.

During a round of golf they actually discussed who "needed a date with destiny," Bradenton told me during his interrogation. No one in particular was bothering any of them at that time. But they were getting bored.

Then Cox said the name Bob Appleby, who had applied for membership at the Olde Naples Country Club. Cox knew that because he was on the membership committee.

They agreed that Appleby and his wife did not fit in to the social fabric of their town and did not belong in their country club. The Funeral Home King of Iowa? A man who'd somehow earned his way into Port Royal by planting stiffs into the Midwestern prairieland? Are you fucking kidding me? Even though it seemed unlikely that Appleby would actually be approved for membership, they were annoyed that he'd even applied to their club.

Boom. Good-bye Funeral Home King, and his girlfriend aboard his yacht, a *Naples Daily News* story reported. Too bad about the girlfriend, but shit happened.

This time, $300,000 was wired into The 305 Man's Swiss bank account. Apparently explosives were an additional expense item in the hit man's fee.

I asked the men if they had somehow learned about my investigation and had decided to end it by having their man kill Charles Beaumont, Wade Hansen, and me, with the mayor heading the list. Bradenton said no, they didn't know about the investigation. He suspected his wife, Paige, of having an affair and assigned a private detective to follow her. She was, with Charles Beaumont. Bye-bye Mister Mayor.

Until that moment, I had wondered if maybe hizzoner did off himself, even with that golf tournament coming up. Running a car in a closed garage to cause death by carbon monoxide poisoning was a standard suicide method. It is said to be painless, but the only people who could confirm that aren't talking. I couldn't imagine how the Miami guy could have pulled that off without leaving a sign of a struggle. With both the golf tournament and Paige Bradenton to look forward to, wouldn't Beaumont have put up a fight? I guess that's why The 305 Man got the big bucks.

Knowland told me what I already knew: Gilbert Merton was in the way of my real estate deal, so he became roadkill. I'd have to find a way to live with that, if I could.

With Charles Beaumont now a confirmed kill, I still wondered about Ash's death. The men denied any involvement. Maybe they were innocent, or maybe they were afraid to tell me—if not her nephew, then her friend—the truth, given that we were out there in the Everglades, where anything could happen. Had Ash awakened (at three A.M.) to find The 305 Man staring down at her, scaring her so badly that her heart stopped?

While on the job in Chicago, I had experiences with sociopaths who felt no remorse for any of their actions. When their behavior turned violent and they hurt people, they were reclassified as psychopaths.

That's whom I was dealing with now: The Three Old White Psychopaths. They were responsible for six, and maybe seven, deaths before we stopped them. That didn't compare with the worst of the worst, men like Ted Bundy, who raped and murdered more than thirty-five women in at least six states; or John Wayne Gacy, who killed at least thirty-three men and boys and kept their bodies buried under his home or in his yard in Chicago; or Jeffrey Dahmer of Milwaukee, whose total was seventeen men and boys in Wisconsin and Ohio, with cannibalism involved.

In some way, our guys were scarier to me than the likes of Bundy, Gacy, and Dahmer. Those three were part of an infamous, deranged brotherhood with abnormal brain anatomy and chemistry, as studies have shown, and, at least for some of them, unpleasant childhoods. They were misshapen Calibans, incapable of leading normal lives. But Cox, Bradenton, and Knowland were successful, upstanding citizens, pillars of their communities, who had turned themselves into stone killers.

I'd run up against plenty of otherwise upstanding citizens driven to murder by sudden and unexpected circumstances, but nobody else like these three, who went looking for it out of sheer boredom and a sense of frustrated entitlement. You had to go back to the case of Leopold and Loeb in 1924 to find anything like that.

Nathan Leopold and Richard Loeb were students at the University of Chicago, with wealthy parents, who murdered fourteen-year-old Bobby Franks, just to show they were smart enough to pull off a "perfect crime," they said. Obviously they were not; even the courtroom skill of Clarence Darrow could not keep them from a sentence of life in the penitentiary, although he did save them from the electric chair.

I asked the self-made psychopaths how long they thought they would have continued. They all said they didn't know, but they'd paid The 305 Man $600,000 so far, and they were discussing that. Should they hammer out a budget for their organization? They could afford to keep going, but did they want to? Maybe there were less expensive, and less risky, ways to get even with people they disliked. A cost-benefit analysis. Businessmen to the very end.

When we were all gathered in the living room, I told them that their thinking was deeply flawed. Four of their victims were old white men, just like themselves, another one was an old white woman, and one was a young woman who was an innocent bystander. You didn't earn self-respect by ordering executions. When you did that, you were a murderer, nothing more.

However, to make certain I was getting the complete story, and that they hadn't been responsible for other murders in Naples or elsewhere, I played Russian roulette with Rollie Cox. This technique seemed appropriate, given that Vasily was my partner.

Cox didn't know that I'd unloaded my Smith & Wesson. I had him sit in a wooden chair in the kitchen and stood behind him so he couldn't see the empty chambers. Bradenton and Knowland could see us from the living room.

Doing the Dirty Harry thing, I asked Cox how lucky he felt and pulled the trigger once. Hearing the click, he shouted, "Hey! Stop! Are you fucking crazy?"

I pulled the trigger again.

Click.

By then, Cox was sobbing and had wet his (Vasily's) grey sweatpants, and I believed he'd told me everything. No need to play the game with the other two. Marisa had a framed print of the Edvard

Munch painting *The Scream* on her living room wall. Chris's and Art's faces looked like that. I guess they didn't feel lucky either.

I led Cox back to the living room. Then Knowland said it: "I'm glad you've stopped us."

There were only two more loose ends to tie up. I asked Cox, who was especially primed to tell the truth, about keeping Vasily off the symphony board, and about bribing a city councilman to gain approval of a marina project. Guilty on both counts. "You should have stuck to your dirty tricks," I told them. They didn't disagree.

I'd never been on a serial killer case before. But an FBI agent with the bureau's Chicago office told me that many of the killers, when caught, said they were relieved that it had ended.

Now it was time for them to make the call to Miami.

42.

Kill Shot

Three nights later, I was alone in Ash's house, in my bedroom on the second floor, with the lights off. I was sitting in an upholstered chair with my feet up on a hassock, reading the *Chicago Tribune* sports section on my iPad.

To my own arsenal of pistols, I'd added Sir Reginald's Mossberg 935 semiautomatic shotgun, which he'd used for bird hunting and I was using for different game. Marisa had picked up Joe because I didn't want to worry about him. I think Joe sensed the impending danger because he didn't object (hissing, biting, threatening legal action) as she carried him out to her car, a nebula grey pearl Lexus LS 600h L sedan (business was very good). Martin and Suzette were in rooms at a nearby hotel. Bradenton, Knowland, and Cox were still at the cabin, with Vasily. They didn't need much guarding, with the airboat gone and their spirits broken.

The three men's wives reported them missing when they didn't come home at their usual time after golf and cards. A country club grounds crew found the two golf carts in the trees, but didn't report that immediately because they assumed that the golfers decided to walk the rest of the way. It happened sometimes.

I'd called Hansen from the cabin to inform him that Vasily and I had the three men, and what we were doing with them. He said that, at this point, he wouldn't be surprised if I'd said we had them hanging from meat hooks in a warehouse somewhere. He agreed to let us play out our hand. Murders trump kidnappings every time.

The chief told their wives that he'd put out a BOLO (be on the lookout) alert to all of his patrolmen and to other law enforcement agencies in the area, but that it would be forty-eight hours before they could be officially declared missing. That wasn't true. With their street shoes and other personal items found in their lockers, and their cars still in the country club parking lot, the forty-eight hour rule would not apply.

At three A.M., I thought I heard a noise. So The 305 Man knew about the witching hour too. I guess it was an open secret among us pros. The Old White Men had told their assassin that I was a trust-fund layabout and heavy drinker who would most likely not hear him even if he kicked in the front door. An easy kill.

My Russian sniper team was set up somewhere outside, scanning the terrain with a night-vision scope, under orders to wound only, not kill. That was a fiction from old cowboy movies: "I just winged him, ma'am." Whenever you sent a steel-jacketed projectile at 3,900 feet per second toward a human body, the distinction between shooting to kill or merely wounding disappeared. Serge's Dragunov didn't have a "gentle" setting. But, unlike Jack Stoney, I wasn't willing to take on a contract killer without backup.

I walked quietly to the bedroom door, opened it a crack, and listened.

Nothing.

Maybe I hadn't really heard anything. Could The 305 Man, no matter how good he was, sneak past the Russians?

Then I heard the sound again. I thought it was the sliding glass door from the kitchen to the backyard.

There are two theories about the best way to handle a situation like that: you can wait for the danger to come to you, or you can meet it head-on. I told Bill Stevens about that once, over beers at the Baby Doll, and he'd used it in one of the books. Guess which option Jack Stoney always chose thereafter?

Like Stoney, I've always been a straight-ahead kind of guy because waiting is boring and I like to call the play. So I picked up the Mossberg, used the barrel to ease the door open farther, and stepped into the hallway. Moonlight through second-floor windows provided enough light for me to see. The other bedroom doors were all closed, so I assumed that the guy from Miami, if he was in fact in the house, hadn't come upstairs yet. He wouldn't close himself into a room.

I moved along the wall to the head of the stairway, looked down, and saw nothing. I made my way down the stairs slowly, swinging the shotgun barrel from side to side, Navy SEAL fashion, and went through the hallway and into the kitchen, which was brightly illuminated by the light of a full moon.

The sliding glass door was open just wide enough for a man to get through. It was locked when I went to bed, to not arouse suspicion. But the lock was easy to pick.

I was thinking about my next move when a nylon rope went around my throat. I clutched at it, as it cut into my neck, and stomped down hard with my bare foot on my assailant's instep. I heard him grunt. That usually shattered bones and ended the fight. But not with this guy. He kept the rope tight, so tight that I wasn't able to get my hand between it and my neck. Soon I'd lose consciousness as the blood to my brain and the air to my lungs was cut off. It is said that your life passes before your eyes at a moment like that. It doesn't. You just panic and hope to see another dawn.

Suddenly the rope slacked and the man behind me slumped to the floor. Coughing and gasping for breath, I looked down at him. He was a big, muscular man, dressed in black, just like my Russians, and like me when I broke into Vasily's office, part of clandestine tradecraft.

I couldn't tell his hair color because the top of his head was gone. I felt a wetness on the back of my head and neck and shoulders. Blood. Fortunately not mine, I discovered, as I quickly checked myself out.

On the floor beside the body was a garrote, a length of nylon rope with a wooden handle fastened to each end.

Then Serge was at the door, holding his Desert Eagle pistol, which was better than the Dragunov in close quarters. Stefan remained outside. Serge came into the kitchen, kicked at The 305 Man with his boot, and watched him for a moment even though there was no possibility a man could survive without the top of his head.

"There was no other way," he said to me, showing no emotion at all. In this encounter, one killing machine had bested another.

"I know," I told him. "Thanks."

Those were the first words in English that Serge had ever spoken to me. Stefan had also said nothing I could understand. I'd assumed that neither of them spoke English. I was glad that I'd never said anything disparaging about either one of them in their presence, such as, "Hey borscht-for-brains, got a match?" The corpse at my feet was evidence of what could happen if you got on their bad side.

Serge had made an amazing kill shot, with my head just inches from the killer's, shooting through the narrow open section of the sliding door so that the bullet wouldn't be deflected by the glass. The rifle must have had a sound suppressor because I didn't hear the shot. The house next to Ash's had been occupied for the last several days. Thus the need for a silent shot.

Serge used his cell phone to call Vasily and spoke to him in Russian. Then he handed the phone to me.

"We've got to let them go," I told Vasily. "Even though I hate it."

Without the assassin's testimony, we had no proof of their crimes.

"I know," he agreed.

I ended the call, handed the phone to Serge, who left, and used my cell phone to call Wade Hansen. When I looked up from finding Hansen in my phone's contacts list, Serge was gone.

Twenty minutes later, Hansen arrived with a crime scene team and an EMS van. I gave him my report as the crime techs examined the house and the grounds. One of the techs, a woman in her thirties with short red hair and freckles, wearing white coveralls that said "Naples Crime Scene Team" on the back, used a piece of white blotter paper to collect a blood sample from the floor. I doubted that a pro like The 305 Man would have his DNA on file with any law enforcement agency, but maybe his fingerprints were.

When the EMS crew loaded the body onto a gurney and took it to the city morgue, Hansen left and I went upstairs to shower and change my clothes, getting rid of The 305 Man's bits of blood, flesh, and bone that had splattered on me. I went into my duffel bag and put on Jack Starkey's blue denim work shirt, jeans, and running shoes. The ghost of Frank Chance, the great Chicago Cubs first baseman, could return to Cooperstown.

I DROVE my Corvette to Everglades City, stopping at that Dunkin' Donuts for takeout nourishment, and parked on the street in front of the one-story pink wooden building that looked like a schoolhouse but was, a large sign on the front lawn said, the Museum of the Everglades. I hadn't noticed it before. What stories that building could tell. Now Vasily and I had added one more, but, with luck, ours would never be on display. I vowed to come back for a tour with Marisa, and maybe an airboat ride.

I walked a block down to the dock, where Elena was waiting for me in the airboat. She greeted me warmly, we were partners in crime now, and ferried me to Vasily's island. I went inside to find him sitting in the living room with the three men who'd set all of this in motion. Serge and Stefan were elsewhere. Maybe it was their routine to clean the Dragunov and then go out for a cold beer after a kill.

"What happened?" Cox asked me as I took a chair and Elena made a fresh pot of coffee. There was one doughnut left on a plate on the kitchen table, but I'd eaten three on the way so I left it there. Now that the investigation had concluded, it was time to start a diet.

"Your man is dead," I answered. "And you're going home."

Upon hearing that, the three who used to be men of privilege and influence, and who had morphed themselves into pond scum, looked like they were deciding whether to cry or faint.

Elena poured the coffee into a Thermos. We all walked down to the dock and got into the airboat.

43.

Camp Knowland

If you always want a happy ending, read a book or go to a movie. But in real life, sometimes the bad guys win, and all you can do is move on and get ready to fight the good fight another day.

I was back to my life in Fort Myers Beach. Marisa sold Ash's house for $35 million to a couple from Dubai. She said that, with her commission, we were going to have dinner in Paris someday soon, and that she was relieved that my case had been completed without me being shot in the groin, or anywhere else. That's two of us.

I was planning a trip to Chicago to see Claire and Jenny. I vowed that I would do that regularly. Claire was engaged to that orthopedic surgeon. A surgeon trumps a cop, every time.

Thanks to Jenny and Brad, I had a fine grandson with the excellent name of Jack James (after Brad's father) Thornhill. I was waiting for him to be old enough to attend a Cubs game with me on Bill Stevens's roof. Maybe by then the team would have a strong bullpen and some batters who could take it long, 400 feet over the ivy-covered brick center-field wall. While I'm dreaming, why not throw in a Golden Glover or two in the infield? Or why not three: the next Tinkers-to-Evers-to-Chance combo.

Wade Hansen had seen that my consulting fee and expenses were paid in full, with the approval of the lame-duck mayor.

Arthur Bradenton, Christopher Knowland, and Roland Cox were back to their old lives too—but not before a come-to-Jesus meeting with Wade Hansen at police headquarters. The men had lawyered up before that meeting and were represented by Phil Weingarden from Los Angeles, the most famous criminal defense attorney in America.

During the meeting, Hansen told them he knew they were all murderers. If there were any more unexplained deaths in his city, he'd come for them and personally "rip off their heads and shit down their necks." No doubt quoting his Parris Island drill instructor. I think I had the same one. Hansen told me that Weingarden had said nothing at all during that session; he knew he'd already won. Clarence Darrow could not have done better by his clients. I'm guessing he remains on a large retainer.

With Knowland's grudging approval, his $2 million from my real estate scam was donated to the Collier County Boys and Girls Club, which was Hansen's idea. In announcing the generous gift, the club said that it would be used to purchase a summer camp for the kids named after their benefactor. Camp Knowland. That was the only positive thing to come out of the whole affair.

Boris Ivanovich of Brighton Beach, New York, was still making above-market returns for his Atocha Fund clients, including Charles Beaumont's widow, his true identity remaining a secret. Holding to the deal he agreed to, Hansen, who announced that he was a candidate for mayor in the upcoming November election, did not alert the FBI or Securities and Exchange Commission about the impostor hedge fund manager.

And why shouldn't Vasily get a pass? In our criminal justice system, all manner of dirty rotten scoundrels are granted clemency for helping government prosecutors, as was our plan for The 305 Man, if he'd survived. Vasily helped to stop the Naples serial killings and to take an assassin off the board.

The 305 Man was identified by his fingerprints as Carl Lewellyn, a former Army Delta Force operative who had gone rogue and worked as a mercenary out of Miami for whatever person or government wanted to pay his fee. There was no evidence in his Biscayne Boulevard penthouse condo linking him to any of his clients, including Bradenton, Knowland, and Cox.

Chief Hansen's official report stated that an unknown person had shot Lewellyn as he was breaking into Ash's house. I was not mentioned. It was a page-one story in the *Naples Daily News,* but by the next news cycle it was forgotten. After all, nobody in Naples cared how a burglar was brought down as long as he was.

Maybe some day Wade Hansen would give me permission to tell Bill Stevens he can use the Naples serial killings as the basis for a Jack Stoney novel, if he disguises the characters and locations.

That would be nice, because I'd like to see how Detective Jack Stoney would handle the case.

44.

Undercover In Paradise

Three A.M. *The Witching Hour. Jack Stoney was sitting in an upholstered chair in the bedroom of a borrowed mansion on the Caribbean island of Saint Kitts. A Mossberg double-action shotgun was propped on a wall within reach.*

The lights in the house were off; Stoney was reading the Chicago Tribune *sports section on his iPad. It was early September, and the Cubs had a lock on last place in their division. So what else was new?*

Stoney thought about the Russian sniper team set up somewhere outside, scanning the terrain with a night-vision scope, under orders to wound only, not kill.

That was a fiction from old cowboy movies, however: "I just winged him, ma'am." Whenever you sent a steel-jacketed projectile at 3,900 feet per second toward a human body, the distinction between shooting to kill or wound disappeared. A Dragunov didn't have a "gentle" setting.

Stoney thought he heard something. He put down the iPad and listened. Maybe it was just the wind rustling the palm trees, or the creaking of the big old house. Could anyone sneak past the Russians?

As they'd been ordered, the men known as The Unholy Three, who were responsible for six murders on the island, had told their hit man that his target was a trust-fund fop and heavy drinker who would most likely not hear him even if he kicked in the front door.

An easy kill.

But it was a trap.

The three old men were prisoners in a fishing lodge on Nevis owned by the brother of Basseterre Police Chief Konris Soubis. Basseterre was the capital of the Federation of Saint Kitts and Nevis.

Stoney wondered why in the hell he'd agreed to become involved in this case. He was retired from the Chicago PD and was living a comfortable life in Key West. He could not care less what happened on Saint Kitts. He'd never even been to the island before. It had to be that, after a life of action on the mean streets of Chicago, "comfortable" translated to "boredom," he concluded.

When his friend, the Key West police chief, approached him with a "consulting assignment" for his pal Konris Soubis—just look at some case files of possible murders, nothing more—the word "murders" translated as "adrenaline."

An old firehorse, answering the bell one more time.

There it was again.

The sound.

Not the rustling of palm fronds.

Not the creaking of the old house.

It was definitely a man.

The man Stoney was expecting.

If Jack Stoney had wanted an adrenaline boost, he was getting it now. He picked up the Mossberg. At close quarters, you always let a shotgun, not a handgun, which was harder to aim under stress, do your talking.

He realized that the sound he heard was the turning of doorknobs. The hit man was checking each of the five second-floor bedrooms.

Stoney waited, saw the doorknob on his bedroom slowly turn, and then . . .

When the fat lady had completed her aria, taken off her horned helmet, put down her spear, and gone out for a brewski, the hit man was lying unconscious on the hallway floor, his wrists and ankles bound with plastic ties.

The hit man was tall and muscular, with a jagged knife scar running down his right cheek. He was wearing a black turtleneck shirt, black military pants, and combat boots.

He was bleeding heavily from the mouth where Stoney had delivered a ferocious blow with the stock end of the shotgun. Maybe he'd had nice teeth. Now there was no way to know.

Stoney went downstairs to the kitchen, made a cell phone call, and then put a pot of coffee on to brew as he waited for Chief Soubis and a crime scene team.

One month later Jack Stoney was back to his life in Key West. It was a good life, Stoney thought, but after retiring from the Chicago police force, he hadn't realized how much he'd missed the excitement of the hunt until getting involved in another murder case. Maybe he'd get his Florida PI license and take on a few cases, just to keep himself sharp, he mused. Or maybe he'd check in with his former Chicago colleagues to see how they were getting along without him.

But for now, Jack Stoney was making the Nirvana *ready for a cruise to the Turks and Caicos with his main squeeze, Miranda, who decided she could take two weeks off from her real estate agency in pursuit of sugar-sand beaches and rum drinks with fruit and little paper parasols in them.*

Sam, Stoney's cat, would come on the voyage too, even though he didn't love sailing. But he enjoyed the fish that Stoney caught and Miranda prepared in the galley. She was a wonderful cook.

When Stoney told Sam they were going on a cruise, Sam looked at him and meowed, which Stoney interpreted as, "Are the tuna biting?"

Stoney met Miranda Lopez when he saw her sitting alone in a booth at the Rusty Scupper. The prettiest girl in the room. She was drumming her long nails on the tabletop and looked annoyed.

He went behind the bar and made a Papa Doble, a rum drink favored by Ernest Hemingway during his Key West years. He carried the drink to her booth, put it on the table in front of her and asked, "Are you waiting for this?"

She looked at him and said, "I'm waiting for my boyfriend who . . ."

Stoney slid into the booth opposite her and finished her sentence: ". . . who just lost the best thing he ever had."

The hit man, whose name was Alex Reyes, out of Miami, had a new set of dentures, compliments of the Saint Kitts government. He now sat in a cell in Her Majesty's Prison, awaiting the trial for murder in Magistrate's Court.

The Unholy Trinity, three wealthy, retired Brits, had hired him to murder four of the island nation's citizens over the past year, just because the victims had annoyed the men in some way or other.

The Saint Kitts attorney general told Stoney he was confident that, on the testimony of Reyes who'd agreed to cooperate in return for a reduced sentence, all three men would be convicted of first-degree murder. Jack Stoney thought he just might sail to Saint Kitts for the hangings.

45.

Dead Solid Perfect

I was aboard *Phoenix* early one Saturday morning, sitting at the table in the galley with a cup of coffee. Marisa and Joe were still asleep in the stateroom. I'd just finished reading the draft of Bill Stevens's latest book, *Jack Stoney: Undercover in Paradise*. It was the semidisguised story of the Naples murders.

Marisa was delighted that Jack Stoney had a girlfriend based upon her, a real babe. And he did base another character upon Lady Ashley Howe, and made her younger. She would have been pleased. I told Joe that Stoney had acquired a cat named Sam. Hard to tell if anything impresses a cat.

Even though the outcome of my work with the City of Naples hadn't been ideal, the murders had stopped. Marisa reported that residential property values there had increased by 25 percent. Life was back to normal—or as normal as it could be in a rarefied world like that.

I had help solving the case from Marisa, Vasily, and Jack Stoney, and I was glad to have had it, given that my detecting skills had been on the shelf since retirement. Only a fool and his ego turned down assistance. And I was alive only because a Russian sniper was able to make a world-class shot.

Naples Mayor Wade Hansen had given me permission to tell Bill Stevens about The Case Of The Old White Men on the condition that nothing in the book would link the story to Naples.

It didn't. Jack Stoney was retired to Key West, not Fort Meyers Beach; The Old White Men were now three ex-pat Brits known as

The Unholy Trinity; and the setting was Saint Kitts, an island in the West Indies, and not a city even resembling Naples, Florida.

Vasily was delighted to have been promoted from Russian gangster to oligarch in the story. All other main characters and settings were properly disguised.

True to form, Mother Nature continued to cull the human herd. The Old White Men's club now had just two members. Recently Arthur Bradenton was riding his horse when one of South Florida's few surviving panthers appeared out of the brush and spooked it, tossing Bradenton out of the saddle, breaking his neck.

If Brother Timothy was correct in his beliefs, Bradenton's immortal soul flew upward for a reckoning with Saint Peter. I imagined that whatever arguments Bradenton might have used to try to justify his earthly behavior to Saint Pete didn't cut it, and he was residing in a considerably warmer climate than we have in South Florida.

Maybe if, before their obituaries were published in the *Naples Daily News*, Christopher Knowland and Roland Cox donated all of their money to the Boys and Girls Club, or to the Humane Society, or another worthy cause, and volunteered to join aid workers in West Africa to help fight an Ebola outbreak, they'd have a better shot at forgiveness and redemption during their final accounting. Brother Timothy would have counseled them to give that a shot.

I'd checked to make certain that Bill Stevens had done his homework for the ending of the new book, and he had. Google confirmed that executions were indeed still done by hanging on Saint Kitts. No problem there with the shortage of the chemicals used for lethal injections like we were still having in Florida. You never ran out of rope. So I had no edits at all for that final chapter.

I got up to pour another cup of coffee and noticed Joe, standing in the doorway to the stateroom, staring at me. Time for breakfast. I opened the refrigerator, took out a carton of milk, poured some in a dish for him, and set it on the floor. He rubbed against my leg and began lapping it up and purring contentedly.

I was scheduled to meet a roofing contractor at The Drunken Parrot later that morning to get an estimate for damage caused by a tropical storm three days earlier—the *Phoenix* escaped harm—and then have lunch with Cubby Cullen at Doc Ford's. Cubby called with the invite the day before, saying he'd like my opinion about "an open investigation" in Fort Myers Beach, something involving alligator poaching and meth cooking, which were somehow related.

I agreed to read the case file and offer any thoughts I had in return for a California burger with onion rings, both of which Doc Ford's did very well. No harm in just scanning the file and offering a few thoughts, right?

I was planning another trip to Chicago in three days. Jenny told me that my grandson, Jack, still wasn't quite old enough to go to a Cubs game on Bill Stevens's rooftop. I wondered how old a kid had to be to eat a Chicago dog. However old that was, I'd be the one to get it for him.

Joe finished his milk and strolled over to the table, milk dripping from his whiskers, ready for the next course. I decided to make pancakes. I always made one in the shape of a little J, just for him. My father did that for my brother, Joe, and me on Sunday mornings.

As I was whisking the pancake batter, I heard Marisa yawn. I poured a mug of coffee for her and took it to her. She yawned again, stretched, and said, "How about something sweet to go with your coffee, big guy?"

Which I took to mean exactly that. The pancakes could wait.

Bill was coming down in a few days for some fishing, so I'd give the annotated manuscript of *Jack Stoney: Undercover in Paradise*, to him then. As with all the Jack Stoney books, the bad guys were brought to justice in a most satisfying way, the hero got the girl, and the future looked bright for Detective Lieutenant Jack Stoney of the Chicago PD Homicide Division, retired to Key West, but, his fans would demand, not permanently.

It was all dead-solid perfect, as only fiction can be.